Bad Money

Jason Vail

Bad Money

A Hawk Publishing book.

Cover illustration copyright Can Stock Photo Inc.
Cover design by Ashley Barber

ISBN-13: 978-1534630406
ISBN-10: 1534630406

Hawk Publishing
Tallahassee, FL 32312

ALSO BY JASON VAIL

The Outlaws

Stephen Attebrook Mysteries

The Wayward Apprentice
Baynard's List
The Dreadful Penance
The Girl in the Ice
Saint Milburgha's Bones

Lone Star Rising Stories

Lone Star Rising: Voyage of the Wasp
Lone Star Rising: T.S. Wasp and the Heart of Texas

Martial Arts

Medieval and Renaissance Dagger Combat

Bad Money

Bad Money

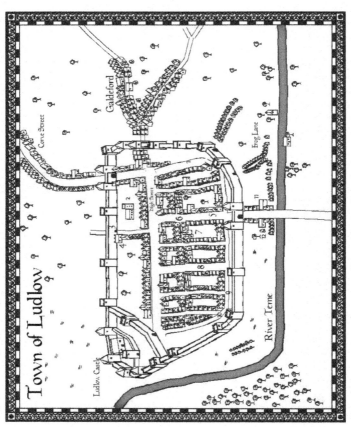

1. Old Street
2. St. Laurence Church
3. Linney Gate
4. Baynard House
5. Broad St.
6. Bell Lane
7. Broken Shield Inn
8. Mill Street
9. Christcroft Street
10. The Trumpet
11. St. John's Hospital
12. Wobbly Kettle

Part One

April 1263

Chapter 1

"Help me! Dear God in Heaven, help me!" a woman cried from the depths of Bell Lane. "Oh, please, please help!"

"What's got into Mistress Bartelot, I wonder?" Harry the beggar said. The carving he had been working on sank to what little he had of a lap. "Has she taken to apprehending miscreants on the street now?"

"I can't imagine," Stephen Attebrook said. He withdrew his left foot from the warm salt bath that Jennie Wistwode had brought out from the kitchen and toweled off the stump of what remained of it and hastily returned the foot to his boot before anyone at the inn just across the yard might spot his shame. "But it sounds more serious than that. I hope no one's died. It's too early for that."

In the past few months, Stephen had more than enough death and grief to fill several lifetimes in his work as Ludlow's deputy coroner. He did not relish the prospect of having to attend another death, and this one across the street and probably someone he knew.

Stephen added, "We haven't even had breakfast yet. And besides, I need to get up to the castle or I'll miss the muster."

Word had come to Ludlow that Llywelyn ap Maredudd, a Welsh princeling, was on the march into Shropshire for a bit of raiding and pillaging. Roger Mortimer and Percival FitzAllan had summoned all Englishmen in this area of the borderlands to gather at Ludlow with their arms to oppose Maredudd.

"It's not like they're going to want you, damaged as you are," Harry muttered, attending to his carving with more attention than before.

"They'll want me now that the Prince has taken the king's army away and left us to fend for ourselves against the Welsh," Stephen said.

"I doubt it. Look what happened last time. Nobody likes a cripple." Harry knew well what he was talking about, since his legs had been taken off above the knees after a wagon had rolled over them. Compared to that, Stephen's injury, his foot lopped off at the arch, was rather minor, although anyone who saw it was as repulsed as much by his stump as by Harry's.

Already people were responding to the cry. Stephen heard the front door to the inn slam open, and several people were rushing out the side door into the yard and making for the gate to Bell Lane, none of them, fortunately, sparing Stephen a glance so that he was able to struggle into his boot, even though his foot was still damp.

"You don't think it's the housekeeper, do you?" Harry asked. "I rather liked Mistress Dungon."

"I don't see why it should be," Stephen said without conviction, setting off across the yard as fast as his bad foot would allow: a rather stumpy, awkward jog. "Try to keep up, will you? You'll miss the best gossip, and I know how much that's worth to you at the gate." The "gate" was Broad Gate down the hill from the inn, Harry's normal post during the day. But this being a Sunday, he was prohibited from begging, his normal work.

"It is unseemly of you to make light of Mistress Bartelot's misfortune," Harry said, drawing on the padded leather gloves that protected his hands from the ground. With his legs off below the knee, he had to use his hands to get around, which he managed with surprising speed and agility.

"I take my example from you, my friend," Stephen said as he reached the gate and entered Bell Lane.

There was a sizeable crowd gathered before Mistress Bartelot's house, which stood just a few doors down on the other side of the street from the inn.

Mistress Bartelot's window on the first floor, from which she spent her day surveying the comings and goings on this little avenue of commerce, was open as usual. But she was not seated as usual, clutching the gold cross that adorned her neck. This morning she stood at the window, hands upon the sill, babbling something that was now indecipherable, her face a study in anguish. She was a gaunt woman, severe in appearance and in dress. Deep lines ran from her eyes to her strong chin, accentuating the boxiness of her face. She always wore black fringed with white lace, as if she remained in mourning for the husband she had lost at least a decade ago.

"Felicitas!" cried Edith Wistwode, the proprietor of the Broken Shield. "Whatever is the matter, dear?"

"Oh, dear God!" Mistress Bartelot replied. "I'm ruined! Ruined! It's all gone! Every scrap!" She shook her hands in the air and then dropped her face to her palms. "Even my bauble!" she was heard to mutter through her fingers.

And it was only then that Stephen noted that she did not have the heavy gilded cross around her neck as she always did, and he began to get a sense of what might have happened.

"Mistress Bartelot!" Stephen called. "May we come in? You must tell me the nature of this misfortune."

Mistress Bartelot sniffed and wiped her nose. "Dungon," she said to someone in the chamber behind her, "will you please go down and let Sir Stephen in."

When Mistress Dungon, the housekeeper, opened the door, the crowd took it as an invitation for them all to enter, curiosity being as irresistible an addiction as wine. But Dungon barred the door with an outstretched arm, making an exception only for Edith Wistwode. She shut the door on the others, who would be left to pry the matter out of Edith, who was not much of a gossip, especially where her friends were concerned. Everyone already knew that Stephen was a lost cause as regards to news, but there was always the hope that he would tell Harry. One fellow, who knew who could be depended on, stopped by Harry at the inn's gate, and patted him on the shoulder. "I'll see you later, eh?"

"Right, Bob," Harry said. "Don't forget to bring a farthing or two."

"It's Sunday!" Bob objected.

"What difference does that make? A man's got to eat," Harry was heard to say as the door to Mistress Bartelot's house swung shut on Stephen's back.

"It's terrible, simply terrible," Dungon said as she led Stephen and Edith through the hall to the stair that climbed to the first floor.

"What's so terrible?" Edith asked, anxious although it was clear by this time that death was not involved in whatever misfortune had befallen the house.

"I'll let the mistress tell you," Dungon said.

Stephen had never been in Mistress Bartelot's house before. They crossed the passage to the hall, Stephen glimpsing what had once been a shop to the left, but which was now empty, shuttered and forlorn. The hall held nothing but a plain wooden table and two stools, not a chair to sit comfortably by the fire on the floor which had gone out. It was a sure sign of poverty that Dungon had let the fire die. The floor itself was hard-packed dirt.

The hall lay in the middle of the house, open to the roof to allow the smoke from the fire to escape, like many such houses. There were sleeping chambers at the front, over the shop, and at the back, over the pantry and buttery. Mistress Dungon climbed the stairs to the forward chamber.

The housekeeper opened the door and stood aside for Stephen and Edith to enter.

Mistress Bartelot stood in the center of the chamber, which was as bare of furniture as the hall. There was only a bed without curtains, a stool by the window, a wardrobe in the corner and a small chest beside it, the top open.

"Felicitas, dear!" Edith exclaimed as she rushed to Mistress Bartelot's side. "What is it?"

Mistress Bartelot pointed to the chest. "It's gone! All of it!"

Edith peered into the chest. "So it is. But what was it?"

"My entire fortune. All I had left. All I had to live on." Mistress Bartelot dropped her face to her hands and shook her head. Edith put her arm around Mistress Bartelot's shoulders, which was a feat as Edith barely stood as tall as the other woman's armpit.

Bad Money

"What am I do to now?" Mistress Bartelot sobbed. "How am I to live?" She raised her head. "The rent is due in only a few weeks and I've nothing to pay it with now." She drew away from Edith. "I'll be thrown out on the streets . . . like that dreadful man!" She waved in the direction of the Broken Shield.

"You'll not have to live like Harry, I promise you," Edith said. "Here, sit down." She guided Mistress Bartelot to the stool and forced her to sit.

"But I have no family left — my husband gone, my children dead! No one! I am alone!"

"You are not without friends. You shall be taken care of. I shall see to it. Now, tell us exactly what happened."

Mistress Bartelot's mouth drew down at the corners, elongating a face that was already square and long, the crevasses that ran from her nose to her chin growing even deeper than normal. "I slept poorly last night, so I was late in getting up. Dungon was already here, and she woke me. I rose to find that!" She pointed to the chest. "Someone broke in during the night and took everything!"

"What did they take?" Stephen asked. "Money?"

"Money? I have no money and have never done."

"What was this fortune then?"

"My husband left me spoons. Silver spoons. He liked to collect them, you see. He spent a good bit of all we ever earned on them. I thought it an extravagance, a lot of nonsense. But when he died, I found I could sell a spoon, or a part of one, now and then, to pay my bills and my rent. It is how I lived. I have nothing else. The guild won't take care of me, you see. Reginald quarreled with them. He was accused of embezzling guild funds, and they expelled him. He hanged himself. Edith knows the story! Everyone does. It is my shame!"

Edith glanced at Stephen, who had not heard this story, and nodded.

"I suppose he used the money to buy the spoons," Mistress Bartelot said. "I never thought about it until now."

16

"Put it out of your mind," Edith said. "It doesn't matter."

"Your cross is missing," Stephen said.

"They took that too. Everything I own is gone. I'm a pauper now. My mother would be so ashamed. She had such expectations, and none of them played out." Mistress Bartelot looked grim. "Lucy! Just think what she will say when she hears the news! She could never forebear from gloating whenever I went there."

"Lucy?" Stephen asked.

"Lucy Wattepas," Edith answered, identifying the wife of one of the town's leading craftsmen, the goldsmith Leofwine Wattepas. "They are cousins, although distant ones, from my understanding."

Mistress Wattepas nodded. "We both came from good gentry families, and have both fallen so low. That's the lot of the youngest daughters, you see. If no one can be found for us among our own class, we are dispatched to some merchant or craftsman. My father had only daughters, an even dozen of us. Reginald was the best my father could do. Lucy was luckier. And she has never let me forget it."

"These spoons," Stephen asked, "did anyone else know you had them?"

Mistress Bartelot shook her head.

"Not even Dungon?"

"She is in my confidence, but she is the only one."

"I didn't even know," Edith said, "and we've been friends since Felicitas came here."

"Where did you sell these spoons?" Stephen asked.

"To Wattepas, of course. Who else? He is the only goldsmith hereabout," Mistress Bartelot replied. "Do you think you can find them? My spoons? I would be ever grateful."

"It is a long shot," Stephen said. "Whoever is responsible is probably well gone by now."

Chapter 2

"Thank you, Sir Stephen for your concern," Mistress Bartelot said. She seemed to be recovering somewhat from her distress. "Dungon, if you would show my guests out?"

Dungon, who had remained just beyond the chamber door, said, "Very good, my lady."

That form of address sounded odd in this house. Mistress Bartelot might have started life out as a lady, but she wasn't considered one after marrying a tradesman. But Stephen let the conceit pass. She wasn't the only person he knew in Ludlow who entertained it.

"Thank you, Dungon," Stephen said as he passed the housekeeper at the head of the stairs and went down. "I would like to see the rest of the house."

"I don't think her ladyship will allow that," Dungon said.

"Why not?"

"Well, she's quite particular about people poking about beyond the hall." Dungon sighed. "It's bad enough there."

"You mean she doesn't want people to see how impoverished she's become."

"Yessir. I'm afraid so."

"It's that bad?"

"A church mouse has got more in its larder than the lady."

"And you? She can afford you but not food?"

"Some appearances must be kept up no matter what. Although I haven't had me wages this month, and it don't look I'll see them."

"What good would it do to poke about?" Edith asked as they reached the hall. "It would only upset her."

"You know as well as I," Stephen said. "We might find how the thief got in the house. There might be some clue to whom it is."

"I shall leave it to you," Edith said turning toward the front door. "I've an inn to run and hungry guests. And I don't want Felicitas to think I've taken advantage of her misfortune to rummage through her cupboards."

"If she only had cupboards," Dungon muttered.

"Thank you for that, Dungon. I shall see you at the inn, Sir Stephen," Edith said. She marched toward the passage to Bell Lane.

Dungon and Stephen stood without speaking. The smell of dust in the air rather than the smoke that permeated a happy house made Stephen sad and reminded him of his own condition.

"The pantry's that way," Dungon said at last to fill up the silence if nothing else, or perhaps to get the distasteful chore over with so she could be about whatever business Mistress Bartelot required, though that could not be much.

"I think I can find it without your help."

"I'm sure you can, sir. It ain't like we've hidden it."

The doors to the pantry and buttery stood across from each other in the passage to the rear garden. Neither was lighted, but Stephen could see well enough that the windows opening at the rear of the house were shuttered and barred from the inside.

"Were any of these windows open when you got up?" he asked.

"I haven't touched nothing here," Dungon said.

Stephen nodded to himself. Whoever had broken in had not used this route. Thieves were never so considerate as to close the door, or in this case a window, as they left.

He went out to the back garden and examined these windows again, and could see no sign that either had been forced just to be sure. He could imagine Gilbert Wistwode asking if he had checked that detail and he did not want to be wanting. He brought his face close to the back door as well. The wood frame was old and had many nicks, but none were fresh.

Stephen dropped to all fours, heedless of the startled expression on Dungon's face, and searched the ground beneath the windows for any sign that a ladder had been used to gain entrance above, or that someone had boosted up the thief, which had occurred in another burglary recently. But the grass and the ground seemed undisturbed.

"These windows," Stephen asked, "you've not touched them this morning?"

"No reason to," Dungon said.

"They were shuttered up tight and barred last night, as they are now?"

"I check them every night before going to bed. They were such as you see them now."

Stephen backed away from the house and looked at the windows of the upper chambers. Both were open.

"Which one is yours?"

"The one on the right."

"Were the windows open all night?"

"I like the fresh air, especially now that it's spring. Helps with the stink."

"And you heard nothing?"

"I'm a heavy sleeper, unlike her ladyship."

"She obviously heard nothing."

"She'd have said so if she did, I'm sure."

"And you had nothing to do with the disappearance of these spoons?"

Dungon's mouth tightened. "Are you accusing me?"

"I'm asking you. You're the only person who knew about them, apart from Leofwine Wattepas. Who else was in a better position? It wouldn't be the first time a servant stole from her master."

"You can search my things, if you care to. You won't find them."

Stephen wondered how much of this was a bluff. "I think I will."

He re-entered the house and passed through to the hall. He paused at the threshold, a thought just having occurred him. "Do you have a candle in the pantry?"

"There is one. We save it for emergencies."

"Fetch it, please, and a striker."

Dungon turned back to the pantry, muttering to herself about the insult and the waste, but returned right away. "Here you go." At Stephen's level and unfriendly look, she added. "Sir."

Stephen took the striker, which consisted of a flint and steel and a small box containing some tinder. He put the box on the floor, struck the flint and steel over the tinder until sparks jumped off and ignited the tinder. He blew on the tinder to give it life and reached for the candle. He entered the hall with the candle while Dungon stooped to blow out the tinder.

He did not get on all fours this time, but bent low as he could, examining the floor. He should have done this before, but he had not thought of it until now. He was always forgetting obvious measures of this sort, and just bungled along. It was a wonder he ever found out anything at all. It was a good thing people had not seen through his façade of competence, or his reputation, little as it was, would be even lower. And like all people, he treasured his reputation more than the contents of his purse.

"What are you doing, may I ask . . . sir?" Dungon asked from the doorway.

"Just being careful."

"Waste of time . . . sir."

Stephen straightened up. "Yes, the dirt's packed hard." Besides, if an intruder *had* passed through the hall to Mistress Bartelot's chamber, Dungon's feet and Stephen's would likely have obscured the marks. He did not say this to Dungon and avoided her eye.

"Mind blowing out the candle . . . sir? It's our only one."

"Right." He blew out the flame and tossed Dungon the candle.

"Now to your room. Yours is the one of the left, I believe?"

"That's what I said . . . sir."

Stephen climbed the stairs, conscious of the proximity of Dungon's nose. A hallway led to the rear of the house, where another window overlooked the garden. It, too, was open to admit the light and what fresh air the spring breeze happened to bring.

He entered Dungon's room. It was an ordinary room with ordinary furnishings, but unlike Mistress Bartelot's room, it looked as though someone actually lived in it: a frame bed with shabby curtains; a chair with a pillow on it by the window for taking one's ease and the view of the yard with its depleted woodpile, privy and expanse of grass that could use the attentions of a few goats to keep it in check; and the similar gardens of the neighbors. A wardrobe stood in the corner. Stephen crossed to the wardrobe and opened it. It was empty but for two folded gowns on one shelf and several lace wimples, one of which looked quite expensive, folded on another. A spare pair of shoes and wooden pattens, the sandals that shielded good shoes from the mud, occupied the bottom shelf.

There was nowhere to hide stolen spoons unless Dungon had fashioned a secret cupboard in the walls. But that possibility seemed unlikely and he had already appeared silly enough that he didn't want the embarrassment of being seen tapping about in a search for a concealed hiding place.

"Satisfied . . . sir?" Dungon asked from the doorway. "Finished prying?

"Everything seems in order."

"Mistress Bartelot is fond of order."

It had grown late by the time Stephen finished at Mistress Bartelot's house, and, with regret, he turned away from the inn and the breakfast that should have been waiting for him.

He was several long strides toward Raven Lane when he heard Gilbert Wistwode's voice calling to him. He paused for Gilbert to catch up. Gilbert unfolded a cloth in his hand and held out several strips of bacon and a piece of cake.

"I thought you might want this," Gilbert said.

"Thank you, Gilbert. That was very thoughtful." Stephen thrust a strip of bacon in his mouth. He had developed a fondness for bacon, although people of the gentry did not eat it. Nor did they eat upon the street like some common person, but he was hungry and there was no one about.

"Jennie was about to give it to Harry, but I thought it best go to you."

"Poor Harry," Stephen said, chewing on his bacon, confident that while Gilbert might think he had intervened to keep Jennie and Harry apart, in all likelihood Jennie would see that Harry did not go hungry. Jennie was not supposed to have anything to do with Harry after he had got her in trouble with the law for an unlicensed business they were conducting together. But the two found ways to spend time together despite the opposition of Jennie's parents. "Had yours already?"

Gilbert patted his ample stomach. "I make it a rule never to leave home without breakfast."

"Even for such a small errand as this?"

"You don't think you're going to the castle alone, do you? You're going to need my reassurances when they reject you again."

"This time will be different. They need every man. Besides, I proved myself at Montgomery." Not long ago, Stephen had ridden out on a raid into Wales from Old Montgomery, the aged timber fortress that guarded a major ford of the River Severn. He felt he had done well enough to put aside anyone's misgivings about his abilities despite the fact things had turned out badly.

"That was a terrible failure. All those men killed! No one wants to remember it. And they won't take kindly to your reminder."

"My reminder?"

"Well, you will no doubt boast of your role."

"I am a modest person. I do not boast. I shall merely state fact — that I can ride in battle as well as anyone. I came through it without being unhorsed."

"And that will be enough to remind everyone that two prominent people died in the debacle."

"That wasn't my fault."

"Yet the fault may be laid at your doorstep. When there is failure, people always look for someone to blame. It doesn't matter if the accusation is true. I should be careful about it, if I were you."

Stephen, who had not wanted to hear this advice, stepped faster, leaving Gilbert a few paces behind. Gilbert broke into a waddling run to catch up. He grasped Stephen's sleeve. "Have a care for a poor old man!"

"You're not that old, not even forty yet." Nevertheless, Stephen slowed his pace.

"Old enough," Gilbert said, panting from his exertion. "I am your elder, and you should heed my wisdom."

"I shall heed it as much as Edith."

"Which means you will pay no attention."

"Exactly."

"I don't know why I bother! There is no hope for you, any more than there is for Harry."

"You bother because Sir Geoff pays you to do it."

"Not enough. Not hardly enough with all the trouble we've been in. And he's late again with my stipend."

"Yes, I'm feeling the pinch as well. I've creditors hiding behind every tree."

"No, you don't. You've only one or two at most. Try running an inn. You'll know then what it's like to be hounded by creditors."

"Unless you're a lord with too much debt."

"True. They're the worst when it comes to dodging creditors. You should avoid that fate when you have your own manor."

"That seems unlikely, the way things have gone."

"There is always hope."

"There is always false hope."

"Don't give up. Some heiress will take pity on a handsome fellow like you."

"You know women don't marry for looks. They weigh a man's purse first before deciding."

"That's not always true. Edith chose me for my wonderful qualities, none of which had anything to do with my wealth. Seeing that I had just fled from my monastery, there was little to recommend me on that score."

"She is the exception."

"She certainly is exceptional," Gilbert said with affection.

Quite so, Stephen thought.

"There is," Gilbert ventured, "Lady Margaret. She seems fond of you. Although now that I think about it, she is a bit calculating."

"I would rather not discuss Lady Margaret." Stephen was not sure what to think of the Lady Margaret de Thottenham. She had been much in his thoughts since they had met and contested over a lost list of supporters of the rebel Simon de Montfort to the point of crowding out of his mind the memory of a woman he had truly loved and wished more than anything he had not lost. Contemplating Margaret seemed at times almost like a betrayal of Taresa's memory, especially as Gilbert was right: Margaret could not be trusted. She looked to her own advantage in everything and damn the consequences on anyone else. Yet she was so lovely that this was easily overlooked.

"Yes, she is a touchy subject," Gilbert said as they climbed Raven Lane to High Street. "Best you not see her again, I suppose."

"I said I would not discuss Lady Margaret."

"Well, it is time you put your grief aside and started thinking of the future. You have a son to provide for, and you've paid scant attention to him."

"You are not my conscience. I will see to my duty in my own time."

"Someone must shake you out of your present doldrums. Harry isn't up to it. So it will have to be me."

"I am doing well enough on my own."

"Of course you are. I'll just give you a needed shove now and then."

"You want me to leave the nest?"

"It's not that I want it. It's just inevitable. You can't remain where you are. We all know the many reasons for that, least of which is our friend Percival FitzAllan. You'll leave eventually and I'll be left to train up another deputy, undoubtedly someone who is far more of a dolt than you are."

"You're calling me a dolt now?"

"Did I? Forgive me if I gave that impression. It's just that all the other deputies have been wanting. It dismays me to have to guide another."

They turned onto High Street and headed toward the castle, which occupied the ridge at the northwest corner of the town. The merchants and shopkeepers who lived here were leaving their houses with their families and heading east toward Saint Laurence's Church for the Mass at Prime, which occasioned the exchange of volleys of good days and how are you's before Stephen and Gilbert got by the crowds and passed through the castle's main gate.

The spectacle within — of tents and the great paddock erected to the north within the outer bailey — warmed Stephen's heart. Here the army of the March was gathering and would march out soon to confront the Welsh.

He and Gilbert hurried through the tent village, and met Sir Geoffrey Randall, Stephen's employer, at the gatehouse to the inner bailey.

"Good morning to you, Attebrook," Randall said, leaning on his cane before he wagged it at Stephen. "Must hurry. The Mass already started."

"Gout bothering you again, sir?" Stephen asked as they clumped across the bridge spanning the inner ditch.

"A touch, just a touch. Not enough to slow me down."

Stephen wasn't sure about this since Sir Geoffrey was favoring his right foot so much that he hardly walked upon it. But it was not tactful to contradict the coroner. "Of course, sir. You look quite fit, actually."

"I do. Yes, I do. Looking forward to getting into the field again. The last time it was just a lot of riding around in the rain. Beastly, it was." The reference was to the recent campaign against the Welsh by an English army brought to the March by Prince Edward. It had wandered into Wales and relieved a few sieges, but the Welsh had melted into the hills and mountains of their miserable country and refused battle. Now word was things would be different. The English, what there was of them now, would give the Welsh the thrashing they deserved.

A familiar figure was in earnest conversation at the chapel doors as Stephen and Randall came up. The two men drew apart when they realized their words might be overheard. The familiar person turned in Stephen's direction, a sardonic and false smile on his lips; the other gazed at the sky as if measuring the weather, although the sky was almost cloudless, an unusual condition for England.

"Well," said the familiar person, "look who's here."

"Good day to you, FitzSimmons," Stephen said. "I belong here. It's you who are out of place."

"We may have our differences," Nigel FitzSimmons replied, "but we have our common enemies. I have as much to lose as anyone in the shire from marauding Welshmen. So I've answered the summons, same as any sensible man with estates here."

People of the gentry often had their differences with those who lived about them, but the differences separating Stephen and FitzSimmons were both small and great. There was bad blood between them arising from the death of one of FitzSimmons' cousins last fall, and there were larger political ones as well. Stephen was allied with Randall who was a supporter of the King. The rule that the lower men embraced the loyalties of those above them required that he also followed the King. FitzSimmons was a supporter of Simon de Montfort. De Montfort, the king's brother-in-law, led a faction of barons determined to diminish the king's power and to substitute members of their own party for the nobles now at the King's elbow. FitzSimmons was also a friend of Margaret de Thottenham's. It had been at FitzSimmon's bidding that she had fought Stephen for possession of a secret list which had set out who in Herefordshire and Shropshire supported the King and who supported de Montfort.

"I say, Crauford," Randall said to the elegant young man beside FitzSimmons, "what are you doing here? I thought you were at Windsor."

"I am under normal circumstances," Crauford said, "but I've come with a contingent of men in answer to the Marcher lords' call for aid."

"How many have you brought?" Randall asked.

"Forty."

"I see. Knights and sergeants, I hope. We can't have enough of them."

"Crossbowmen, actually."

"Oh." Randall looked disappointed. "Mercenaries, then."

"I am afraid so," Crauford said.

"I am forgetting my manners," Randall said. "Forgive me. Attebrook, this is Maurice Crauford. Crauford — Attebrook."

"So you're Attebrook," Crauford said. "I've heard about you. You're the fellow who knocked Nigel off his horse."

"Yes," Stephen said, glancing at FitzSimmons who was frowning at this reference to a duel they had fought last autumn in which Stephen had emerged the victor, more by luck than skill.

"How did you manage it, owing to your condition, I mean? Without a foot one can hardly ride properly, can one."

"Oh, you know about that."

"Well, it's hardly a secret."

"Nothing is, it seems."

"Tell me, did it hurt? Losing your foot, I mean. I heard it was chopped off by a Moor."

"I only lost part of the foot, not all of it. And no, I hardly felt it. The infection that came afterward was worse."

"Well, in any case, congratulations on your victory," Crauford said with a smile.

"Shall we go in?" FitzSimmons said, and without waiting for an answer, for none really was expected, he entered the chapel.

"I suppose we should," Randall murmured, for the tension in the air at the mention of the duel had been so thick one could barely breathe.

"How do you get away with saying such things to FitzSimmons' face?" Stephen asked Crauford.

"Oh," Crauford said, "we're cousins. On opposite sides, it seems, over de Montfort and his reforms, but still family. You know how it is: Every family has its black sheep."

"Indeed," Stephen said as he followed Crauford into the chapel, for he was the black sheep of his own family.

Stephen and Gilbert stood at the back of the crowd in the round chapel and did not go forward at the end when many took communion. Stephen wanted to avoid making contact with Percival FitzAllan, who was near the head of the line with Roger Mortimer. They were almost brothers now that FitzAllan's son had married Mortimer's daughter. Mortimer, one of the most powerful men in the March, probably had not cared a fig about Stephen, although Stephen's home and where his brother still lived was only a few miles from Wigmore, but FitzAllan surely had poisoned his mind by now, or would, given a reminder.

The crowd went into the hall after mass. Planning for the coming war could not be put off by the fact it was Sunday.

Stephen and Gilbert were the last up the steps to the hall. As they entered and took a place at the back of the crowd of leading men, Gilbert murmured, "So that was Crauford."

"What about him?"

"You haven't heard? Wattepas has betrothed his youngest daughter to him. I'm surprised that a dandy like Crauford would take such a wife, the daughter of a craftsman."

"I've heard she's a beautiful girl."

"That's true, but you were just saying that people of your class don't rest their marriages on simple attraction. There must be a substantial dowry, as I hear that Crauford has the gentry's disease."

"Mountainous debt?" Stephen guessed.

"Exactly."

"Well, Lucy Wattepas is a Mortimer, though from a minor branch. Perhaps that was an enticement."

"I wouldn't think it was an enticement as much as a mark in her favor to weigh along with the money she should bring to the arrangement."

"I suppose you're right."

The senior men gathered about Mortimer, a broad-shouldered man with a receding hairline and a perpetual scowl.

"There are only a thousand of us!" one of the senior men exclaimed. "What can we do?"

"There a thousand foot, two hundred archers and two hundred horse, to be precise," Mortimer said.

"But we'll be outnumbered!"

"We're more than enough for that rabble," another man said.

"The Welsh aren't a rabble," Randall said. "Any more than our foot are a rabble."

"Well, they are that," someone said.

"Randall is right. We cannot underestimate the Welsh. As long as our foot don't run away we'll be fine," Mortimer said. "You officers will see to that."

"I wish Prince Edward had remained," said a voice from the back of the pack. "He left too soon."

"Well, I for one was glad to see the back of his mercenaries," said another in the crowd. "They're nothing but trouble."

"But we've got more, damn it. Unreliable scum!"

"I shit more scum than the King's deigned to send us in help. No good at all, what he's sent. Might as well have done nothing!"

This sparked a chorus of *"Oui's"* for here French was spoken rather than the rabble's English. Nobody liked the army of mercenaries the King kept about him rather than depending on the local men raised by his loyalists. It was as if he didn't trust the English to keep him safe, and this was one of Montfort's bones of contention: Not only the presence of the mercenaries and the trouble they caused among the people with their bad behavior, but their cost, for their wages were a drain on an already taxed treasury. People were tired of being taxed to pay for them when the kingdom had so many other needs.

"But it means we have to fend for ourselves!" someone objected.

"When has it been otherwise?" Mortimer asked. "Our safety has always been our own responsibility. We've never been able to depend on Westminster to look out for us. They're too far away, and let's be frank, they don't care. Now, enough of this. We've real work to do. We will march on the morrow and there isn't time to waste."

When it was clear that Mortimer was finished with his leading men and they began to disperse to their encampments to make ready for tomorrow's departure, Stephen approached Mortimer as he settled into a chair by the fireplace, a mug of wine newly thrust into his hand.

"What do you want?" Mortimer asked, his scowl more pronounced.

"I have a request, my lord," Stephen said.

"I hope you don't want money, or anything like that."

"No, I was hoping you'd find a place for me in the army."

"You're Attebrook, aren't you?"

"Yessir."

"The one with the missing foot."

"Not all missing, my lord. Just a piece. I can ride as well as anyone."

Mortimer stroked his chin. "There is a way you can be useful."

"Yessir," Stephen said hopefully.

"Crauford there will be taking over as constable for the duration of the campaign. He needs men to hold the castle while we're gone. You can assist him. There's not much likelihood of Ludlow being attacked. You two ought to be able to manage."

"I see."

"Is that a problem?"

"No, my lord."

"Good, then. Off you go."

Chapter 3

"We've forty-two men, sir," reported Philip Dainteth, the senior sergeant of the garrison, an old man in his fifties with a beard shot through with gray and deep wrinkles about his brown eyes. He had been left behind to work with Crauford's Flemish and Dutch mercenaries when the rest of the garrison had marched off with the army. "Damned foreigners! You can't understand a word they say. God help us if we are attacked."

"It's a big castle," Stephen agreed, running his fingers along a crack in the table in the guard commander's chamber of the inner gate tower. "But we'll do what we can. I doubt there will be trouble." His mind turned momentarily to what to do if the castle were attacked. The outer bailey was vast and it would be a challenge to hold it with forty-two men. He half made up his mind that if the worst happened they would retreat to the inner bailey, which was a castle within a castle, and hold out there until help arrived.

"You think we'll win the battle?" There was worry in Dainteth's voice, even though he affected a light tone to conceal it. He had a son and two grandsons in the army that had marched northwest that morning to confront the Welsh.

"Of course."

"You're just saying that."

"Well, battles are risky things."

Dainteth nodded. "I've heard that. Never been in a battle, myself. A skirmish or four, and a few raids. But never a pitched battle in all these years of soldiering. What about you, sir?"

"I've been in a few."

"Won them all, eh, sir?"

"No, not all of them. Let's figure out a watch list. This isn't peace time, and we'll have to make sure the walls are manned throughout the night."

"Christ's blood, I don't even know all their names yet! Nor do I care to. Can't pronounce most of them, anyway."

"Call a muster. We'll sort them out. I'll get a wax board and we'll write down their names and the hours they're to stand."

"You mean the clerk will write them down. But we've no clerk."

"I'll do it."

"Ah. It's true then, you were a lawyer once?"

"Almost, but luckily I avoided that fate."

"Can't stand lawyers. They're worse than clerics, arguing how many angels fit on the head of a pin. Fussy bastards."

"Not a life I craved. Now, keeping these lads awake through the night won't be easy. I'll stay up. You'll have them during the day. I want them working at the posts three hours in the morning and three in the afternoon. No laying around, drinking."

"You're sure about the night watch, sir?" Night watch was hard duty and usually fell to a lesser man than the deputy constable. "I don't mind."

"It will serve to keep the boys on their toes. Put a scare into them every time I show up."

"You'll do that, sir, I don't doubt," Dainteth said. "You're scary enough in daylight. I can't imagine you coming up on me in the dark. Pity the army wouldn't take you."

"You know what people think about cripples."

"Yes, but your wound hasn't slowed you down that much."

"Not everyone sees that. Let's call the men together and get started."

Most men would chafe at being left behind while their fellows rode off to battle, but Crauford's sentence as temporary constable of Ludlow Castle did not seem to bother him. Mortimer and FitzAllan had hardly cleared the gates with their followers when he ordered a full cask of wine be brought up from the cellar. He had a servant fill a mug and settled by the fire until one of the whores from the Wobbly Kettle, making a house call, answered his summons. Then he repaired to the master's chamber with the girl and was not seen for the rest of the day, supper being delivered to his chamber as well as a constant stream of wine.

Although Stephen was supposed to be his deputy, Crauford had not spoken a word to him about how he wanted affairs conducted. So the watch lists stood undisturbed, and the castle's business went on unaffected by the change in leadership, as well-run castles were prone to do.

"Sir," one of the younger Dutch mercenaries said in badly pronounced English, "you're wanted."

Stephen squinted, palm over his eyes, irritated that someone would awaken him at this time of day. It was nearly noon from the angle of the slices of sunlight that made it through the cracks in the shutters. He had been up all night again to keep the watch on its toes, sleeping through most of the day.

"What is it?" Stephen snapped more sharply than he should have done. It wasn't the boy's fault he was being awakened. It could be a Welsh attack, but that seemed unlikely. More likely some spat between the guards that the elder sergeant could not handle.

"Someone's died, sir."

This was news that Stephen had not hoped to hear. Although he was deputy constable, he was still deputy coroner and had to deal with any deaths that might happen in the vicinity of the town. "That is inconvenient. Who, do you know?"

"No, sir. Only that it happened on Lower Broad Street. A Thomas Tanner is in the yard asking after you."

Tanner was a member of the parish jury. If he had been sent to fetch Stephen, it meant that the jury had already been convened. "Can't Gilbert take care of it?"

"Master Thomas said you should come right away."

Stephen flung off the blanket and swung his feet out of bed. "He did, did he?" He could hear Gilbert's voice in that summons. There was no avoiding what had to be done now, no matter how much he wished to pull the blanket over his head and get what sleep he could during the remainder of the day. "There's no shirking duty, is there. Tell him I'll be right down."

"Very good, sir," the soldier said. He retreated from the sergeant's chamber to allow Stephen to get dressed.

Thomas Tanner had his hat in his hands, twisting it out of shape so that it no longer had any semblance to a hat, when Stephen finally emerged from the gate tower.

"Ah, sir," Tanner said. "There you are."

"Unfortunately, yes. What's this about a death?"

"At Sprunt's, sir, it is."

"Sprunt's?" Stephen struggled to remember who that was. "On Lower Broad?"

"Right, sir. Found this morning, quite early, actually. But Master Gilbert said not to disturb you until the jury could be brought together."

"That's thoughtful of him."

"He said you'd been sleeping late these days. Lucky you, sir. Wish I had the luxury."

"I am a lucky one, Thomas. There is no doubt about that. Well, let's not keep our corpse waiting."

"Yes, sir. They do go foul quickly now that it's getting warmer."

Sprunt's house lay on the east side of Lower Broad Street about halfway between Bell Lane and the gate. Stephen remembered something about Sprunt as he neared the house, the sign of a glove hanging above the door. Sprunt was a glover. That in itself was not extraordinary, but he also made hats. The combining of these two professions — glover and hatter — had caused some controversy in the town, since craftsmen were supposed to stick to one thing. But Sprunt was a younger son of the gentry who had been set up by his father, who had the connections and the stubbornness to overcome the guilds' resistance. These dual professions plus an inheritance from his mother had made Sprunt one of the wealthiest men in Ludlow, to rival the goldsmith Leofwine Wattepas who stood at the economic pinnacle.

Gilbert met Stephen at the door. "You do not look the least bit rested."

"I would be if it weren't for these interruptions. What do we have?"

"A puzzle."

"I hate puzzles. Especially when they keep me from my sleep. I was up all night again."

"You should delegate that chore. Isn't that what leadership is all about?"

"I wanted to delegate this business to you, but Tanner informed me that would not be possible."

"This time, I'm afraid not. Especially since it's Sprunt's house. He will expect more than a clerk to manage this business."

Gilbert led the way through the house, which was deserted, both shop and hall, an unusual thing for any house, to the back garden. Everyone in the household was there from Sprunt himself, a tall thin man with a long neck and a big head that bent forward as if too heavy for his body, to all his journeymen and apprentices, servants, his wife and children, and a few people who looked to be neighbors. Other neighbors were peering over the fence on the sides and back of the garden.

This crowd parted at Stephen's approach. There on the ground by the wood pile was the body of a boy of thirteen or fourteen, his face obscured by tangles of curly red hair that in life would have fallen to his shoulders. The body lay upon its stomach, one arm above the head. There were no obvious marks that indicated a cause of death.

"Has he been moved?" Stephen asked.

"No," Sprunt said. "We left him as we found him."

"Who is he? One of your boys?"

"I have no idea who he is."

"Anybody else know him?" Stephen asked, surprised at this answer.

Sprunt answered for everyone. "Nobody knows him."

"That is odd." Ludlow was a small town. In any given circle of people, you were bound to find that among them they knew everyone in town.

"I'll say it's odd," Sprunt snapped. "Wait till you see the rest of it."

Stephen glanced at Gilbert for some clue what this meant. But Gilbert was looking into space, his hands in his sleeves.

Stephen knelt by the body. This close he could now tell that the lingering scent of excrement was not from the privy nearby but from the body, which had voided upon the boy's death, one of those unpleasant occurrences that made the job even less enjoyable than it was. He noticed now that the boy's head was twisted at an odd angle that it could never assume in life. One eye was open, the eye itself having that odd flatness eyes attained after death. The lower half of the boy's face was blue, as was half of his forehead and neck, the upside waxy looking. One arm was splayed above the head, the fingers of the gloved hand bent in a claw shape, the other arm under the body. Stephen felt the boy's cheek with the back of his hand. The cheek was cold. When Stephen tried to turn him over, he found that the body had gone completely rigid.

"He's been dead quite a while," Stephen said to no one in particular.

"We found him this morning. He must have died sometime during the night," Sprunt said.

Stephen flipped the body on its back. There were marks on what had been the underside of the face: stones and dirt embedded on the cheek, the underside eyelid, and the lips.

Stephen glanced upward. The body was directly under the projecting eave of the roof, which was four stories above the ground. The marks on the face and the proximity of the eave seemed to lead to only one conclusion. "It looks as though he fell off your roof. But what would a strange boy be doing up there in the middle of the night?"

"I don't know," Sprunt said. "But I can guess. Come inside and I'll show you."

"Show me what?" Stephen asked, bewildered.

"You'll see."

Sprunt led the way into the house. He climbed the stairs leading to the rear chambers, reaching the top floor, where he unlocked one of the back rooms. He stood back to allow Stephen and Gilbert to enter.

It was a small room. Expensive looking clothes hung from pegs on the left. There was a chest so large in the back right corner that it would need two men to pick it up. The lid stood open. A padlock lay on the floor beside it. The window on the back wall was open, giving a view of the rear garden and those of the neighbors.

"What was in the chest?" Stephen asked, suspicions stirring in his mind.

"The family silver," Sprunt said. "My inheritance from my mother. A full twenty pounds of it."

Stephen stepped to the window. The dead boy, surrounded by the circle of the curious who looked up at Stephen, lay beneath the window.

"You think he was one of the thieves?" Stephen asked Sprunt.

"What else could he be?" Sprunt snapped.

Stephen noticed that the bar that should have secured the shutters lay by his feet. "You kept the window closed and barred?"

"Of course. All the time. Unless I have business here, when I open it for the light. But no one comes in here but me or my wife. All our precious things are here."

"And only the silver is missing?"

"Only the silver."

Stephen bent down to examine the bar. There were nicks in the center where a sharp object might have probed to lever up the bar. He rose and closed the shutters. There was enough of a gap between the panels to allow the passage of a knife. "It seems you may be right."

"Of course, I'm right," Sprunt said. "I am always right."

I wonder if your wife thinks so as well, Stephen said to himself.

"The question is, what are you going to do about it?"

"Me? I doubt there is anything I can do."

"What good are you, then?" Sprunt growled and stomped out of the storeroom.

"I wonder how he got up there in the first place?" Stephen mused as he and Gilbert stood on the street outside of Sprunt's house after the jury had returned a verdict of death by misadventure and fined the hundred the cost of Sprunt's roof, which was a very expensive roof.

"Assuming that he actually fell from the roof."

"You don't think he did?"

"I admit that the evidence points in that direction," Gilbert said. "But you've been wrong before."

"You agreed. You said so."

"I yielded to the pressure of public opinion."

"You mean you surrendered to the force of my irresistible logic," Stephen said.

"If you prefer to think of it that way. But it would be nice to have more evidence. I am particularly interested in how the thieves broke into the storeroom, assuming that they got in through the window. It's so high up that the whole thing seems impossible."

"Yes, it does," Stephen said. "It's certainly not something I'd attempt. Although I think Harry might have been mad enough to try it, when he was whole."

At the thought of Harry, Stephen glanced toward Broad Gate, where Harry sat watching them from his nook, his begging bowl on what remained of his lap. Stephen strode down Broad Street to the gate.

"Morning, Harry," Stephen said.

"So, what's the verdict?" Harry asked.

"It seems the boy fell off Sprunt's roof during the night."

"You don't say." Harry's eyes drifted away from Stephen's and his lips pressed together as if he was having a thought. Whatever it was he did not share it. "Any of Sprunt's hoard missing?"

"Yes."

"From an upstairs chamber?"

"Yes. News gets around fast."

"Well, it is a small town. And you think this child was one of the robbers?"

"That is the prevailing opinion."

"Rather like Bartelot's."

"That thought had occurred to me. Have there been any other mysterious disappearances of silver that you've heard of?"

"Now that you ask, I heard of one theft. But it wasn't in the town."

"Oh?"

"It was a manor called Bockleton, south of here."

"I've heard of it. What do you know?"

"Well, it isn't much, just what some travelers said in passing. Someone broke into the manor house and made off with the silver while everyone was sleeping. You know, you might ask Will Thumper about it. He's got his fingers on the pulse of local criminality."

"A good idea. Meanwhile, I wanted to ask you something else."

"Ask away. I am a font of knowledge, except when I'm not."

"If you were going to get up on Sprunt's roof, how would you do it?"

"As I have no legs, there is no way I am getting on Sprunt's roof."

"Imagine that you have legs."

Harry squinted up the street toward Sprunt's house. "That's easy." He pointed to the town wall above their heads. "If you had half a brain you'd figure it out for yourself."

Stephen followed Harry's finger and saw what he meant. The roof of the nearest house abutted the wall. And going up Broad Street, the houses were built shoulder to shoulder, one roof touching another.

"Come on, Gilbert," Stephen said entering the gate tower.

"What?" Gilbert exclaimed. "You're not thinking of taking a stroll on the rooftops? That's insane!"

"You wanted your other evidence!" Stephen called back. "This is how we must look for it."

"I've got to see this!" Harry scooted away from his nook as Gilbert reluctantly entered the gate tower and climbed the stairs after Stephen.

Gilbert sat down on the peak of the roof nearest the town wall and would go no farther. He tried to say something, but his words came out an inarticulate yelp.

"You are the funniest thing I've ever seen!" Harry called from the middle of the street.

Stephen glanced back at Gilbert. He regretted goading Gilbert into coming along. The roofs, which ran back from Broad Street creating a series of peaks and valleys that had to be climbed to reach Sprunt's, were quite steep. But as long as you stayed in the center, there was no danger of falling off, only perhaps of getting stuck in one of the valleys if you could not manage the climb out. "Stay where you are!" Stephen called to Gilbert.

Gilbert waved. Then he slid out of view, back to the wall walk, where they had gained the roof in the first place.

Stephen had broken out into a sweat and was panting with the effort by the time he reached the peak of the fourth house. And he still had quite a way to go. By resting frequently in the valleys, however, he finally managed to reach Sprunt's.

He wasn't sure what he was looking for and stood on the slope of the roof, peering around. There wasn't much to see: a few loose shingles were the only thing of interest, and it was hard to tell if they meant anything for there had been skewed shingles on the roofs of the houses he had crossed to get here.

He went to the rear of the house and looked over into the back garden. The boy's body had been removed and there was no one in the yard but a servant who was chopping wood, one of those chores that was never done like dishes and the making of beds. One of the shingles had what might be a gouge worn in the edge, but that could have been an old mark, an imperfection in the wooden shingle when it had been put up. In any case, it wasn't directly over the window of the storage room but slightly to the side.

Stephen sat down to think, hoping that some observation might surface from the muck of his memory and reveal its illuminating importance. He heard voices through the roof: servants discussing the finding of the body. A servant's room must be straight below. It was not uncommon for the lowest members of the house to be quartered at the top floor, not unlike he was at the inn, for the chamber he inhabited had been a servant's before he showed up. Pigeons landed on the peak of the roof above Stephen and examined him. He made no sudden moves to frighten them. They flew away.

Nothing emerged from the muck. After a considerable time, he rose and made his way back to the wall.

Chapter 4

Although no one at Sprunt's had recognized the dead boy, Stephen had arranged for the body to be cleaned and set out at Saint Laurence's Church. A linen sheet covered him, as the boy's clothes had been cut off so that his entire skin could be viewed for marks that might have given some indication of the reason for his death. The town bailiffs were ordered to go throughout the town and the suburbs and command everyone to come by during the day to see if they could identify him. This had to be done straightaway, since the body would quickly foul in the warming weather. It was a great deal of effort for what promised to be little return, but Stephen thought it was worth it.

The body lay on a board stretched between two trestles in the same nook of the church where another victim of an untimely and unfortunate death had lain so that the town could view her. No one this time, however, cried out that the corpse was that of a saint.

Stephen and Gilbert waited on a bench by the body throughout the afternoon as people came and went, hoping for some exclamation of recognition. But there was none of that, only callous and vulgar jokes at Sprunt's and the dead boy's expense. It was boring work, and Stephen was almost crazy with it. Pacing and stretching did not relieve his discomfort.

Toward sundown, when the stream of visitors had trickled out and there was no one in the church but Stephen and Gilbert, Harry and one of the inn's servants, the boy Mark, showed up.

Mark seemed indisposed as he halted before Stephen. "He won't pay, sir." Mark had been sent to bring Harry up in a hand cart. No one in town, not even the beggars, were exempt from the view.

"You won't?" Stephen asked Harry.

"This is a waste of time," Harry said. "I'm sure I don't know him if nobody else does."

"What makes you think nobody does?"

"Mark said so."

"Pay up, Harry. It will include a ride back to the inn, won't it, Mark."

Mark's feet pawed at the dirt. "Very well, sir. If you insist."

"There," Stephen said.

Harry dug into his purse and tossed Mark a farthing. Mark bit down on it. Harry said, "You can't tell good money from bad that way, you idiot."

"If you insult me again, you'll have to crawl back to the inn," Mark snapped. He stamped toward the door.

"That boy needs to learn to keep his temper," Harry said. "Always flying off." He glanced up at the body on the board. "Well, are you going to bring that thing down to my level, or what? It's not like I can jump up."

"You take one arm, I'll take the other," Stephen said to Gilbert.

"I don't think my back is up to it," Gilbert said. "I think I pulled it out with all that climbing around."

"You only made it up to one roof," Harry said. "I wouldn't call that climbing around."

"It was a steep roof, and dangerous," Gilbert said. But nonetheless he grasped Harry's right arm and what remained of his thigh while Stephen bent down on the other side.

"One, two, three!" Stephen said and they hoisted Harry into the air.

"I would never have thought half a man could be so heavy," Gilbert grunted, for Harry was much heavier than he looked.

"It's me head," Harry said. "So full of brains, unlike yours which is likely to float off your shoulders."

"You know, my grip is weakening," Gilbert said. "I might drop you upon those brains. I would hate for them to foul this holy place."

"Sir Steve!" Harry cried. "You aren't going to let him get away with that?"

"With what? Hurry up. Tell us if the boy is familiar. I'm about to lose my grip as well," Stephen said.

"No, he don't look familiar. Now you can put me down, and be gentle. My noble flesh bruises easily."

Stephen and Gilbert were stooping to return Harry to the floor when a familiar voice said behind them, "Well, will you look at that!"

Stephen glanced back. There stood Will Thumper at the head of his considerable brood: uncles, cousins, a pair of brothers, a sister or two, a wife and at least a dozen children ranging from a babe in arms to Tad, who was thirteen or fourteen, Stephen couldn't remember which, and who was growing to be as broad and as powerful as his father.

"Hello, Will," Stephen said. He had managed to lift Harry up several times in the past, but without anyone seeing. Now it was going to get all over town. He almost burst out crimson at the embarrassment. "Good of you to come, and your lovely family."

"What's this?" Thumper asked, pointing at the dead boy.

"It's a dead boy."

"I can see that. We heard he fell off Sprunt's roof."

"That's what we think. Do you know him?"

"Hmm." Thumper bent close to the dead boy's face, pretending to examine it closely. "Don't think I do. What about you?" he asked his great family and got murmurs of No, Never seen him, and a round of shrugs and head wagging.

Thumper was about to go when he hooked his thumbs in his belt and regarded Harry. "What's that brother-in-law of yours been up to these days?"

"Nothing!" Harry answered quickly. "Nothing at all."

"Is he still in the business?"

"Don't know what you mean. He's a servant at Hereford Castle, and has been for years. You know that."

"I've heard that," Thumper said, "but I don't know it. You're the only person who's told me that. Not sure I trust you, anyways." He said to Stephen, "We don't know him, and have no reason to. He isn't from around here."

"You do business with a lot of people who aren't from around here," Stephen said.

"I don't like to foul the nest, so to speak," Thumper said. "Safer that way."

"In any case, you won't mind if I come back with you and have a look at your storeroom."

Thumper stroked his chin. "Don't suppose it matters. You've already seen all there's to see in there anyway."

Thumper claimed to be a handyman and day laborer, as did everyone else in his family. Most days they were seen to make their living at odd jobs about the town and countryside, and in the fields at sowing and harvest time. But other days, things were different. Neighbors often witnessed odd comings and goings at the Thumper house, a ramshackle residence east of Lower Galdeford, often involving packhorses and carts, and there was talk of stolen property being kept there for later sale in distant parts. But no one had ever taken the trouble to investigate, for word of these suspicions did not circulate beyond the neighborhood.

The Thumper brood straggled ahead toward Galdeford Gate while Thumper and Stephen paused at Spicer's wine shop for a cup on the street at Stephen's expense.

"You really don't know him?" Stephen asked as he put down his empty cup.

Thumper shook his head.

"You know about the break in at Sprunt's," Stephen said.

"I heard about it."

"And you have no idea who might be involved."

Thumper looked at a spot over Stephen's shoulder. "No idea."

"If you hear anything, I want you to tell me about it."

"That would be breaking my oath," Thumper laughed.

"What oath?"

"The thieves pledge! Don't you know!"

"You admit you're a thief, then."

"Never stole anything in my life. I'm an honest man. But you know I've a business to run."

"Just so long as it doesn't involve property missing from around here, as you said."

"It don't. Now, thanks for the cup of wine. You want to see my storeroom, or not?"

"Just to be certain."

They were stepping away from Spicer's as a cart train rounded the bend at the Beast Market, the wide open spot where Corve, Galdeford, and Old Streets came together.

The pair and the train approached each other. What was in the carts caught Stephen's attention as they came together. The carts were not full of goods, but of the bodies of men, some of them wounded, but many clearly dead.

One of the men in the second cart was Geoffrey Randall, the coroner of northern Herefordshire and Stephen's employer. His face was slack but did not have the waxy color of the dead. There was a bloody bandage around his head, and one on his thigh.

"Sir Geoffrey!" Stephen cried. "Are you all right?"

Randall raised his head and looked at the source of the noise, then let it fall back on the corpse supporting his back without any sign he had recognized Stephen.

"The army has returned, I see," Thumper said. "I hope it was victorious."

"I shall see about you later," Stephen said.

He fell in behind the cart and followed it to the castle, all thoughts of missing silver, lost crosses and dead boys vanished from his head.

Part Two

May 1263

Chapter 5

"Good God in Heaven!" a voice cried from the privy.

Harry looked up from his bowl of porridge at Stephen Attebrook, who sat on the bench above him. "I say, that must have been a rewarding experience."

"I'd rather not talk about such things at breakfast," Stephen murmured, stirring his porridge to break up some of the lumps of oats the cook had missed. "It is distasteful."

Harry opened his mouth to make some rejoinder, no doubt vulgar and cutting, as Harry dealt in the vulgar and cutting like a skilled swordsman, but the appearance of one of the inn's guest from round the corner of the stable forestalled any attack on Stephen's reluctance to address this morning's first point of interest. The guest, a cloth merchant from Bristol on his way to Carlisle, appeared agitated. He held up his braises with one hand to keep them from falling to his knees, a task any well-mannered person should already have accomplished out of sight in the privy. His lips quivered and the other hand pointed in the privy's direction.

"Come on, man, get a grip," Harry said when the merchants quivering lips delivered inarticulate blubbering. "It can't have been that wonderful."

"There's a dead man in the privy!" the merchant said to them at last, glad he had someone's attention. He turned to the inn and shouted loudly enough to be heard at Ludlow Castle, "There's a dead man in the privy!"

Stephen shot to his feet. His bowl flew out of his hands, spewing porridge, some of it striking Harry on the face.

Harry paid no attention to the indignity, for both he and Stephen knew there was a dead man in the privy. He had been there since last autumn, and they both thought they had taken sufficient steps to ensure he would not be discovered.

"A dead man?" they both gasped at once.

"There's a dead man in the privy!" the cloth merchant shouted again, backing into the yard. Now that he had raised the alarm, his pointing finger sank to the drawstring at his braise. He tied them up and pointed again round the side of the stable, where the privy stood between that structure and the kitchen, almost barring the way to the wood pile and back garden.

"Gilbert burned it out," Harry muttered. "There shouldn't be any sign."

"Shut up, Harry," Stephen said, as alarmed at this development as Harry. He paused. "You have porridge on your face."

Harry wiped his face. "So I have. Is it raining porridge today as well as dead men?" He glanced from the porridge on his fingers, which he wiped on the stumps of this thighs, to the fallen bowl. "Well, breakfast is ruined, at least for you, eh? Get to work, will you, and clear this up in a way that is satisfactory to all concerned. I love having friends in government. It solves so many of life's knotty problems."

By that Stephen understood Harry to mean in a way that pointed the finger of suspicion away from those who had any responsibility for the presence of the dead man in the privy, that is, him, Stephen and their landlord, Gilbert Wistwode, the proprietor of their lodgings, the Broken Shield Inn.

Harry was right, as he often was, although Stephen did not like to make such admissions even to himself. As deputy coroner of this little fold of Herefordshire, it was his duty to take charge immediately. He strode toward the cloth merchant, who was beginning to calm down.

"A dead man?" Stephen asked with as much nonchalance and unconcern as he could muster. "In the privy? You can't be serious."

By this time, the guests and staff of the inn were spilling into the yard, eager to learn more about this curiosity, a babble of questions and statements of disbelief filling the air, along with some rather vulgar comments and rude jokes. A good portion of the crowd did not bother with the discoverer, but made their way to the privy to see for themselves.

Stephen hurried to the corner of the stables and ordered: "Get away from there!" but not before two or three forced themselves into the shed covering the privy.

These lucky few emerged as if scalded, for Stephen had a good command voice, which he had developed during the days, now long gone and never recoverable, when he ordered soldiers around. But they had seen enough, and informed the crowd, "It's true!"

Stephen stood at the doorway to the privy, heart pounding, frightened of what he would find, despite the power he had to direct suspicion elsewhere if need be. He'd had one brush with the law as administered by the undersheriff here, Walter Henle, and had come off the poorer for it. He did not wish to repeat the experience.

Gilbert and Edith came up to Stephen. "A dead man?" Gilbert asked, unable to conceal his worry and concern.

"Yes," Stephen said. "Apparently."

"What's he doing there?" Gilbert asked in a voice that he meant to convey innocence but did not sound convincing.

"Yes," said Edith, who had no idea there had ever been a dead man in the privy, "what's he doing there?"

"I suppose we shall have to see," Stephen said, although he had no wish to see at all. "It's dark in there. I wonder how anyone can see anything." It was rather dark yet, being just sun up, with the yard still in shadow, the air cool and, except near the privy, fresh with spring. While people were accustomed to such smells, it was sharper than usual in the privy's vicinity, and Stephen wished for a scented rag to hold over his mouth. As the inn was the better sort, there was a bowl of such rags by the door for that purpose, but as quite a few of the spectators were armed with them, he doubted any were left.

"I'll fetch a candle," Edith said. "Mark!" she called to one of the grooms. "Fetch a candle!"

Mark did not move from his spot near the privy door. "Jennie!" he called to Gilbert's daughter. "Fetch a candle!"

"Fetch it yourself!" Jennie snapped. "You've no leave to give me orders."

"You're a girl!" Mark said.

Jennie crossed her arms and glowered.

Realizing that Jennie would not be moved and seeing a similar glower on Edith's face, Mark slipped away toward the inn.

Gilbert sighed, slid his hands into his sleeves and rested them on his ample belly, which gave him a monk-like appearance. He leaned close and whispered in Stephen's ear, "I suppose it would come out one day, you know. I always did. I laid up nights worrying about it."

"Say nothing, Gilbert," Stephen said. "We don't know who he is or how he got there."

"Ah, yes, of course we don't. How could we, after all?"

Mark returned from the inn bearing a lantern, a candle burning inside. He handed the lantern to Stephen. "There you go, sir. Enjoy."

"Mark is spending too much time with Harry," Stephen said to Gilbert.

"That's your fault, not mine. I've told you time and again, Harry's a bad influence. Look at the trouble he's caused Jennie."

Not wishing to debate this point, wishing instead that he was miles away, but not having any choice in the matter, Stephen stepped to the privy's threshold. He removed the candle from the lantern and held it up to illuminate the interior, although even as he did so, he saw there was enough light to see into the privy pit. A pale hand was clearly visible down in the foul muck. As Stephen bent over for a better view, he made out an arm attached to the hand, a shoulder, and part of a face, only the jaw and lips, long hair concealing the rest.

Stephen took a deep breath despite the choking odor, and stepped back into the comparatively cleaner air of the yard. "He's fresh," he said to Gilbert.

"Oh, thank God!" Gilbert gasped. The fellow they had put in the pit should be nothing but bones by now.

"Thank God?" Edith asked, incredulous. "You're glad we've a dead man in the privy? Think what that might mean for business!"

"Before we worry about that," Gilbert said, greatly relieved, "we shall have to determine how he got there. We might have no fault in it."

"Well then," Edith said, ever practical, "you'll have to fetch him out, won't you."

"I am afraid we shall," Gilbert sighed.

Pulling a dead man from a privy pit was not the sort of chore men relished, so it took some time to round up anyone willing to do it. After some negotiation, John Hapgood and his son Ralph agreed, but only if they were paid. As they were night soil collectors this business did not seem too far removed from their usual work. Then there was a dispute over who should pay, but it came down to the fact that it was the Wistwodes' privy, so they should bear the burden, not the neighborhood. Edith did not like this solution, but having been overruled by the collective will of her neighbors, she went back to the inn to fret over the expense after paying John and Ralph more money than they earned in the normal week.

John and Ralph went at it with surprising efficiency. With a pair of ropes and iron hooks, they had the corpse out of the pit without much fuss, having only dropped it once on the way up, and laid on the ground before the privy threshold, and were calling for soap and buckets of water to clean themselves up that had been laid nearby for this purpose.

More buckets had been prepared to wash the filth off the body. This chore fell to Gilbert and Mark, who applied the contents of the buckets to the dead man in an almost dainty way, careful not to splash themselves, and dancing to avoid the nasty rivulets that drained away from the body.

The body, now somewhat clean, lay on its back. The man appeared to be in his forties from the gray shot through his black hair and the lines around his nose and mouth. The face itself was lean and long, the neck lean as well with a prominent Adam's apple. He wore a blue tunic, which had buttons at the shoulders which could be undone so the arms could be freed from the sleeves, a woolen shirt beneath the tunic, and green stockings. A tooled belt secured the tunic and shirt at the waist. The belt held a knife, but there was no purse, which normally would reside beside the knife, only what appeared to be the strings to support the purse. His boots were stout and made for walking. It was the sort of ensemble worn by the craftsmen of any town.

"All right then," Stephen said, his voice muffled by the scented rag he had commandeered from a spectator. He flicked strands of hair from the man's face with a short stick. "Anybody know him?"

An elderly man in the assembled spectators held up his hand.

"And you are?" Stephen asked.

"Edward Shapley is my name, of Hereford." Shapley gestured to the body. "And that's Nicholas Feyn, without any doubt. And I for one am not surprised that he met his end in this way. If any man deserved it, he did."

"You did not get along, I take it?"

"Feyn never got along with anyone. He was a quarrelsome, angry man who blamed everyone else but himself for his misfortune."

"I suppose he had a great share of that, then."

Shapley nodded. "It wasn't for want of talent. He had a great store of that, but he squandered what God gave him through gambling, drink and chasing other men's wives."

"What sort of talent?"

"He was a goldsmith, though he never rose higher than journeyman. The masters of the Hereford guild never trusted him as a fellow."

"Was he a guest?" Stephen asked Gilbert, whose expression, concealed behind a scented rag of his own, hid his reaction to Feyn's identification.

"He was," Gilbert said. "Came yesterday. You don't remember him?"

"I don't keep track of every guest," Stephen said.

"I am surprised. He was quite loud. Don't you remember the uproar during the dice game?"

"I think I'd gone to bed, but I heard there was a commotion. Just a lot of shouting, I thought."

"Well, it did die down pretty quickly for a game where cheating was alleged."

"Feyn was cheating?"

"No, he was the accuser. It was another fellow. But nothing came of it. Or so I thought." Gilbert pushed aside Feyn's hair with a stick of his own. "Look there. He's got a knock on the head."

There was a cut on Feyn's left brow at the hairline. Stephen bent down to examine it, holding his breath against the stench. "It doesn't seem to have bled much." Scalp wounds of that kind usually bled copiously, even when they were minor. Stephen had received and inflicted enough wounds like that during fencing practice to know.

"Which could mean it knocked him silly. The killer dumped him in the privy right after, and he died straightaway."

"Or he slipped, hit his head, and fell in."

Gilbert shrugged, admitting the possibility.

"Did anyone see him come out here?" Stephen asked.

No one, especially the staff, who had remained, recalled it.

"It was probably early in the evening," Stephen mused.

"Why? Gilbert asked.

"Because if he had to relieve himself after he retired, he'd have used the chamber pot inside." Stephen added, "He had a purse, and it looks like it has been cut."

"A robbery?" Gilbert exclaimed, alarmed. "In my house?"

"I suspect so," Stephen said. Some impulse made him put out his hand to the wound on Feyn's forehead. He gently pressed the skin beside the cut. The skull should have felt solid, but instead, the bones beneath the skin yielded to the pressure. "Whoever struck him hit hard enough to break his skull."

"Oh, dear. Not an accident at all."

"I think not. Missing purse, broken skull. Hard to explain that except as robbery and murder."

Gilbert sighed. "I suppose we should have his clothes off, just to be sure that's all there is. I do so hate this part. When will it ever be your turn?"

"We've been over this before. I am the officer. It's lowly work."

"A good officer shares in the toils of his men."

"That depends upon the nature of the toil. What about Mark, there?"

Gilbert knelt by the body and took out his knife. "No, he'd just make a mess of it. And we'd have to listen to him complain the entire time." He glanced around. "It's too bad Harry's gone. We might've got him to do it."

"You'd have had to pay him. Edith might balk after what the Hapgoods cost."

"Oh, yes. I hadn't thought of that."

There being no other apparent alternatives, Gilbert, a grimace spreading across his face, grasped Feyn's collar and began to cut through his tunic and shirt.

Chapter 6

While Gilbert bent over the corpse, Stephen thought about the quarrel of the previous evening. Quarrels were the most frequent reason for homicides. If the outburst subsided without blows it usually blew over. But some people nursed grudges that they acted on later.

He disengaged from the circle of spectators and made his way to the inn. As it was Friday, washing day, Edith Wistwode was upstairs on the first floor superintending the stripping of the linen covers from the mattresses in the common sleeping room, the large, long room where most guests spent the night. Single rooms were more expensive. This was a menial chore that she did not ordinarily superintend, and she was pacing about snapping at the maids. They all seemed quite grim, the maids for being under Edith's tongue and Edith for something else.

"I cannot believe this has happened in my house!" Edith burst out when Stephen emerged from the stairway and she caught sight of him. "We shall never live it down! It's hard enough getting people in as it is! When word gets around, no one will come! No one wants lodgings where their persons or effects are not safe!" She shook a finger at Stephen. "I want you to find the culprit! Without delay!"

Stephen, who had been thinking about doing no more than finishing the inquest and passing the matter off to the undersheriff, blinked at Edith's attack. "I will do what I can."

"'I will do what I can.' Gilbert says that all the time, and usually I have to have someone clean up after him." Edith turned and snapped at one of the maids for some transgression in the stacking of the mattresses, although the girl's mistake was not apparent to Stephen, and apparently not even to the girl, whose eyes and lips narrowed in a sulk. Edith asked Stephen, "What are you doing here? Go out and find the killer!"

"You've been listening at the window," Stephen said.

"What if I have?"

Stephen shrugged, having suspected Edith's retreat to the inn had been a display of false unconcern. "I need to know who that fellow was who exchanged words with Feyn last night. I'm sure you know him. Nothing escapes your attention."

Edith drew herself up, which was a feat, owing to her short stature; the top of her head did not even reach Stephen's shoulder and she seemed almost as wide as she was tall. "His name is Albert de Brereton. Last I saw him, he was headed for the stable." Her eyes narrowed in thought. "Now that I think about it, he seemed remarkably unconcerned about the discovery of the body. Never went close to see what was up. Went straightway to the stable. Hurry! He might be gone already! Do you think it was him?"

Stephen crossed the yard to the stable limping more than usual from the pain from his bad foot. A riding horse and six pack horses had been tethered to the rings along the stable wall. Four men were tying panniers to the pack horses, one box on each side. The riding horse had already been tacked up, and a fifth man dressed in the decent but worn clothes of a middlingly prosperous merchant stood beside it, an impatient look on his face.

"Are you Albert de Brereton?" Stephen asked.

"What if I am?" the fellow replied, wiping the crumbs of a barley cake from his lips. Brereton's eyes gave Stephen the up-and-down, weighing and measuring what he saw.

Stephen was used to being assessed like this, conscious of the tattered state of his clothes — the battered maroon hat, green tunic with fraying cuffs, fading blue shirt, patched red stockings — as Brereton tried to guess where he fell on the social ladder. Class distinctions were often subtle, but made a great difference in how people treated each other, for even poor gentry like Stephen were entitled to deference from the richest merchant, although such deference might be colored with disdain, carefully expressed, of course, in ways that were calculated not to give outright offense.

"I would have a few words with you," Stephen said.

"I'm busy," Brereton said as he turned to the men loading the pack horses, having decided that Stephen was not worth his notice.

"I want to ask you a few questions about that fellow over there, the one found in the privy."

"You are being bothersome. Go away."

"Nonetheless, you will take the time to answer. I am the deputy coroner here."

"You? It must not be a lucrative position if you're all they've got to fill it." Nonetheless, because Stephen represented the crown despite his tatty appearance, Brereton turned back, arms crossed, lips downturned. "What do you want?"

"You had words with the deceased last night."

"I'd hardly call them words."

"Over a game of dice."

"He was a little upset at his losses. Threw a tantrum."

"And you answered him with hard words."

"I told him to fuck himself, if that's what you mean. But that was the end of it. I retired for the night and it was over."

"He accused you of cheating."

"Losers often do that. How often have you found men willing to take ownership of their own mistakes?"

"I'll admit, it is a common fault. Nonetheless, he leveled the accusation."

"And it blew over. These things do, you know."

"And you never went outside after?"

"Went straight to bed, as I told you. We've got to make Shrewsbury today. It's a long way and we planned to get an early start, which you and all the commotion have now ruined. Can we get back to work?"

"Do you have anyone who can corroborate you?"

Brereton waved at the four men, who had paused in their work to listen to the conversation. It was more interesting than the loading of pack horses. "We all slept together in the common room, there. Are you quite finished?"

"Do you have your own dice?"

Brereton looked taken aback at the unexpected question.

Stephen went on, "I know you have your own. You've the look of a gambling man."

Brereton's lips compressed. "What if I do? What's that got to do with anything?"

Stephen held out a hand. "Let me see them."

Brereton glanced at the four laborers. His hand dipped into his belt pouch, fumbled around, and emerged with a small leather tube that was topped with a leather cap.

Stephen uncapped the tube and upended it. A pair of ivory dice fell into his palm. He rolled the dice in his hand. One of the pack horses wore only a saddle blanket, its saddle and panniers on the ground beside it. Stephen swept the saddle blanket from the horse and spread it on the ground. He knelt and cast the dice. The first cast turned up a seven and a five, but the next ones came up snake eyes.

He stood up. "I'll be keeping these, and I'll be letting every tavern and inn within ten miles know about you, Brereton. You get in a game in my territory and I'll have the skin off your back."

Brereton's lips compressed even more than they had before, and he trembled with rage. But he had been caught out and he said nothing.

"And," Stephen said, holding out his hand again, "I'll have your winnings from last night. Although we can't truly call them winnings, can we?"

Brereton's hand drifted to the dagger at his hip, and Stephen thought he would refuse and there would be trouble. Stephen's hand slipped to his own dagger.

"The man no doubt left a widow and children," Stephen said. "They are entitled to compensation for your cheating."

Brereton's nostrils flared, but just when Stephen thought he might draw the dagger, Brereton dug into his pouch for his purse. He loosened the strings and poured silver pennies into his hand. He upended the hand and let the pennies cascade onto Stephen's palm. "Now get out of my way."

There were so many pennies that Stephen needed two hands to contain them all. For a moment, he thought with some alarm that this might have been a ruse to tie up his hands for a sudden attack, which he had fallen for like an idiot. But Brereton turned away and snarled at his laborers, "Get those nags loaded!"

A few of the pennies had fallen to the ground. Stephen retrieved them and retreated to the inn.

Gilbert had carved the corpse out of its clothes down to the braise, which Gilbert left intact since there were women in the much diminished crowd, by the time Stephen returned to the privy. Those having meaningful work to do had long since got to it, leaving the gossipmongers to see and report anything of interest.

More unpleasantness awaited, which could not be avoided, for it involved a close examination of the body for other signs of injuries that might have contributed to the death. The examination revealed no marks other than a few old, healing bruises on the arms and an injured thumb, the sort of wound one often saw upon careless carpenters.

There was, however, a thong around the victim's neck and looped under the left arm: a circlet of leather, which was an odd thing, as people did not wear such things as decoration. Stephen removed the thong from around Feyn's neck and discovered that it was attached to a leather pouch, which had evidently hung down the man's back when he was alive. It was a large pouch, and quite heavy.

Stephen worked the mouth of the pouch open and poured the contents on the ground; or rather, he expected it to pour. But instead of money two iron cylinders about two inches thick by four inches long plopped onto the ground.

"What the devil?" Stephen asked no one in particular. He had never seen anything like these cylinders and had no idea what they were, or why a fellow like Feyn would be carrying them in a hidden purse.

A design had been engraved on one end of each cylinder. Stephen held them out to Gilbert. "What do you make of that?"

Gilbert's eyes narrowed as he bent for a closer look. He ran a finger over the designs. "These are the dies for minting money. No one should have these. No one, but with the proper license from the king."

Chapter 7

Stephen and Gilbert had hardly passed through the door to the inn, the inquest having concluded with the inevitable verdict of death by homicide, when Jennie confronted them.

"Dad," she said, "you've got to see this."

"What have I got to see, dear? Can't you see that we're very busy? We've got to question as many people as we can while their memories are fresh."

"Mum said to come upstairs. She's something odd to show you."

"I've had my fill of odd things today. Can't it wait?"

"It's about that dead man."

Gilbert glanced at Stephen. "Very well. Let's be quick."

Stephen should have let Gilbert handle this oddity and gone on to begin the search for possible witnesses. But that was such a tedious and usually unrewarding business that he let his curiosity pull him up the stairs to the first floor after Jennie and Gilbert.

Jennie led the way to the front room overlooking the street. It was the most expensive chamber in the house, and had a cupboard for clothes, a night table and even a chair. It was well lighted with two great windows that were thrown upon to admit the morning's air and light. Edith stood in the open doorway, a thunderous expression on her face.

"What is it, my dear?" Gilbert asked.

"Look at what that fool did before he died," Edith said.

Gilbert and Stephen stepped around Edith into the chamber. Gilbert gasped at what he saw. A plain cloth satchel lay in the middle of the floor. It was empty and its contents had been strewn about. But that wasn't what had Edith upset. The chamber, in addition to its other furnishings, had a poster bed with curtains and a feather mattress and feather pillows. The mattress had been pulled off the bed, its linen bag cut open and the feathers dumped out. There were feathers everywhere. The pillows had received the same treatment.

"Why would he do that to a perfectly good mattress?" Edith demanded.

"I don't think Feyn did this," Stephen said. "It was someone else."

"But why? What's the point? Other than sheer vandalism and love of destruction?"

"Someone came here after Feyn died," Stephen said. "Someone who was looking for something he had."

Gilbert looked thoughtful. "I think you have that right."

Stephen feigned shocked. "Mark this day, Edith. Gilbert agrees with me on something."

"The dies perhaps?" Gilbert said.

"That could be the only thing."

"Companions in crime who had a falling out?"

"That is a likely possibility," Stephen said.

Gilbert prodded the empty satchel, while looking about the room. "These are his only effects. That's odd."

"Why?" Stephen asked.

"He came on foot, without a horse."

Stephen blinked at this seeming change of subject. "So?"

"Most people who take this room are men of substance. They usually have a horse and more baggage than a simple bag."

"Perhaps he stabled his horse elsewhere."

"Perhaps so. But how do you explain the bag?"

"Perhaps he stored his effects elsewhere."

"You don't believe that."

"I don't know what to believe. I am suspending judgment until I have more facts."

"That is unlike you, Stephen. You are learning."

"With all your pestering, you don't give me any choice. He had no obvious companions, either. What man of substance travels alone?"

"Perhaps he stored them somewhere else as well."

"Or perhaps he was trying to elude them."

Gilbert nodded. "That seems most likely. A falling out, they pursued him, and found him here."

Stephen strolled into the chamber, kicking the piles of feathers, trying to capture a thought that raced about the edges of his mind. "It's odd that he would take this chamber, a man of little apparent substance spending so much for a single night's lodging."

"What are you doing!" Edith cried. "You're making the mess worse!"

"Sorry, Edith," Stephen said. "I thought perhaps there might be something underneath that might be important."

"I'll have the girls clean it up," she said. "If they find anything, they'll bring it to you straightaway."

"Have the girls collect these things," Stephen said, indicating Feyn's effects, "and bring them down to my table in the hall."

Stephen sat at his usual table by the hall's great stone fireplace looking down at Feyn's satchel and belongings. There was an extra pair of braies, a pair of stockings, some loose ties for the stockings, and a linen shirt. There was also a hammer and a pair of shears.

Stephen ran his fingers along the hammer. "Odd things to carry about in your satchel."

"Dies, hammers and shears go together," Gilbert said.

"How so?"

"Let's see those dies."

Stephen produced the iron cylinders from his belt pouch.

"Hold this," Gilbert said, returning one of the cylinders to Stephen. "Keep it up, that's it, engraved part toward the ceiling."

Gilbert poised the other die over the one in Stephen's hands. "You first cut a blank coin with the shears from a flat sheet of pure silver. You heat the blanks over a fire until they are soft. Then you put the blank there, upon the lower die." Gilbert touched the spot. "You then put the upper die upon it, like this." Gilbert rested the die in his hands upon the lower cylinder. He took up the hammer. "Then you strike the upper die so." He tapped the die in his hands with the hammer. "And *voila*, now you have money. That's why it's called striking money."

Stephen smiled slightly. "Almost like out of nothing."

"Well, not exactly out of nothing. You have to have the silver. That's hard to get. And expensive, even in ingots."

"This is odd knowledge for a mere innkeeper."

"One my brothers at the monastery had been a moneyer when the Shrewsbury mint was open at the time the Long Coinage was being minted. It's a simple process, really, except for the engraving of the die. That takes talent and experience."

"So you're told."

"Of course. I've never seen it done."

Stephen placed the die on the table and spun it slowly with a finger. He put the die in his pouch and retrieved the other from Gilbert's hands, which he also returned to his pouch. He stood up.

"Where are you going?" Gilbert asked.

"I need to speak to Harry."

"Good Lord, what about?"

"I am not quite sure."

Harry was at his usual place just within Broad Gate, a blanket wrapped around him for warmth since he was in shadow, his begging cup before him. As there were no people in sight having the intention to pass through the gate, he was whittling on a block of wood, where someone's face was beginning to take shape.

There was no bench or other place to sit while conversing with him. Stephen squatted and put his finger in the cup, stirring the few farthings within it like so much soup.

"What's the matter?" Harry asked. "You hard up for money again?"

"I'm always hard up for money," Stephen said, removing his finger from the cup.

"I've told you time and again that you should sell one of those horses of yours. Useless things, horses, spreading shit everywhere and eating you out of house and home. You only need one, anyway. But you're too pigheaded to take advice."

It was true that Stephen had resisted this advice. He had not sold any of them because he had already fallen so low as a result of his misfortunes in Spain that he could not bear the feeling of sinking any deeper by giving one up. Until recently he had had three horses, but he'd been forced to surrender his best horse, a specially trained Andalusian stallion, to buy his way out of a homicide charge. Now he had only the two mares, ordinary riding horses unfit for battle. A knight needed a warhorse to call himself a proper knight, and he longed more than anything to climb out of the pit afforded by his current employment. The pit seemed deeper now, and he had acquired certain enemies hereabout that made the selling of a horse more urgent as he needed money to get away from Ludlow. Yet he had nothing but excuses to put off what needed to be done.

"I shall probably have to do so soon," Stephen allowed.

"Well, get on with it, and keep your hand out of my cup."

Stephen fished into his belt pouch for the pennies he had taken from Brereton. "I need your advice on another matter, Harry."

"Always ready to oblige if the price is right."

"As this is official business, it is your duty to oblige without cost."

"Is this about that dead fellow in the privy? It's a relief folk found only him. It caused me quite a scare."

"Me too, and yes, it is." Stephen held one some of the pennies. "Can you have a look at these?"

Harry peered at the pennies in Stephen's palm. "Why? Where'd you get those? I've never seen you in possession of such riches at one time, except the time I loaned you my savings." His eyes narrowed. "What have you been up to? I'll have you know that I'll not be a partner in crime. I am a well behaved fellow. I want no trouble."

"I just want your professional opinion."

"Professional opinion about what?"

"You're a connoisseur of money. I'd like you to have a look at these."

"What's a connoisseur? I don't speak Dutch."

Stephen smiled. "It's a person with special knowledge."

"Oh, well, why don't you just speak plain English, then? Of course. I am knowledgeable on many subjects. I have nothing to do all day here but to think great thoughts — the nature of the universe, God's plan for us, what is the best and most fit form of government." He raised his arms heavenward while speaking, then let them drop to his lap. "And why should I look at this money?"

"You're a collector of money. I've never met anyone so obsessed with it."

"You're forgetting Edith."

"I wanted to hear your opinion before I confront her."

Harry's eyes narrowed. "You suspect there's something wrong with this money."

"I fear it might be bad money, some of it anyway."

"You can't usually tell bad money from good money just by looking at it."

"You can't?"

"No. Usually it has to be tested on a scale — weighed against the equivalent weight in silver."

"Why is that?"

"Because forgers, if they know their craft, get the imprints right. It's the materials they skimp on, cutting the silver content, using lead, copper or iron instead."

"If copper or iron was used, couldn't that be easily spotted?"

"Not necessarily. That would be the core, but the surface would be faced with silver. Enough certainly to fool the eye."

"What if we clipped them," Stephen suggested, shaking his palm. "Could we tell then?"

Harry's mouth formed an upside down U. "We might."

"You're not sure."

"I've never thought to do that. Never had the need. False coins are rare. The penalties for possessing them are severe enough to discourage people."

"It does happen, though."

"Perhaps in the bigger towns, but Ludlow? I've never worried about it."

"But you have given the matter some thought."

"Anyone in my position does. It's a matter of professional interest, after all. We beggars discuss these things at our conclaves."

"I am glad you do," Stephen said. He closed his fist over the coins. "I haven't anything to clip them with here. But I'll have some for you to look at after supper."

Gilbert was waiting in the hall when Stephen returned from Broad Gate with word that they had been summoned by the undersheriff, Walter Henle, to the castle.

"I think he's upset that we didn't report immediately to him about the fellow in the privy," Gilbert said as they hurried out to Bell Lane and up the hill to High Street.

"I would say we've been rather busy investigating the death, wouldn't you?" Stephen said. "Can't he understand that we must act quickly before the witnesses disperse? By the way, you've interviewed everyone who might have seen or heard anything, haven't you?"

"All but Harry. I trust you've taken care of that."

"Of course," Stephen lied. It had not occurred to him to ask Harry if he'd seen or heard anything last evening, although he should have done. "And what did you learn?"

"No one saw or heard anything untoward."

"I wonder how much of that is true."

"I doubt we shall ever know."

"We've done all that could be expected of us, at any rate. It's a matter for the sheriff anyway. Not our affair. Time to pass off the unrewarding business."

"Certainly the matter of those dies are. You have them still? His messenger asked after them."

Stephen patted his pouch. "They're safe here."

Henle received them in the castle's hall, a great timber building over a stone undercroft that stood between two towers on the north wall of the inner bailey.

Henle steepled his fingers when Stephen and Gilbert stood before him. "I've been led to understand that this fellow Feyn had the dies for making money in his possession," Henle said. "Where are they?"

"Here," Stephen said. He put the dies on the table.

Henle rolled them on the table top and inspected the engravings at their ends. "I wonder how he came by them," Henle mused, a question that did not seem to call for an answer so Stephen and Gilbert said nothing. "This is no ordinary death. It is a matter of great importance. We must find out how he acquired them. And he must have had accomplices. I made inquiry about the fellow and he did not seem the sort to have acted alone." Henle directed a finger at Stephen. "I shall need a full report from you on what you've learned. In writing, right away. The sheriff will want to know everything." Henle took up one of the die. "I shall dispatch your letter and these to Hereford first thing tomorrow."

"Of course," Stephen said, glad that Henle seemed eager to take over this unpleasantness.

"Meanwhile, you shall continue your inquiry," Henle said.

"I shall?" Stephen asked, his relief punctured.

"Of course you shall. This is a crown matter. You are the person best suited for it." Henle said this, however, with some reluctance and a dash of distaste, for he had no affection for Stephen. "I want you to find out how Feyn got these dies and what he proposed to do with them. You shall report all your findings directly to me, and to me alone. Do good work and perhaps you will redeem yourself."

"I have no need for redemption."

"Percival FitzAllan thinks otherwise."

"He is mistaken."

"He says you conspired with the enemies of the king to do harm to his grace's friends."

"I was engaged to find the killers of some salt merchants, nothing more." There had, in fact, been quite a bit more, and FitzAllan was right, although Stephen would not say so.

"If you find out what Feyn was up to and we catch his accomplices, I will put a good word in for you. The king will be much concerned about the counterfeiting of his coin. He will reward those who put a stop to it."

"I shall be pleased to assist," Stephen said, doubting that Henle's word carried much weight with either the king or Prince Edward, and not being pleased at all. It was bad enough that he had to pursue work that he found distasteful, but worse that he would be under Henle's thumb while he did it, since Henle was sure to grab the greater part of the credit for himself. "What about my expenses? This is likely to be a costly undertaking."

Henle pursed his lips, taken aback at the question. He had clearly not considered the ramifications of his order. "Just don't be profligate."

"I shall do my best, your honor," Stephen said.

"See that you do."

"I am surprised you agreed," Gilbert said as they descended the stairs to the bailey.

"I don't know what came over me," Stephen said. "It was the scent of blackmail, I suppose."

"I for one am glad. I have been worried that we might not have an answer for the matter, and that it will reflect badly on the inn. It's bad for business to have guests murdered in the yard, the sort of thing that could put us out of business if not resolved. If we left the inquiry to Henle, he'd just bollix it up."

"That's why he's forcing us to do it, while he takes the credit. Just like the business with the emeralds."

"We are too good for our own good."

"With no reward at the end."

The writing of the letter took longer than it should have. People of Stephen's class never wrote down their own letters, but instead dictated them to clerks. However, the chief clerk was ill and his adjutant was nowhere to be found. The letter had to be in either Latin or French because no one wrote letters in English except merchants. Stephen could speak French, of course; his mother had taken pains to ensure that, although the business of the manor and the household where he grew up had been conducted in English, for fluency in French was one of the great distinctions of the gentry from those below them who labored. Gilbert's French was not up to the task despite his long association with the coroner, Sir Geoffrey Randall; it was just good enough to take orders or get by in casual conversation but not practiced in the formal phrasing required for such a letter, nor was he sure about the spelling, which was more complicated than Latin. But Stephen was wary of his Latin and did not want to rely upon it, for making a good impression on the sheriff seemed a good idea. So he dictated in English, which Gilbert then put down in Latin, a halting process that involved much thought-gathering and false starts. Then the draft had to be copied over in clerk hand.

By the time they finished, the sun had started its course toward the horizon and was casting lengthening shadows from the walls into the bailey.

A spring breeze greeted them as they emerged from the castle into the broad expanse of High Street, carrying away the aromas of horse manure, smoke and privy that were the signature scents of the town. Stephen breathed deeply at the momentary freshness; it was a luxury enjoyed mainly by those wealthy enough to have a house here, such as the goldsmith Leofwine Wattepas, whose tall house loomed at the corner of Mill Street. Like all houses in town, its shop occupied the ground floor, the windows' shutters down to admit light and

Bad Money

the fresh air, Wattepas' apprentices and journeymen visible within hard at work.

"Don't goldsmiths know how to spot false coin?" Stephen asked, nodding toward Wattepas' shop.

"I would think so," Gilbert said. "Metals are a goldsmith's business."

As Stephen veered toward the shop, Gilbert added, "You don't think that Feyn was actually passing false coin?"

"I don't know. I want to find out."

"Oh, dear!" Gilbert exclaimed. "You don't think he paid for his chamber with bad money, do you?"

"He might have," Stephen said.

Gilbert shook his head. "Dear me, it will mean we have to inspect every penny we've taken in to spot them!"

"I suspect you may have to. I wouldn't want you or Edith to lose a hand, after all," Stephen said, for the penalties for passing bad money were harsh and the court often made no allowance for the innocent who came into possession, particularly if a large number of coins was involved.

One of the journeymen at Wattepas' put aside the bowl he was shaping with a hammer on a wooden dish, and came to the window. Stephen recognized him but could not remember his name. "Can I help you, sir?" the journeyman asked.

"I'd like to see the master," Stephen said.

The journeyman frowned. "He's not in."

"When will he be back?"

"I don't know, sir." The journeyman hesitated. "He went out this morning and hasn't come back yet."

"Who's there, Oslar?" called a woman's voice from the interior of the house, which Stephen recognized as belonging to Wattepas' wife, Lucy.

"It's Sir Stephen Attebrook, madam!" Oslar called over his shoulder.

Lucy Wattepas emerged from the rear of the house. There were few people in Ludlow who presented a more severe image than Mistress Wattepas, her major rival being the gossip

Felicitas Bartelot. She wore an expensive embroidered wimple that made her face seem larger and more severe than it might have done without it, emphasizing her receding chin and overbite, her nose appearing large and dominating. But it was her eyes that one was most drawn to, piercing and judgmental, a cold gray, eager to find fault and assess social position, always in a way that might put her on a rung above whomever she dealt with.

"My husband has gone out," she said crisply in a tone that seemed intended to dismiss all further questions about the matter. "If you have business, you shall have to come back later."

"Perhaps one of his boys could help," Stephen said, indicating Oslar and the other two journeymen, one of them a recently promoted apprentice who had taken the place of a journeymen caught up in an affair of stolen emeralds and murdered last month.

"What is your business, then?" Mistress Wattepas asked, in a way that suggested Stephen could not possibly have business with a goldsmith, since he teetered on the edge of pauperhood, where by rights he should have fallen long ago and no doubt properly belonged. "I am as capable of handling matters as anyone here."

Stephen was surprised she would offer her services. "I need to find out if this is good money."

Mistress Wattepas regarded the pennies in Stephen's hand. "Oslar, fetch the scales and the weights."

"Right away, madam," Oslar said. He hurried to a cupboard to the right, and came back with the scales and a small box, which he put on the counter and stepped back.

Mistress Wattepas made no move to take the money, and continued to look at Stephen with pursed lips. He realized that she had no intention of plucking coins from his palm, for that might force her to touch him. He dribbled the coins onto the counter top. Mistress Wattepas selected half a dozen pennies, which she deposited upon one pan of the scales. She opened the box and removed several small weights which she put on the other pan of the scale. The pans teetered up and down and finally came to rest, the one with the money only a tad beneath the other.

"Inconclusive," Mistress Wattepas sniffed, leaning close to peer at the pennies in the pan. "Could have been clipped, but that doesn't make them bad."

"I had been so sure ..." Stephen said, disappointed.

"Wait!" Mistress Wattepas commanded. She took up one of the pennies and held it up to the light, turning it about and rubbing it with her fingers. She contemplated the penny. "Michael! Go get a jar of vinegar and the salt bowl from the kitchen! And an empty bowl!"

The apprentice so addressed rushed back into the depths of the house. Stephen could hear him calling to one of the servants for the items Mistress Wattepas wanted.

It wasn't long before Michael came back to the shop. He put a clay jar and the salt bowl on the counter by the small pile of pennies along with an empty wooden bowl.

Mistress Wattepas poured vinegar from the jar into the empty bowl and added two pinches of salt. She stirred this mixture with a long, bony finger on which there was a ring with a large blue stone. She wiped her fingers on a cloth, careful not to get any of the vinegar on the ring. Then she dropped the penny she had inspected into the vinegar. "We shall let it rest a moment," she said.

When she judged the moment had passed, Mistress Wattepas recovered the penny from the vinegar and wiped it on the cloth. What Stephen had thought was the dull gray of tarnished silver had been replaced by the sheen of copper.

Mistress Wattepas put the false penny on the counter. "Bad money, all right."

"What about the rest?"

"You've seen the trick of it. I shall leave it to you."

Chapter 8

"You want vinegar," said Baldwin, the inn's chief cook, perplexed. "Are you ill?"

"And salt," Gilbert said.

"Salt? Salt and vinegar? I've never heard of that kind of remedy. What is the matter?"

"Nothing is the matter, except perhaps for a little sickness of heart," Gilbert said. "Now off with you. We haven't time to waste."

"It might not be that bad," Stephen said as the cook went off to the pantry.

"I fear the worst," Gilbert said. "Wait until Edith finds out."

The cook returned with a pot and a wooden box. He put them on the kitchen table. "There you go." It was now late in the afternoon, almost supper time, but instead of backing away to prepare dinner's leftovers for supper, Baldwin stood and watched.

"Don't you have work to do?" Gilbert asked.

"Certainly," Baldwin said, not moving.

"People are hungry," Gilbert said.

"I know," Baldwin said.

Gilbert took up the pot of vinegar and peered inside. "Not much here." He fetched a bowl from the shelf, poured the vinegar into the bowl, and added a couple of pinches of salt from the box as they had seen Mistress Wattepas do.

"Now you," Gilbert said.

Stephen fished in his pouch for the pennies, which he plopped into the bowl. He stirred them with a finger, now and then taking up a penny and rubbing it.

"Washing money," Baldwin murmured, watching at this operation as if he was witnessing alchemy. "Or are you trying to turn it into gold?"

"A cloth," Stephen demanded after some time.

Baldwin hastened to sacrifice his apron, eager to see the results of this alchemy.

Stephen rubbed the pennies, one at a time, and deposited each on the table. When he was done, he had thirteen gleaming copper pennies and three silver ones.

"Damn it," Gilbert said. "Damn it to hell."

Stephen's brows rose at this unaccustomed profanity.

"What's going on?" Baldwin asked.

"None of your business," Gilbert said.

"This has to do with that fellow in the privy, doesn't it?" Baldwin asked.

"Never you mind. Forget what you've seen. Tell no one."

Stephen sympathized with Gilbert's upset. Once it got around that the inn had accepted bad money, it might be hard for the inn to pay its bills, since its creditors would fear the coin it offered in compensation.

"We'll have to check every penny," Gilbert sighed.

"I'm afraid so," Stephen said. He slid the three good pennies toward Baldwin. "Have one of the boys run up to the wine shop for more vinegar. We're going to need a lot of it."

Edith Wistwode received the news that they would have to wash every penny the inn possessed better than Stephen or Gilbert expected. There was no stamping, shouting, cursing or hair pulling. No frothing mouth or rolling on the floor. There was but a grim frown, crossed arms and a tapping foot as she gazed at the copper pennies on the kitchen table.

"Well, that's it then," Edith said, surrendering to necessity. "There isn't time to do it today. We've supper to get out. And there won't be time in the morning. We'll have to do it tomorrow afternoon. You and I, and no one else. Can't trust the staff around so much money."

"What about Stephen?" Gilbert asked. "We should have a witness."

Edith eyed Stephen as if he was a rat who had slipped into the kitchen. "I suppose he will have to do."

"I appreciate your trust," Stephen said.

"You're welcome," Edith said before she stalked out to the hall.

As the discovery of the false money was supposed to be a secret, it didn't take long before the entire town knew about it. At dinner the following day, some of the craftsmen and shopkeepers in the neighborhood who stopped by for a bun and cup of ale, suggested that the inn be renamed the Bad Penny or something similar. Other jokes were uttered at the front window, none of which Edith found to be funny or tasteful, but there was nothing she could do to stop them.

Consequently, Edith was in an even more foul mood as her daughter Jennie and the servants cleared away the dinner plates and wooden trenchers, and applied themselves to sweeping the floor, while Edith superintended to ensure the capture of every speck of dirt tracked in.

"Fetch the box," she ordered Gilbert at the foot of the stairs, which mounted to the upper floors of the inn to the left of the great fireplace.

"You know how heavy it is, dear," Gilbert said. "I don't think I can manage by myself. I shall have Mark fetch it."

"You'll do no such thing," Edith snapped. "I'll have no one else near the money but us."

"Very well," Gilbert said, head drooping, which lowered his inconsiderable height even more. He turned to climb the stairs.

Stephen slipped around Edith and followed Gilbert to the first floor and down the hallway to the rear of the house, where the master bedchamber occupied the corner overlooking the yard.

Gilbert fumbled with a ring of keys at the chamber door. He found the appropriate key and unlocked the door. "I don't think you should come in."

"Is it really that heavy?"

"There is quite a lot of money, I'm afraid."

Stephen remained in the doorway while Gilbert crossed to a cupboard by the bed, which was also locked. He unlocked the cupboard. There was a large chest at the bottom of it. Gilbert grasped the handles and lifted it with a groan that became a gasp as the chest slipped from his fingers and crashed to the floor.

"Oh, dear," Gilbert said. "My poor back."

Stephen entered the chamber. "Go down and clear the hall. I don't anyone to see."

Gilbert nodded and left the chamber.

Stephen bent down and lifted the chest. It was, indeed, extraordinarily heavy, and a grunt escaped his lips as he stood up with it.

He lumbered out into the hallway to the top of the stairs. "Is it clear?" he called out.

"It's clear!" Gilbert called back from the bottom.

Stephen contemplated the stairs with indecision and some dismay. They were almost as steep as a ladder, and he wasn't sure that he could get the box down without falling or dropping the box. It was this obstacle that had prompted him to offer his assistance, since he had been sure that Gilbert could not have managed it. He hit upon the solution of backing down the stairs, depositing the chest on one stair at a time, until he reached the hall.

"There you go, Edith," Stephen said, panting at the struggle and glad there was no one about to see him performing manual labor, grateful that Gilbert had thought to close the shutters as well. "Where do you want it?"

"In the kitchen," she said.

Edith threw a table cloth over the kitchen's largest table to prevent any coins, which were no larger than a man's fingernail, from falling into any cracks and being lost as pennies left about were prone to do.

With the chest on the table, Gilbert began counting the money and separating it into one shilling piles. Edith took one pile at a time and washed it in the vinegar and salt solution in a cooking pot. This was a time-consuming task, especially since each coin had to be rubbed dry to ensure that any tarnish, should it be false money, came off.

No one other than Stephen was allowed in the kitchen while this went on, not even Jennie, although Gil the younger, Gilbert and Edith's son, raced through a couple of times despite his mother's sharp orders to stay out.

Toward the end of the day, Baldwin stuck his head in and inquired what he was to do about supper. Although Gilbert had joined in washing money after he had counted it, they were only half way through, and Edith told him to take what bread and cheese they had in the buttery and use that.

While Baldwin and his helpers fetched food, with Edith standing between them and the kitchen table to impede their view, Jennie came to the doorway.

"Mistress Wattepas is here," Jennie said, drawing her mouth down in an effort to elongate her round face in imitation of Mistress Wattepas. "She wants to see Sir Stephen."

Stephen roused himself from his stool where he had been napping. Who would have known that washing money was so tedious? He rose and stretched. "What does she want?"

"I have no idea," Jennie said. "She didn't say. Just ordered me to fetch you out. 'Fetch Sir Stephen, if you please.'" Jennie's voice gave a good imitation of Mistress Wattepas' upper class accent even down to the sharp, dismissive tone.

"I'm to be fetched, eh? Let's go see what she wants."

Mistress Wattepas was seated at Stephen's favorite table near the fireplace, gazing into the fire. She did not rise when Stephen came up, as she should have done, given their differing social positions, but Stephen did nothing about that. The girl with Mistress Wattepas did stand, however, and it took all Stephen's self-control not to gape at her. She was perhaps sixteen or seventeen, which meant of marriageable age, but her auburn hair fell down her back in a single thick braid, signifying she was not yet married. She might have been taken for a maid, since Mistress Wattepas was not the sort to go about without a gaggle of them. But there was something about the girl that suggested she was something more. Perhaps it was her shift, a fine maroon with long sleeves. Or her face, which bore something of a resemblance to Leofwine Wattepas' in its squareness, the cleft in the chin and the same eyes, although there was nothing blockish or masculine about her appearance. This girl had the look of a daughter, and so must be Adele. Stephen had heard about her but had never seen her. Stephen slipped onto his bench opposite the two and the girl sank down as well, her eyes toward the floor so there was no chance their gazes might meet.

"Good afternoon, Mistresses," Stephen said, "or I should say good evening." He hoped there would be an introduction to this girl, but none was forthcoming.

"Is it?" Mistress Wattepas asked. "Good, I mean? I suppose it is for someone."

"Is something the matter?"

Mistress Wattepas' mouth turned down, becoming more severe than ever. "Yes, there is." She took a deep breath, as if what she was about to say took some effort. "My husband — he has disappeared. I should like you to find him."

It took Stephen a few moments to digest this declaration. People, especially prosperous craftsmen who were pillars of the town, did not just disappear. "I don't understand," he said.

Mistress Wattepas' fingers twined and untwined and then twined again. "He went out yesterday morning. He always goes out at dawn. He takes walks, you see. Every day, first thing, as the boys open the shop. For his constitution, he says. Who ever heard of such a thing!"

"I had no idea."

"Of course you didn't. We never speak of it. It is so . . . unconventional. He isn't gone long, an hour at most, I suppose. Yesterday he did not come back."

"And you're only now searching for him?"

"I had the boys look everywhere yesterday evening!"

"I see."

"I don't know what to do! Something has happened to him! Something terrible, I'm sure!" Mistress Wattepas blinked as if there might be a tear coming, but none appeared. Her lips were a thin line.

"And you want me to find him?"

"Him or what befell him. But him, if he still lives, by the grace of God."

Stephen nodded. "I would like to, but I've been ordered by Walter Henle to attend to another matter."

"I don't care what Henle wants. I will pay. I'm sure he will not."

Stephen hesitated, torn between his desperate need for money and the obligations of honor dictated by his position.

At that moment, the girl met his gaze. Her eyes were arresting, the color of slate. "Can you not help us, sir? There is no one else who can!"

Chapter 9

The women had gone by the time Harry returned from his post at Broad Gate. The sun was nearly down, the yard was in shadow, and night's chill was setting in.

Stephen saw Harry clump through the gate on his board with its rockers, propelling himself with his arms, his fists clad in thick leather gloves to protect them from the hazards of the street. He almost went out there, but instead he went back to the kitchen to see what progress had been made. He was glad to find that Gilbert and Edith had finished washing the money, the air still thick with the fumes of vinegar. Gilbert was counting the pennies to compare his concluding tally with the one made at the beginning to ensure that no penny went unaccounted for, except for the pile of copper coins that lay on the tabletop.

"How much?" Stephen asked.

"Two shillings, almost," Edith replied with disgust. "I should have suspected something, a man like that spending so freely. I let myself be taken in."

"Don't be so hard on yourself, dear," Gilbert said, finishing up his tally. "It could have happened to anyone.

"It should never happen to us," Edith said grimly. "Such a mistake could ruin us."

"What did Mistress Wattepas want?" Gilbert asked, shutting the lid on the chest.

"Leofwine Wattepas has gone missing," Stephen said.

"What?" Gilbert and Edith burst out together, for it was an astonishing notion, and perhaps even more astonishing that they were just now learning about it, Ludlow being such a small town that one man's business, no matter how private, was soon known to everyone, as one could see from the matter of the bad money.

"And she asked you to find him," Edith said.

"She seemed quite upset," Stephen said.

"I would be too if my sole base of support suddenly vanished off the face of the earth," she said.

"Now, Edith," Gilbert said, "perhaps she does care for him."

"I cannot imagine her caring for anything but herself and her position," Edith said. "Let's get that thing upstairs where it belongs."

The chest seemed no lighter for its loss of two shillings, but going up was easier than coming down, and in the darkness of the hall few, if anyone, noticed that the person carrying the load was the one who should not have done.

Stephen went no farther than the top of the stairs. Gilbert and Edith between them were strong enough for this chest on a level floor, and they did not seem eager for his assistance beyond this point.

So he left them and went out to see Harry, to ask the question that he had forgotten to ask before.

Harry was eating his supper, grumbling about the fact that it was only bread and cheese, the sort of thing one usually had for breakfast, instead of the delightful leftovers from dinner.

"Have you solved the mystery yet?" Harry asked through a mouthful of bread.

"Swallow before speaking," said Jennie, who was seated on the bench beside him. "You don't want to embarrass yourself before his honor."

"He's seen me eat before."

"And no doubt been appalled at your lack of manners."

Harry swallowed. "Sorry."

"That's better." Jennie stood up. "I suppose they're done, then?"

Stephen nodded. "Just took the chest back to the bedchamber."

"I'd better go." Jennie hurried toward the house, glancing at the windows to the master bedchamber, which were shut but might be thrown open at any moment for the last light of the day so that expensive candles or smelly lamps fueled by pig fat did not have to be lit. Harry watched her wistfully, taking another bite out of his cheese.

Stephen opened his mouth to ask about Feyn when Harry, first remembering to swallow his cheese, said, "What were the Wattepases doing here? Lucy Wattepas would rather be struck dead before showing her face among the common folk."

"Master Wattepas has disappeared. The Wattepases, you said?"

"He's gone missing? What rot. Probably dead drunk at the Pigeon stretched over some whore. Yes, the Wattepases, Lucy and her youngest whelp."

Stephen gazed across the yard. "So the girl was Lucy's whelp and not a maid."

Harry opened his mouth to speak, paused and cocked an eyebrow. "I detect a bit of salacious interest."

"What? Nonsense. They came on business."

"Ha! They want you to find Wattepas! And you agreed?"

Stephen shrugged without speaking. In point of fact, he had agreed, although it was against his better judgment, since the Feyn matter should, by rights, take precedence. He had not worked out how he would address both at the same time.

"Did she show you any leg as an enticement?"

"Shut up, Harry. She is a decent girl."

"You *are* interested."

"I am not. I can't afford to be interested. Besides she ..."

"Is beneath you."

"I didn't say that." This was true, however, although he had not thought such a thing until Harry suggested it.

"And she's a Wattepas. Who'd want to marry into that family?"

"Maurce Crauford, or so I heard. This conversation has gone well beyond where it should."

Harry laughed. "My favorite kind. Most people are so boring, but you're always full of surprises, and pulling your third leg is so easy. But you did not come out to wax lustily about the comely Adele Wattepas."

"No, I wanted to know if you heard anything the other night."

"Like what?"

"Like murder."

"What does murder sound like? The last time I was involved in such a thing, I remember it being rather silent, apart from a few gasps." Last autumn Harry had strangled a man to death at the doorway to the stable. He and Stephen had disposed of the body in the privy pit, and that was the body they had thought had been discovered.

"You heard no sounds of argument? No shouting?"

Harry frowned. "I heard voices, I think. But they were in argument, but not all that angry. I went to see what was the matter, but no one was in the yard."

"When was this?"

"An hour or so after sundown? I don't know."

"But you had not yet gone to bed."

"I like to sit up, thinking about things."

"You're not still making carvings for sale?"

"My fingers like to keep busy. I don't know what happens to them when they leave my hands. There is one thing, though."

"What?"

"You promise not to tell anyone?"

"What possible secrets could you have that might interest anyone, except perhaps Edith?"

"Well, I did part with a carving to that fellow who died."

"Of Rosamond?" Stephen asked. Rosamond was the name of a girl found dead at Christmas in Saint Laurence's churchyard. Many people thought she was a saint, although Stephen had found that she was an ordinary girl who had fallen into terrible misfortune that had eventually led to her death.

Bad Money

"He'd heard about her. Like everyone, he thought her likeness might bring him luck. Apparently he thought he needed it. He seemed to be in some sort of trouble."

"Did he say what?"

"No, he just seemed fretful, worried about something."

"When did this happen?"

"After I'd had my supper and retired for the night. Not long before I heard that argument, now that I think about it."

"He came to your stall?" Stephen asked. Harry lived in the last stall on the left which was otherwise reserved for storing hay.

Harry nodded. "Don't know how he found me."

"Jennie tell him?"

"She might have. Though everybody knows where I live. Now that I think about it, I heard the voices right after he left."

"How much did you get for it? The carving?"

"A full penny."

"It was probably bad money."

"Shit!"

Stephen stood up. "All the money Feyn lost at dice was bad, and Gilbert and Edith have almost two shillings that's nothing but copper."

"I've been cheated!"

"Apparently you're not the only one."

"I'd kill him myself if he wasn't already dead," Harry fumed. "You think that Feyn's killer is among his circle of victims?"

"That seems the most likely possibility."

"You've had a look at his room, I suppose."

Stephen nodded.

"Did you find my carving? I'll have it back, if you don't mind."

Stephen paused in midstep. "You know, we didn't find any carving. That's odd. Good evening, Harry."

"If it turns up, you know where to find me!"

Stephen hardly heard. His mind was on Adele. Adele — he said the name several times to himself as he crossed the yard to the inn.

Chapter 10

Stephen sat on his window sill despite the chill, naked except for his braises, dismayed at the prospect of the tedious inquiries that awaited him this morning, the limping from one witness to the next, the same questions and the same useless answers that more often than not led nowhere but to sore feet, especially for his bad one, and an aching back and frayed temper. He had no idea what to do about Wattepas and doubted he would find out anything, and he was at even more of a loss in the Feyn matter. At least the Wattepas matter promised a fee, which took him in the direction he wanted to go, which was as far away from Ludlow as he could get before Percival FitzAllan denounced him as a traitor. Then it occurred to him that Lucy Wattepas might not be inclined to pay anything if he came up empty, and it would be unseemly for him to press for payment then. He regretted taking the commission now. What had he been thinking?

"I am an idiot," he said to himself, realizing that today being Sunday there was likely to be racing on the meadow north of the castle, a time when many bargains were struck over horses. Yet he still shrank from that course. He had already sunk so low from his heady days of success in Spain, where he had acquired a fortune only to have it snatched away with the fall of Rodrigo's castle, that he could not bear the thought of slipping any lower. But despite his hopes and best intentions, no matter how desperately he clung to what he had, he seemed to slip lower down the slope with each day. It was a waking nightmare which he could not escape.

Then Harry swung out of the stable on his board and paused at the bench by the door where Jennie had set his breakfast, and Stephen was reminded that the bottom of the pit was far lower down than where he stood. That reminder frightened him more than he cared to admit.

Harry looked up, a square of cheese suspended before his mouth. "You thinking of jumping?" he called. "Go ahead! It will end the misery! Just don't expect me to speak at the wake!"

"I know you'll have nothing good to say."

"Oh, I could talk about what a devious rascal you are, but your reputation's so bad now that I doubt I could drag it any lower." He waved a hand. "Anyway, jump or get out of that window before some of the good wives of the town see you. You are indecent. Have a care! People will start to say this is a bawdy house. Then I'll have to move to a more respectable establishment."

Stephen laughed. "It's good to see you, Harry. Try to stay out of trouble."

"Trouble? Me? Before you came to town my life was uneventful!"

Harry took out his whittling knife and applied it to the bench while he chewed on his cheese, and Stephen noticed for the first time that he had already made some progress in carving one corner with an interesting, Celtic design. Stephen wondered why he hadn't noticed that yesterday.

No one should try to get the last word with Harry, so Stephen withdrew from the window, for Harry was right. The tongues of the good wives of Ludlow would waggle if anyone caught a glimpse of him in the window, and there was a good chance that if he lingered one of them down the hill might do so, for it was a glorious morning, marked by an achingly blue sky, fleecy clouds, and a golden sun that promised to warm the greening countryside this spring day, which meant that at any moment one of those wives would emerge to tend her garden, and there were quite a few such gardens between him and the city wall below. It was too fine and rare a day to waste in the pursuit of answers he would never find: better to put together a picnic and take it down by the river and watch the swans and ducks in the current, get drunk before noon and dream of having his own manor house with its little stretch of river.

But he had work that could not be avoided.

Stephen met Gilbert in the hall, where they collected their breakfast and went out to the yard, neither of them enthused about the task ahead, but Gilbert a little more so than Stephen, for it allowed him to avoid the chores that Edith might heap upon him if he stayed home, even though it was Sunday. There was no escaping chores at an inn.

Rather than head straight out the gate, Stephen paused to inspect Harry's work on the bench. As he knelt for a close view, Gilbert wiped his hands on his coat, and said, "So Harry's taken to defacing our property, now? I will have to have a sharp word with him. This can't be tolerated."

Stephen stood up. "If you're worried about the value of your bench, I'll take it off your hands."

"What do you want a mere plank bench for?"

"I want to see where Harry takes this."

"I don't know. It is such a fine bench. And you can't afford a decent pair of stockings at the moment, let alone a bench like this." Since Randall's wounding at the second battle for Clun, neither of them had seen a penny in wages.

"Quit being difficult. It's only a few planks pegged together. No one uses it but me and Harry."

"I suppose," Gilbert said, turning toward the gate. "Although I don't see what good a mutilated bench is going to be to you."

"I am fond of the bench. I shall miss it when I go. Perhaps I will take it with me as a reminder of all the good times we have had together while sitting upon it. Perhaps I will ask Harry to add a likeness of you upon your mule. That is a sight I do wish to remember."

"It is unseemly to make light of someone's suffering," Gilbert said as they turned the corner onto Broad Street and headed up the hill.

"You have to admit, it is a funny sight."

"Yes, clinging for dear life with death on either side. It is a long way down."

"I know. I've fallen many times."

"Really? I would never have thought."

"Even the best take a spill now and then, you know."

"I suppose that's true. I attended the death of a lord who broke his neck in a fall from his horse some years ago." Gilbert wagged a finger at Stephen. "Which is why I am opposed to getting about upon a horse."

"Or in your case, a mule."

"I do it only because I am forced to do so, and would appreciate it if you would not make fun."

"Well, I've never laughed out loud at your misadventures with the mule."

This conversation might have gone further, but they reached John Spicer's wine shop at the corner of Broad and High, where they turned toward the castle. John the Younger, who ran the shop, waved at them from the doorway and called "Good morning!" which required them to answer.

If Stephen or Gilbert expected the exchange to consist of mere civilities, they were disappointed, for John asked, "Have you learned anything yet?"

"Not yet," Stephen said. "We're still making our inquiries."

Gilbert suppressed a grin, since they had not made any inquiries yet.

"Ah," said John, disappointed at not being the first to learn some new gossip.

"You wouldn't perhaps have seen Wattepas Friday morning, would you?" Stephen asked, stabbing in the dark.

"Why, yes, in fact I did. He went by the shop, like he did every morning except Sundays. I hardly remarked upon it at the time. Is it important?"

"Where did he go?"

"That way." John waved toward the east.

"Toward Galdeford Gate?"

"Well, I don't know if that's where he was going, but in that direction." John frowned, remembering a detail. "Always in a hurry in the morning, rushing so."

"What do you mean?"

"He always seemed to be in a rush. He'd hurry by, said good morning, of course, but only out of politeness, and distracted like, as if his mind was on something."

"I see," Stephen said, although he didn't see what this had to do with anything. He let silence fall to encourage John to go on.

John did. "When he came back, he didn't seem so much in a hurry. Not glad to be getting to work, I guess. Although, I must say, it must be good to have journeymen and apprentices who can put out the work and all you have to do is watch them. That's hardly work at all."

"I think Wattepas did more than merely supervise."

"I suppose. Say, do you think I'm the last person to see him alive?"

"I hope not."

A tailor from down the street on his Sunday stroll stopped to gossip and inquire about wine prices, so John turned away to pursue profit over gossip.

Stephen paused in the street. He gazed toward the Wattepas house, where he had been intending to begin the search, but he reckoned that he had enough from John to get started, which was too bad. He had been hoping to catch a glimpse of Adele Wattepas. The last time he had felt a pull of such intensity was with Margaret de Thottenham, and his relations with her had brought as much trouble as pleasure. Desire was such torture. He wished that he did not have such feelings. He had still not gotten over Taresa's death, even though more than a year had passed since a fever had swept her away leaving him with a small child he hadn't seen in months, another thing that gnawed at his conscience and that he needed to set right. Better to stay away, he decided.

Now the tedium began in earnest, as Stephen and Gilbert passed down High Street by the drapers' and grocers' shops and into Butcher's Row and at last to the crossroads where High met Corve and Old Streets, the broad open space known as the Bullring. On market days, the place was crowded with animals and their sellers — sheep, goats, chickens, cattle and horses in their temporary pens of wicker thrown up to confine them — and the buyers wandering about, examining a potential purchase, haggling over prices or swilling ale at the taverns around the Ring. But today it was deserted and all the shops closed so that they had to bang on the doors to get anyone's attention.

At every shop they passed they confirmed what John Spicer told them: that Wattepas went by early in the morning heading this way, as was his usual practice; no one thought anything about it or paid much attention since they were used to seeing him. Now that Stephen and Gilbert had reached the Bullring, they split up to question the tavern keepers round about since Wattepas could have taken any one of the three routes out of the Ring.

Stephen worked his way around to the right while Gilbert went to the left. They met at Galdeford Street, which left the Bullring only a short distance from Galdeford Gate.

Gilbert, who was chewing on a sweet bun, shook his head as they came together. "You?"

"Nothing," Stephen said.

"I suppose there's nothing for it but to work our ways down the streets," Gilbert said, sweeping his arm to encompass Galdeford, Old and Corve streets. He seemed no more enthusiastic than Stephen felt about the trudging and repetitive inquiries that would be necessary.

Stephen heard a rattling behind him. A voice asked, "You fellows mightn't be able to spare a farthing, would you?"

Stephen turned to see you had spoken, for the voice was close by and seemed to be directed at him. When he turned, the speaker said, "Oh, it's you two. Never mind. Away with your bad money."

"Hello, Dick," Stephen said. "Aren't you out of place?" This was One-eye Dick, one of the beggars of the town who normally worked at the Galdeford Gate. He was dressed in rags almost as frayed and worn as Harry's. Whereas Harry lacked legs, Dick was missing an eye, a feature he used to good effect when begging, for he flipped up his patch so passersby could see the empty socket, the flesh within wrinkled and pink. He often walked with a crutch, although he was not crippled, his stockings down to reveal a seeping sore when he had one. But today he was without his crutch or a sore, and was seated on a box at the entrance to the Black Lion tavern at the corner where Galdeford Street emptied into the Bullring.

"Nah," Dick said. "I'm all legal. Got a license to beg the market. What you done for Harry gave him an unfair advantage. The rest of us got to keep up, or he'll snag all the good charity." Some time ago, Stephen had obtained a license for Harry to beg the weekly market on High Street, a very coveted location. "Say, got any good money to spare? What about you, Gilbert? You're a rich fellow. You must have at least one good penny."

Gilbert peered into Dick's cup. "It looks like you've been doing quite well for a Sunday. Isn't it illegal to beg on Sundays?"

"It ain't been a bad day," Dick said, ignoring the suggestion of illegality. He rattled his cup and winked his good eye. "It could be better if you'd help out. No?" He sat back, disappointed. "Say, I saw you snooping about the Ring. What's going on? It about that dead fellow in your privy? Bad for business, people getting murdered like that."

"No," Gilbert said. "It's not. It's about Wattepas."

"Leofwine Wattepas?" Dick asked. "I heard he'd disappeared. Run off to get away from that wife of his, I don't doubt."

"You didn't happen to see him Friday morning?" Stephen asked.

"Don't know if I did," Dick answered. "That's so long ago. My memory don't go back that far." He rattled his cup again. "But it might be encouraged, if I think on it hard enough."

Stephen sighed. He and Gilbert exchanged looks. Gilbert put his hands in his sleeves and gazed into the distance. Stephen dug out his purse and dropped a farthing he could not afford to spare into the cup. Dick plucked out the farthing and examined it closely, licking it and rubbing it on his sleeve.

Dick closed his good eye, his face compressed by a grimace.

"All right, then," he said, relaxing the grimace and grinning. "I believe I did see him."

"Early in the morning?" Stephen asked.

"Just as I was getting to the gate."

"Galdeford Gate."

"That would be the one."

"Did you see him every day?"

"Actually, yes. Odd thing, isn't it? A rich man like that walking about when he should be getting ready for work."

"I suppose he passed through the gate."

"You'd be an idiot if you didn't — no offense meant, sir."

"Which way did he go?"

"Which way? I'm such a busy man I don't have time to note such trivialities."

"Don't give me that, Dick. You know. Not much happening around this town escapes you."

Dick rattled his cup again.

"Forget it. You've got from me all you're going to get."

Dick looked sour.

"If we find him, especially if it results from your help, there might be something more for you," Stephen said, surrendering to the demands of the marketplace.

"Most generous of you, sir," Dick said. He stuck a finger into the empty eye socket and scratched an itch that broke out there. "He took the left fork in the road."

"The left fork, you say?"

"I only know of one left fork. It's the one opposite the right."

"Thank you, Dick." Stephen stepped away, about to draw off toward Galdeford Gate.

"There's a widow outside Upper Galdeford," Dick said. "You might want to seek her out."

"Why would I want to do that?"

Dick shrugged. "Don't know. She's a great gossip. Name's Gwenllian."

"I'll do that. Come on, Gilbert."

"A full penny!" Dick shouted at their backs. "It's worth a full penny!"

Four women with buckets were drawing water from the Galdeford village well, which stood behind the stone cross at the crossroads where Upper and Lower Galdeford Streets parted ways. Stephen called to them since they looked like prospects for interrogation. One of the women paid no heed to him, and took her buckets toward Lower Galdeford, but the others waited for him to draw up.

He established straightaway that they lived along Lower Galdeford, so there was no use asking them about Wattepas, but he did inquire about the gossip Gwenllian. This provoked a few chuckles. Stephen had the sense that the women were laughing at him, as if he was the butt of some secret joke. One of the women waved toward Upper Galdeford. She said, "Last house on the left after the chapel. You can't miss it. Nobody does. Good day to you, sir."

There was another round of sly smiles, while the women collected their buckets and set off into Lower Galdeford.

"Mistress Gwenllian does not seem to be very popular," Gilbert said. "I wonder why."

"Her popularity is not our business."

"Shall we head up there first?"

"No. We might as well ask if anyone along the way saw anything. You take the right side. I'll take the left."

Gilbert eyed the stretch of road that lay before them. "It's almost dinner time."

"Sacrifices must be made."

"I would have you make them. Not I. Especially not my dinner. It is the happiest time of the day, except for bedtime."

"Let's get on with it. Or it will be sundown before we're through. Do you want to miss supper as well?"

"I am growing tired of this line of work," Gilbert grumbled, but set off toward the first house on the right.

The line of houses was not long; they ended after about a hundred yards or so, not far beyond the close of St. Stephen's church. Yet as with most inquiries of this sort, much time was lost before they reached the little chapel that marked the end of the village. Across the street stood the great oak shading the house of Beth Makepeese, a woman of Stephen's acquaintance. Neither Beth, her children nor their many goats were in evidence. He thought, nonetheless, about knocking on her door as well to get a sense of what he might expect of this Gwenllian. But since the last house on the left stood only a few yards away, he went straight there.

Gilbert sat down on the plank bridge separating the yard from the street. "My feet are sore. I hope you don't mind if I wait here?"

"Suit yourself," Stephen said. He pushed through the gate into the front garden, which was overgrown with grass.

Someone spotted him through an open window, for Stephen heard a voice calling, "Mum! Someone's here!" as he crossed the yard, and he didn't have to knock on the door. It opened as soon as he reached the threshold.

A woman of uncommon attractiveness stood in the doorway. You could not say she was beautiful; her nose was too large for that, her chin too square, her lips too full. Yet the full effect of these features, along with cool, appraising eyes that were a fetching green, made her pleasing to look upon. A man could get lost in those eyes. Her hair, plaited beneath a linen wimple, had only a few strands of white among the blackness, which gave her age away in a manner in which her face, which had only the smallest of lines about the eyes and mouth, did not.

"You are the Mistress Gwenllian?" Stephen asked.

"I am," Gwenllian said with only a trace of a Welsh accent. "What brings you to my door. Not wool, I'm sure."

"Wool?" Stephen said, a bit startled at that.

"Wool is our business, my daughters and me. We are spinners. It is how we make our living, such as it is."

"I see. I didn't come about wool."

"Something else, then?" Gwenllian leaned against a door post, arms crossed under breasts that pushed interestingly at the fabric of her linen shift.

"Uh," Stephen said, trying to keep his gaze on her face. "I am here about Leofwine Wattepas."

The slightest of tremors shook the corners of Gwenllian's mouth and eyes, so slight that if Stephen had not been staring directly at her face he might have missed it. "I don't know a Leofwine Wattepas," Gwenllian said.

"You don't know him?"

"I know of him. Everybody does, I suppose, as he is the richest man in town. But I don't *know* him. Why?"

"He has gone missing. He was last seen heading into Upper Galdeford."

"What business is this of yours, if I may ask, sir?"

"I've been asked to find him."

"By whom? Certainly not Sir Geoffrey. I doubt he would care."

"No, not Sir Geoffrey."

"His wife, then, eh?" Gwenllian came off the door frame and stepped back into the house a pace.

Stephen did not answer this question. Instead, he said, "I have been told that you are a good source of information on what happens in the village."

Gwenllian smiled, but not in a friendly way. "You've been to the well, I see."

"I stopped there."

"Those women are full of spite. They'll say anything."

"Nonetheless, did you see Leofwine Wattepas come this way Friday morning?"

"No."

"Or any other morning?" Stephen persisted.

Gwenllian shook her head.

One of the daughter, out of sight behind her, said, "Mummy —"

Gwenllian's head snapped around. "Quiet!" She turned back to face Stephen. "Is that all? We have much work to do. It is hard enough as it is to make ends meet without a husband without having to waste time on missing goldsmiths."

"That did not seem to go well," Gilbert said, rising from his seat on the plank bridge as Stephen came through the gate.

"You heard?"

"I am not deaf, you know."

"A rather more sharp denial that I would have expected from a mere spinner."

"You think she was lying?"

"It felt like she was being less than candid."

"Should we go back and put the question to her more vigorously?"

"I've the feeling that she could stand up to whatever we threw at her."

They strolled down the street toward town in silence until they reached a spot three houses down from the crossroad. A path came in from the north at this place. Stephen contemplated the path.

"Where does that go?" he asked Gilbert.

"Plainly, into that field there." For a barley field was visible beyond the gardens, which were bordered by a thick hedge of hawthorn.

"I wonder," Stephen said. He walked the path to the point where it entered the field. The path continued north toward St. Mary's, the village next to the River Corve Bridge. Another path skirted the field by the gardens lying along Upper Galdeford Street.

"You think he took this path?" Gilbert asked. "It seems unlikely, doesn't it?"

"Dick said he entered Upper Galdeford Street. Yet no one here reports ever having seen him. If he took this path, that might explain why. He goes up to St. Mary's and comes back by Corve Street, a circle of sorts."

"A very long shot."

"Yes, it is." Stephen bent to examine the ground, although he was not hopeful that any sign of Wattepas' passing would remain after two days. He straightened up and was about to turn away when he spotted a pile of horse manure a few paces along the way behind the houses of Upper Galdeford Street. A pile of horse manure was, by itself, nothing extraordinary. The world was brimming with horse shit. But as Stephen's eyes followed the path, he saw at last four more piles. That was a lot of piles for one horse, which meant that more than one horse had taken this path in the last couple of days, for when he cut open the nearest pile with his dagger, he could see that although the outside had begun to dry and turn brown, the inside was still green and moist.

He was about to dismiss this mystery as having nothing to do with Wattepas when six horsemen came at a fast trot down the alley behind them and arrayed themselves in a semi-circle around Stephen and Gilbert, hemming them in against the hedge. They were a tough looking bunch, hard and muscular: men-at-arms at the very least, all with swords and dressed too well to be the ordinary highway robber.

If either Stephen or Gilbert had an impulse to run, that intent died quickly, for one of the horsemen, who regarded them over a drawn crossbow, said, "Don't think about it."

"What do you want?" Stephen asked, measuring the gaps between the horses and wondering how thick that hedge was. Some hedges were as sturdy and impassable as a wall.

"You're Attebrook," said the man with the crossbow, who had a harelip that made it look as though his face had been split open, crooked teeth showing.

"So? Have we met? If we have I don't recall it."

"You've something we want."

"I don't see how that is possible."

"That fellow in the privy. You took them from him."

"The dies for making coin?"

The man with the crossbow nodded.

"I gave them to the undersheriff. He's sent them on to Hereford by now."

"I want you to get them back."

"Don't be daft."

"Oh, you'll get them, all right." The fellow gestured to one of the others, who dismounted. "Take that fat fellow."

The man who had dismounted grasped Gilbert by the collar and dragged him away from the hedge, while the man with the crossbow trained the weapon on Stephen in case he interfered.

"I know he's a good friend of yours," said the man with the crossbow. "If you don't get those dies, we'll cut off his head. You have one week. We'll be in touch to let you know where."

Chapter 11

Two of the ruffians bound Gilbert's hands and feet with leather thongs. They boosted him upon the hindquarters of a horse and, with another set of thongs, tied him to the saddle, as if he was a rather bulky bedroll. Stephen stood by, helpless under the crossbow.

The burden secure, the men mounted, and the horsemen trotted along the path behind the hedges, Gilbert bouncing and groaning, eyes clamped shut and face livid, but unable to utter a protest because he'd been gagged with a strip of rag. They swerved across the barley field toward a copse to the east of St. Mary's. Riding across someone's plowed field was a serious trespass, but the offense was minor compared to the kidnapping and threats.

Stephen watched them go, rage mingled with shame that he had done nothing but stand there. He followed the path along the back gardens to keep the horsemen in sight as long as possible. The hedge bordering the path was as tall as he was and thick, so that he could not see through it, and only realized he had passed the little chapel and Gwenllian's house when the large oak in the Makepeese yard across the street loomed into view.

An object in the tall grass caught his attention: a small block of wood with a carving at one end. Stephen stooped and recovered the carving. It was unmistakably Harry's work: the head of Rosamond, the girl in the ice. He tapped the carving on the palm of his hand. This was must be the carving Harry had sold to Feyn the night he was murdered. One of the killers had picked it up at the Broken Shield, and must have dropped it here.

There was a gap in the hedge at this spot, concealed by overhanging hawthorn branches. Someone had cut a passage with a pruning knife. Pushing the branches out of the way, he saw through into the back of a house, where a vegetable garden of cabbage, carrots, turnips and beans had been planted by the usual privy pit and woodpile. Two goats lifted their heads from the grass to inspect him.

It was Gwenllian's house.

Stephen crossed the yard. One of Gwenllian's daughters spotted him through a rear window and called out, "There's a man in the garden!"

Stephen heard rushed movement in the house as he neared the back door. He stepped over a pile of dried horse manure and was about to knock when he thought better of that idea, and pushed the door open. He entered the hallway separating the living quarters from the bier, where the goats were kept. No one met him in the hallway. He passed at the door to the living room. Two girls peered fearfully down at him from the loft. Gwenllian stood at the foot of the ladder, a hand ax over her shoulder, poised to strike.

"Get out of my house!" Gwenllian snapped. "I'll split your skull if you take another step!"

"No, you won't," Stephen said, drawing his dagger in case Gwenllian decided to rush him.

"Not in front of the children, please," Gwenllian said, sounding less confident.

"Not *what* in front of the children?"

"My murder, or rape."

"I've no intention of committing either."

"What do you want, then?"

"Same as before. The truth."

Gwenllian's mouth quivered. Her chest heaved. "They said they'd kill me if I talked."

"Those fellows, the same as went by just now? I'm sure you heard the commotion and saw their heads over the hedge."

Gwenllian nodded.

"They came for Wattepas, didn't they."

She nodded.

"And they took him away."

She nodded again.

"He's been coming here every morning."

Bad Money

"Yes."

"I doubt it was for your cooking."

"Of course it wasn't. What does every man want more than a good meal?"

"Do you happen to know any of them?"

"Never seen them before in my life before Friday."

Stephen glanced up at the two girls, both black-haired like their mother. "Is that the truth?" he asked the girls.

Both nodded. The blue-eyed daughter said, "They dragged Master Wattepas away and said they'd cut off mum's face if she said a word about it." The girl burst into tears. "Mum's going to die now!"

"No, she isn't," Stephen said. "No one will ever know she said a word."

He sheathed his dagger and backed out of the house. He left by the backdoor and the hole in the hedge so that none of the neighbors, who would otherwise be sure to note the event, could see that he had been here.

Stephen hurried back to the Broken Shield. He climbed to his room at the top floor where he put on his gambeson, then struggled into his mail. He slipped on an arming cap, but left the coif down for now. His surcoat went over the mail, and then the sword belt and the second one for his dagger, small hand ax slipped into the belts at the small of his back beside the dagger. He put his barrel-shaped helmet under one arm and draped the strap of his shield over the other shoulder. He paused at the doorway, contemplating his bow which stood in the corner in its linen bag beside another linen bag full of arrows. He grabbed the straps of the bags and clambered down the stairs, at risk of tumbling the whole way, given the steepness of the stairs and the cumbersome burden.

Edith spotted him in the hall and rushed over, alarmed at his appearance and at the thunderous expression on his face. "What's the matter?" she cried "What's going on?"

There did not seem to be any point in withholding the news or softening it. He said, "Gilbert's been taken by the same fellows who killed the fellow in the privy. I'm going to get him back."

"Taken!? What do you mean?" Edith stammered, disbelieving, hand flying to her mouth. "Why?"

"Long story. No time."

Edith followed Stephen to the stable, stammering one question after another. He did not send her away, yet he did not answer any of her questions, either, which only prompted her to press harder. Still, he ignored her while he threw a saddle on one of the mares and slipped a bridle over her head. He mounted and rode out of the stable, the other mare on a halter and lead rope.

"I'll get him back," Stephen called to Edith over his shoulder. "Don't worry!"

But she had every reason to worry. He had only two hours of sunlight left, at most, if he was to catch them before nightfall. And while he tried to sound confident for Edith's sake, he felt only dread and the bitter sense that he had failed his best friend.

Stephen had only a vague notion of what he would do when he caught up with the kidnappers: something like plunge into their midst and take out as many of them as possible in the first onslaught. They were unarmored and lacked shields, while he was fully armored. So the odds at first impression did not seem too daunting. But as he followed the track across the barley field behind Gwenllian's house and his panic began to subside, he thought better of this plan. It was more likely to fail than not and he would be overwhelmed. Yet he was committed, so he kept onward.

A narrow road suitable only for a single cart at a time ran east from St. Mary's and marked the northern edge of the field. The tracks turned east upon the road. There was a fair degree of traffic on this road, and with nothing to distinguish the hoof prints of the enemy from those put down by any other horse, the enemy became hard to follow, especially once the St. Mary's Road joined Upper Galdeford to become the road to Titterstone Clee. Stephen was reduced to watching the margins of the road for signs that the enemy had left it, but by sundown, when he had covered perhaps six miles and reached the turn off to Tenbury which was halfway to Cleobury Mortimer, he had seen nothing that indicated where they had gone.

A sliver of moon lighted Stephen's way back to Ludlow, the night quiet except for the thudding of the mares' hooves and the hum of insects. It would have been a pleasant ride if Stephen's mind had not been in such turmoil.

He rode around the town to Broad Gate, following the town ditch, startling a group of homeless people taking refuge under the bridge at Old Street Gate.

Broad Gate was closed, of course. The voice of one of the town watch came faintly over the wall, calling out all was well. Stephen wished that were true.

He banged on the gate with his helmet, but there was no response, not even a voice calling to find out what was the matter. Gip, the chief warden of the tower, lived on the first floor behind windows shuttered against the night. Stephen contemplated those windows, then went searching for some stones, which he had to dislodge from the road bed with his toe. He stood back and threw one stone after another at one at the shuttered window. The stones glanced off the shutters with loud knocks.

He was about to throw his last stone, when the shutters cracked open and an angry voice said, "If you don't stop that, I'll call the watch!"

"I need to get in!"

"It's after curfew! No one gets in but a royal messenger. I doubt you can claim to be that!"

"I represent the crown well enough."

"Who is this?"

"Me."

"I don't know anyone named 'Me.'"

"Stop it, Gip. It's Stephen Attebrook."

"Well, why didn't you say so straightaway?"

"Because I like standing in the cold and the dark. Now open up and let me pass."

"Don't be in such a hurry. I've got to be sure. Can't grant admittance to some troublemaker."

The shutters closed. Some time passed before the sally door in the gate opened. Stephen stepped through, leading the mares.

Gip was just inside, rubbing his hands. He held out a palm. It was customary to enrich the palm for an unauthorized night passage of the gate.

"I've nothing for you, tonight, Gip. Sorry," Stephen said. "I'll make it up to you."

"Promises are thin gruel," Gip grumbled. He went back inside the tower.

The gate to the Broken Shield's yard was latched as tightly as the town gate. Stephen got in the way he had done before at a similar late evening arrival, standing on the back of his horse to pull himself to the top of the wall and dropping inside to unlatch the gate and lead the horses through.

He crossed a yard. All the stalls in the stable were occupied, so he tethered the mares to rings on the wall outside and removed the saddle and tack from the one he had ridden. Despite the desperate situation, he thought about the dinner and supper he had missed that day and considered slipping into the kitchen for whatever might have been left lying about by Baldwin, the cook.

But first he had to water and feed the horses. Water he got from the well, setting buckets before the mares, which they ignored. Hay had to be got inside the stable. Stephen groped his way to the last stall to the left. He heard Harry, who shared the stall with the hay, breathing wheezily. Stephen slipped in and gathered an armful of hay.

Harry stirred. "Who the devil is that?"

"Just me."

"You're back! Did you get him?"

"No, I lost the trail."

Harry was quiet for a moment. "Does Edith know?"

"I haven't seen her yet."

"She was up and waiting for you when I retired."

"I am not looking forward to seeing her."

Stephen went out to the mares. Harry followed, pelting him with questions so that soon he had the whole story.

"Do you really think they'll kill him?" Harry asked.

"I have a feeling they were not joking."

Stephen deposited hay before each of the mares. He took the carving out of his pouch and gave it to Harry. "I found this. Is it the one you sold Feyn?"

Harry examined the carving in the moonlight. "I wish the light were better. You haven't a candle on you by any chance?"

"Sorry, no."

Harry ran his fingers over Rosamond's face. "I think it's the same one. How did you come by it?"

"I found it near where Gilbert was taken."

"What was it doing there of all places? Oh! One of the *mon-theofas*? Dropped it getting away, eh?"

Mon-theof . . . Stephen hadn't heard that word, the old word for kidnapper, in a long time, not since an incident when he was a child and several young girls from a neighboring manor had been stolen by the Welsh. He said, "Dropped it, but not when he ran away with Gilbert. Earlier."

"They came to the same spot twice to do crime? What are they, fools?"

"No, I think one of them lost it when they kidnapped Wattepas."

"You are making my head ache. Why would anyone kidnap Wattepas?"

"I have no idea. Yet somehow his disappearance is connected with Feyn's death."

"Well, you have more important things to do than look into that matter."

"Yes, they want those dies in exchange for Gilbert."

"But you gave them to the sheriff! He won't give them to you for the asking. Not for Gilbert."

"No, I'll have to steal them."

"I guess I'll have to start preparing my speech for the wake."

"That might not be a bad idea. They're probably in Hereford now, if not on their way to London."

"Hereford, you say?"

"Henle was planning to dispatch them straightaway to the sheriff. Last I heard, Hereford is where he spends most of his time."

"Hmm. That means you have to get into Hereford Castle, find out where those gems are kept, snatch them and escape . . . without anyone being the wiser."

"That's right."

"I know someone who works at the castle."

"So?"

"He knows all the goings on, who's humping whom, who hates whom, who owes money to whom."

"That's not going to help."

"He should know where your little treasures are put for safekeeping. Assuming they're there, of course."

"What's his name?"

"Theobald."

"Thanks, Harry."

"There's one thing, though."

"What's that?"

"He's not likely to help you, especially in something this dangerous."

"That's not unexpected."

"But he might if I ask him."

"And how would we manage that?"

Bad Money

"I'll have to go with you, of course."

Chapter 12

It took the better part of a day to reach Hereford, even though it was only about twenty-five miles away. Had Stephen been traveling alone, he would have covered the distance in half the time in the manner he was used to riding on Spanish raids: an alternate series of walks and trots of the horse that ate up ground. But Harry could not stay aboard the other mare at a trot, even when tied to the saddle, which was the only thing that kept him secure.

Harry elicited stares as they ambled the last length of the journey down Frenschemanne Street, but not as if he was clad as a beggar: a legless beggar upon a horse would have been an extraordinary sight and difficult to explain. So this was a new Harry, bathed, shaved and coifed at first light and clad in Stephen's spare coat and shirt, transformed into minor gentry until he opened his mouth, spoke and betrayed his real class. It was easier to explain a sorely wounded gentry man.

"That way," Harry said as they reached the end of Frenschemanne Street, where it dumped into Wydemarsh, the street leading northward to Wydemarsh Gate, which was visible a hundred-fifty yards away. "He lives on Jews Street. It's just ahead."

"I know where it is," Stephen said.

He had some familiarity with Hereford, although in truth he could not recall ever having been down Jews Street. There were only half a dozen families of actual Jews on the street who lived in fine stone houses; the remainder of the residents were poor Christians. As they turned the corner and entered it, they met a cart with a broken axle lying tipsy against a wall, piles of garbage big enough to impede traffic that should have been cleared away, lines of washing hanging from ropes stretched from house to house.

A fellow with a clay drinking pot poised before his lips — some of its contents evident on his shirt front — watched them with an open mouth. The man raised a finger to draw attention to the spectacle of Harry tied to his horse, and his lips twitched with the words that bubbled upon his tongue.

Harry, who was quicker than Stephen to detect an insult, snapped, "One word out of you, boy, and my friend will have your head off!" in an unexpectedly good imitation of a gentry accent.

One might doubt that threat. But still, one could never tell with the gentry; many were hot-headed and thought themselves above the law. This and the sword slapping against Stephen's thigh as he glowered gave the pot-man pause, and they got by him safely, without insult or injury to anyone.

"Here we are," Harry said at a nondescript timber-framed house indistinguishable from its neighbors. "Sarah!" Harry called out, as Stephen dismounted. "Sarah! It's me! Harry!"

Moments later, a pretty blonde woman, her hair escaping from her wimple, came to the door.

"You don't look like Harry," Sarah said. "But you sure sound like him. What are you doing up there, dressed like that?"

"I've come up in the world," Harry said, as Stephen began to untie the leather straps that held him in place.

"I doubt that," Sarah said.

"Really. Literally. I can see for miles up here."

"With your head stuck in the clouds, I'm surprised you can see anything at all. All I can say, is careful you don't fall on your head. Not that that's likely to do any harm, hard as it is."

"It runs in the family, I see," Stephen said as he finished with the straps and carried Harry to the ground, while Harry muttered, "Gently, sir! Gently!"

"What does, sir?" Sarah said.

"Sharp talk," Stephen said. "It's a wonder you never murdered each other when you were young."

"Oh, we came close many times," Harry said, propelling himself across the threshold without being invited as Stephen untied the board with rockers on the bottom Harry sat on while begging. "But mum was too fast for us."

"And too tough," Sarah said.

"She was that, God rest her soul," Harry said. He called back over his shoulder, "We'll put the horses up in the yard."

"You're volunteering my yard?" Sarah asked. "What gives you the right to do that? Think of the mess they'll cause!"

"Come on, sister dear," Harry's voice came from the bowels of the house. "The least you can do is help us in our hour of need. Besides, they'll fertilize that rat patch you call a garden."

"I offered to take you in when that bitch left you with nothing, you ass. That was offer enough," Sarah said to herself. She realized that Stephen had overheard this. "He said he didn't want to be a burden. Come on, sir," she added, grasping the halter rope of the mare Harry had ridden. "I'll show you the way."

The way happened to be straight through the house. There were three boys who appeared to range from four to eight playing in the hall, racing about and shouting at some game only they understood, but this activity stopped at the appearance of the horses. The boys watched the procession in astonishment, then fell in behind, prancing about and renewing the shouting, Sarah admonishing them to stay away from the back hooves of the horses. "Don't startle them! That's a good way to get killed!" she kept saying without effect. "Behave!"

However, everyone reached the rear garden without injury. Stephen unsaddled the horses while Sarah sent all the children for hay, which got them out of the way.

"May I ask, sir," Sarah said, "what you are doing with this great lump?"

"Trying to save a friend," Stephen said.

"We need to talk to Theo," Harry said. "We need his help."

"He'll be home at sundown. I don't like the sound of this. Why is that?"

Bad Money

Supper was before sundown in the ordinary house, but the family waited for Theobald to come home. When he arrived, it was evident why they had this custom, for he carried a cloth satchel full of leftovers from the castle kitchen.

"One thing I'll say about my job, sir," Theobald said as Sarah set out what he'd brought — a small round of ham, herring, shelled peas, cheese and bread — "we don't go hungry. Stop that, Harry!" he commanded. At first Stephen thought Theo meant the Harry he knew, but the order was directed toward the middle son, who had reached for the herring. Harry the younger snatched his hand back. "We'll say our prayer, first," Theo said, bowing his head.

The prayer finished, the boys were unleashed to eat, although Sarah shot an admonishment at them now and then to mind their manners on account of their guests.

"Uncle Harry don't care," muttered the oldest boy, Mike.

"Think of his friend, then, who is a gentleman," Sarah said, "and wipe your mouth. I've known wolf packs that were better behaved!"

"There ain't no wolves in England."

"That may be," Stephen said, "but there are in Scotland, which isn't that far off. I've seen them."

"Really?" Mike and Harry the younger said together, which led Stephen to a story about how he had been pursued across the moors by a pack of wolves, an entirely made up tale as far as the wolves and the location were concerned; the wolves in the true story had been human and the chase had occurred in Spain.

That story and a few others concluded and the last morsel consumed, Sarah packed the children upstairs to bed, where the family slept in the loft at the rear of the house. Theo put the soiled trenchers, platters and bowls in a bucket in the kitchen to soak overnight, and returned to the table in the hall.

"Sarah said you need my help," Theo said. "It's about a friend of yours, or something."

"Our landlord," Harry said.

"Why anyone would want to help their landlord, I cannot imagine," Theo said. "Greedy lot, they are. Worse than millers."

"This fellow's not so bad," Stephen said.

"I suppose. But what does this have to do with me?" Theo asked.

"He's been kidnapped," Stephen said. "The kidnappers will kill him if I don't give them a set of dies I found on a fellow murdered at our inn."

"So give them to them."

"I don't have them. I turned them over to the undersheriff and he sent them to Hereford."

"Ah," Theo nodded. "Yes, a messenger came the other day from Ludlow with a set of dies for minting money. I recall that now. Seized from a counterfeiter, or something like that."

"Are they still here?" Stephen asked.

"As far as I know. I reckon they should have been sent on to the mint at London, but I think I heard the undersheriff mention he was holding them for our new sheriff, fellow named Arundel, to dispose of them. Should be here any day."

"The Earl of Arundel? Percival FitzAllan?" Stephen asked, alarmed.

"Yeah. Why?"

"He and Sir Stephen don't get along very well," Harry said. "Something about the beating of some of the earl's supporters, and the murder of one of them. There was also an accusation of a castle burning thrown in as well." At Theo's astonished expression, Harry added, "Sir Steve's a talented fellow."

"Talented for getting in trouble, it seems. Can't say I envy you now that FitzAllan's our sheriff. But what about these dies? If the sheriff's got them, they're no use to you."

"I need to take them back."

Theo was quiet, contemplating the implications. "You mean you want to steal them."

"That was my thought," Stephen said.

Bad Money

"Well, then, you can get out of my house right now," Theo said. "I'll have no part of such a scheme, or put my family at risk for it."

"At least, tell me where they've been put," Stephen said. "And we'll trouble you no more."

"They're in the treasury, in the tower on the motte. You've no chance in hell of getting in or out of there. Only those known to the wardens are allowed in and there are two on watch all the time. Give up this mad plan. Go to the sheriff. Explain your need. I'm sure he'll help you on something as serious as a kidnapping."

"We don't think that's likely," Harry said. "The authorities have no love for either Stephen or Gilbert." He glanced into the darkness in the corners. "I'm afraid Gilbert is as good as done for."

Chapter 13

Stephen and Harry said their good-byes to Sarah and Theo the next morning, the sky low, fog filling the streets and obscuring the tops of the houses and the city wall behind them.

Theo helped lift Harry to his saddle, then with a "See you around, Harry," he set off toward the castle. He paused briefly, eyes narrowing as he regarded them, lips pursed as he pursued some thought. But he did not express whatever was on his mind. He turned away toward Bishopsgate Street which was out of view beyond the curve of the street.

Harry watched Theo over his shoulder as they went in the other direction toward a cheap inn Theo had told them about next to Wydemarsh Gate.

"I actually thought he might have some idea what to do," Harry said.

"Why would you think that?" Stephen asked, leading the horses.

"He was a master burglar before he married my sister. No place was safe from him. He could steal the shit out of a lord's ass with no one the wiser."

"I'll have to do it myself. At least I know where the dies are kept without having to ask."

Stephen put up the mare Harry had ridden and left Harry at the inn by Wydemarsh Gate, taking the second horse with him. Pulling up the hood of his traveling cloak against a misty rain, he set out down Wydemarsh Street, walking on the margins as much for the shelter the houses' overhangs afforded as to avoid the mud churned up by the passage of feet and carts. Walking in deep mud was a good way to have a boot sucked right off your foot.

His objective was the castle, at least to have a look around and hope some brilliant plan presented itself. But inquiries along the way revealed that the goldsmiths were quartered along Broad Lane, which was close by and proved to be broad only metaphorically: it was hardly wide enough for two carts to pass each other, Saint Ethelbert's Cathedral visible as he rounded the bend at the lower end, where the goldsmiths were concentrated.

There were six of them, more than you'd expect for a town of Hereford's size.

He stopped at the first one on the left and asked the journeyman who answered his knock on the counter about Nicholas Feyn. The journeyman poked a thumb in the direction of the cathedral. "Worked next door. Although you won't find him there. We heard he drowned in a privy." The journeyman smirked. "A fitting end, I'd say, after the trouble he caused around here over the years."

"Not well liked, I take it."

"Not by most. What's your interest in him? He owe you money? If he did, you're out of luck. He's left no fortune, I'm sure. Every penny that passed through his fingers went for drink or whores."

"It's strictly professional," Stephen said.

"Professional how?" the journeyman asked.

"I am the deputy coroner for Ludlow."

"Really? Are you conducting some sort of inquiry?"

"I am interested in what he was doing in Ludlow. It seems a strange place for him to be."

"Perhaps not that strange, when you know something about him. But it's not my place to tell the tale of his life." The journeyman called over his shoulder to a someone who could be heard moving about in an interior room of the shop, "I'm going to Fretgoose's for a moment." He disappeared from the counter and emerged through the doorway a moment later. "Let's go straight to the horse's mouth."

The journeyman had to go only a few feet to put himself at the counter of his competitor. He called into the shop, "Can you fetch Master Fretgoose? There's a fellow here who wants to know about Feyn!"

"What for?" came the reply from someone who could not be seen. "The bastard's dead! Did that ass owe him money?"

"He says not!" the journeyman answered. "He claims to be the coroner from Ludlow —"

"The deputy coroner," Stephen muttered, but the journeyman did not take notice.

"— and he's conducting some sort of inquiry!"

An apprentice who had been listening to this exchange while he smoothed kinks out of a sheet of what appeared to be gold put down the sheet. "I'll fetch him, Meetham."

"So good of you, James," the journeyman Meetham said.

James retreated into the house and came back a short time later followed by a man in his late thirties.

"I am Fretgoose," the man said, looking Stephen over. "The Ludlow coroner, eh?"

"Deputy coroner," Stephen said.

By this time, everyone in the house had been alerted to this curiosity and the shop filled to overflowing so that some of the curious had to spill out the doorway into the street. This caught the attention of some passers-by as well as the occupants of the neighboring shops so that within moments a considerable crowd had gathered round to participate in the inquiry.

"What do you want to know?" Fretgoose asked, hooking his thumbs into his belt.

"But first, tell us," someone in the crowd called out, "did he really drown in a privy?"

"He was knocked over the head first," Stephen said.

"Someone that bastard cheated, I've no doubt!" called out someone else, rising above a general babble of agreement.

"We thought that might be the case," Stephen said. "But it turned out he was the one cheated."

"That son-of-a-bitch got what was coming to him!" yet another voice called out.

"But," Stephen went on despite the interruption, "there is reason to believe that he was killed for another reason."

"Couldn't have been about a woman, could it?" Fretgoose asked. "He had a habit of annoying the wives of other men."

"We don't think so," Stephen said. "A set of dies for striking money were found on his person. We think the killer or killers were after them."

This revelation caused Fretgoose to grow thoughtful, although many in the crowd again started talking at once about what this news might mean. Fretgoose raised a hand for silence and the crowd gradually quieted.

"A set of dies for coining money, you say," Fretgoose said. "Curious."

"Why would you say that?" Stephen asked, although he was ready to agree it was curious indeed.

"Back when I was an apprentice under old master Bysouth, we contracted to the bishop to produce the coin during the Long Coinage."

Stephen frowned. "You mean when the Long Cross coins were minted."

Fretgoose nodded. "Fifteen, twenty years ago, it is now. Feyn and Leofwine Wattepas engraved the dies for the Hereford mint. Well, Feyn did mostly, for his was the better work. Wattepas' was decent enough but not up to standard."

"Wattepas?" Stephen asked, surprised.

"Yes, we all worked together for Master Bysouth, I as an apprentice then, and Feyn and Wattepas as journeyman."

"Tell him the story about the dies, Fretgoose!" someone called from the crowd.

Fretgoose nodded. "A set of dies went missing from the mint. They were found in Feyn's chamber." He pointed above. "Naturally there was an accusation made that he stole them with an intent to make false money. But Wattepas came forward and admitted that he had mistakenly taken them from the mint instead of returning them to the chest where they should have been kept. People had doubts about that — that Feyn meant to steal them and Wattepas covered for him."

"Why would they think that?" Stephen asked.

"They were fast friends," Fretgoose said. "Wattepas was the only person in the world who could put up with Feyn, you see. That's why they shared the same chamber. It must have been the bowls. They made a formidable pair. Never beaten on the pitch. Made quite a lot of money bowling, too. Wattepas saved every penny, while Feyn drank and gambled his away."

"Wattepas wasn't punished?" Stephen asked.

"He was fined, of course. Could have lost a hand. But he was very well liked. The upshot of it was he had to leave town. That's how he ended up in Ludlow."

"I see," Stephen said, although he really didn't. The doings of the guilds was outside his experience. "And Feyn remained here?"

"He could have taken the same route as Wattepas, since he was never accepted by the masters here, but he never managed to accumulate enough money to buy himself in elsewhere. He resented being passed over for master when old Bysouth died. Never got over that, and being subject to my discipline. I finally had to let him go a couple of months ago. Then he disappeared. No one had any idea where he'd gone until a traveler brought word of his death in Ludlow. We thought he'd gone up there to see Wattepas. Wattepas himself was down here a couple of months ago on a visit about the same time Feyn disappeared."

"Wattepas came to visit Feyn? Wasn't that unusual?" Stephen asked.

"I'd say it was. They hardly had anything to do with each other after Wattepas left, as far as I know. Anything else we can help you with?"

"Thanks," Stephen said, his mind in a whirl as he tried to make sense of what he had just been told. "I don't think so."

Stephen stood in the street for a few moments digesting what he'd heard as the crowd broke up and people returned to work.

Chapter 14

One of the two gate wards rose from his stool as Stephen rode across the wooden bridge from the town. He stood in the way and said, "Who might you be, sir, if you pardon my asking?"

"My name's Stephen Attebrook. I'm the deputy coroner for Ludlow. I'd like to see the undersheriff."

"A moment, sir," the ward said. He disappeared through the doorway to the gate tower.

He emerged a few moments later behind a knight who had to be the captain of the guard.

The captain looked Stephen over with an appraising eye. "You're Sir Stephen? I've heard of you. I know your brother."

Stephen nodded. "I am he."

"He says you're crippled. I don't see any sign of it."

"I hide it well. And you are?"

"I am Roger de Thornhill. What is your business with Sir Hugh?"

"I've been sent by Walter Henle to inquire about the business of Nicholas Feyn and how he came into possession of a set of dies for minting money."

"I doubt Sir Hugh can shed any light on the matter."

"Nonetheless, I feel bound to see what he might know."

Stephen walked the horse across the great bailey, taking in as much detail of the castle's layout as he could. The bailey itself was one of the biggest he'd ever seen: at least two-hundred yards across from the base of the motte, a great mound of earth capped by a round stone tower, to the east wall. A monastery occupied the southeast corner, cut off from the bailey by its own low wall. There even was an orchard and spacious vegetable garden to the left beside the monastery. Two great halls stood within the bailey across from the main gate, a grim building of red stone like Saint Ethelbert's

Cathedral, tall and long, with high narrow windows, the ones flanking the main door giving the appearance of an elongated face and gaping mouth, chimneys poking upward. There were also buildings for a prison, a large garrison and workshops for the manufacture of mangonels and catapults.

The motte was enormous to match the bailey, at least ten times the height of a man, so steep and deep in high grass that it seemed impossible a man could keep his footing upon it. Steps encased by stone walls taller than a man descended from the tower's entrance, a squat forebuilding, to a point not far from the great hall where they ended in another stone gate flanked by square towers. An armed storming party would be hard pressed to pry open that tower.

Stephen left the mare in the hands of a groom at the foot of the stairway to the great hall. He climbed the steps and entered the hall. There were men about the fireplace to the right at the far end of the great chamber. Stephen recognized Hugh de Breton among them by sight. They had never spoken or been introduced. Now that he was here, he had to go over and say something.

De Breton was more careworn than Stephen remembered. He had to be nearly fifty and his hair had gone fully gray. His face had begun to sag. Gray eyes peered at Stephen over a broken nose and drooping mouth.

"My lord," Stephen said when he reached the group at the fireplace. "Good day to you."

"Who are you?" de Breton asked. "I don't think we've met."

"I am Stephen Attebrook."

"Attebrook? Attebrook? Ah — the one who's been causing so much trouble at Ludlow. All those murders! What are you doing here?"

"Sir Walter sent me to inquire about Nicholas Feyn, and how he came to be in possession of dies for minting money."

"Yes, I read your letter." De Breton's hand fluttered in Stephen's direction. "You did not have to come. I have an inquiry underway. Never you mind."

"Nonetheless, sir, I have my orders. I cannot report back to Sir Walter that I've learned nothing."

"I appreciate your dilemma, but I shall take care of it." De Breton blinked, eyes narrowing. "Have you learned anything?"

"Only that Feyn disappeared two months ago, and no one knows where he went or why."

De Breton grunted. "That is hardly helpful." He went on then, with a hint of slyness, "And I already have some idea what Feyn was up to in any case."

"Might I know that to share with Sir Walter?"

"No, you may not! We shall take care of things!"

"Very good, my lord."

"Henle ought to mind his own lands and not poke about in the business of others. You can stay the night, if you please, but you'd best be off for Ludlow in the morning." De Breton turned back to the other men about the fire.

"Thank you, my lord," Stephen said to the back of de Breton's head. It had been an uncomfortable interview, without any real purpose other than to be seen to have some business even if that business was imaginary, and he was glad it had ended. He withdrew across the hall.

He walked down to the stable which lay some distance from the great halls along the west wall. A groom sat on a stool by the door on watch in case he and the others were needed. The groom rose as Stephen arrived. Stephen waved to the groom to return to his stool. "Where's my horse?" he asked.

"To the right," the groom replied. "Third stall."

"Thanks.

"Your servant, sir."

The mare's saddle had not been removed, but the bridle was hanging from a hook outside the stall. Stephen draped the bridle over a shoulder. He was about to untie the rope across the doorway when someone entered and came up behind him. Stephen glanced about to see who it was; he didn't like people sneaking up behind him.

It was Theo.

Theo checked left and right. He whispered, "You've a chance to stay the night. You should take it."

"Why should I do that?"

"Hush! Keep your voice down. We can't have that lad," he nodded toward the door, "overhearing."

"All right, then," Stephen went on in a whisper, "why should I do that?"

"Because I've been thinking about your problem."

"I thought you wanted nothing to do with it."

"I've reconsidered."

"Why would you do that?"

"Well, there's got to be a profit in it. Those things aren't worth much by themselves, but there's got to be a price you're willing to pay."

"There might be. Do you have something in mind?"

"One of those horses of yours. I've always fancied having one of my own. But even the cheap ones are so expensive."

"And if I promise this horse, you can get me in the tower?"

"Oh, yes. I've had harder jobs in my day. Lord, I do miss it so. It was such fun."

Chapter 15

Stephen struggled to stay awake in the chamber where he had been allotted a bed among the younger knights and squires. It was hard to tell the passage of time in the dark. The air smelled of rain. Now and then a flash of lightning illuminated the cracks in the shutters, and thunder grumbled in the distance.

He drew off the blanket and swung his legs out of bed, the ropes holding up the straw-filled mattress and the frame creaking.

Stephen stood up, tensing for the slightest sign that one of the sleepers had heard. Unlike everyone else, he had gone to bed fully clothed even down to his boots. Although it was the practice to sleep naked, no one had remarked upon this, and he hoped that no one would remember it. He collected his cloak, which he had rolled up and used for a pillow, and, dropping to his hands and knees, felt his way across the floor to the doorway.

A flash of lightning provided enough light that he could see he was headed for a wall. He changed direction, crept between two cots, and reached the doorway without anyone waking up and without upsetting the chamber pot by the door. He rose, lifted the latch, and slipped into the stairway.

Stephen felt his way down the stairs to the tower's undercroft which was filled with barrels and sacks and smelled musty.

He pulled the cloak over his head and went out to the yard.

The knights' quarters were across the bailey from the hall, but even with the dark and rain, which had driven the watch to shelter, Stephen did not dare take the direct route. He skirted to the wall of the monastery, passed the cattle pen, tiptoed by the pig-sty so as not to startle the pigs which were prone to a commotion if disturbed, and stopped at the barn, which stood against the south wall. A flash of lightning, followed immediately by a blast of thunder, lit up the bailey such that Stephen could see his own shadow and burned into his eyes the image of puddles across the bailey spattered by raindrops. A voice spoke from above his head: "I'll be right there."

Some uncomfortable moments passed with the rain dappling on his hood and no shelter anywhere. Then the barn door opened and Theo slipped out. He had a thick rope coiled around his shoulder. "Lovely evening, isn't it?"

"Very. I love a good rain. I could do without the lightning, though."

"We'll have to make the best of it. Best put these on," Theo said. He handed Stephen a pair of thick leather gloves while he pulled a pair on his own hands. "Helps protect the hands."

"From what?"

"The rope can be nasty."

Theo led the way past the stable and hall to the ditch separating the motte and tower from the bailey. The ditch was deep and steep-sided, V-shaped, and the grass slick so that they nearly lost their footing as they slid to the bottom. They made their way to the gate tower, which stood upon the slope above a wooden drawbridge over the ditch. Stephen glanced up through the pummeling of the raindrops to the top of the tower for any sign of the watch but it was so dark that he could barely make out the outline of the crenellations let alone a man who might be lurking up there.

Theo climbed the motte to a point just above the gate tower. "We'll do it here."

Stephen put his back against the wall and cupped his hands. Theo stood on those hands and stepped to Stephen's shoulder. Stephen raised a hand above his head. Theo stepped upon that hand, and then the other. Stephen strained to raise Theo as far as he could. Just when he thought he might collapse, the weight was gone. He looked up and saw Theo crouching at the top of the wall.

Theo wrapped the rope around his waist, then dropped an end to Stephen and braced himself. Stephen took hold of the rope, gave it a tug to see if it was secure enough, and clambered up to the top of the wall beside Theo, who coiled the rope about one arm.

They ran up the stair wall to the tower's forebuilding at the crest of the motte. They repeated the exercise where Stephen boosted up Theo to the top of the forebuilding. Theo then dropped the rope so that Stephen could join him.

There was a doorway into the tower that gave access to the top of the forebuilding, for in the event of an attack it was expected that defenders would rain stones and arrows on any attackers from this vantage point. The door sat in an alcove that provided shelter both from the rain and from view. They crouched in the alcove, breathing hard from the effort to get this far.

Stephen tried the latch. It rose and the door opened a crack.

"Not worried about intruders," Stephen murmured to Theo.

"This is as far as you go," Theo whispered. "I won't risk you blundering about in the dark and waking the watch."

"You're sure?"

"I don't need you anymore." Theo slipped through the door and closed it behind him.

A long time passed. Stephen kept an ear pressed to the door, alert for the slightest sound, his heart pounding, head spinning in disbelief at what he was up to. Life was supposed to take a certain trajectory; certain events were supposed to happen and certain things were supposed to be done: a younger son either entered the clergy, took up a profession or craft, or sought his fortune at war. Having made that fortune, a fellow was supposed to come home, marry a girl with some property, and settle down to lord it over his manor. None of those things had worked out for Stephen. He had been forced into a profession by a father who disliked him, and, having rebelled against that life, had chosen arms in Spain, where there was constant fighting and quick fortunes were more likely to be made than in England. But he had lost the fortune more swiftly than he had acquired it, and so now here he was, lurking on a castle's roof, a thief in the night. He would never have imagined this fate for himself.

Footsteps sounded in the corridor beyond the door, not furtive steps, but a thumping approach that was the exact opposite of stealth. A glimmer of light from a lantern or candle flickered at the foot of the door.

Stephen's breath caught in his throat as the steps and voices got closer.

It was the watch. It had to be, up and about on rounds — in the rain.

Stephen and Theo had counted on the watch's usual tendency in peacetime to take shelter from the weather. These fellows were too disciplined.

Stephen rushed out of the alcove, panic welling at the possibility of discovery. Thieves and burglars were entitled to no more mercy than a murderer or rapist.

He leaped to the parapet and hung from it by his fingers as the latch rattled, too afraid to let go for fear that the watch would hear him crash to the ground.

There were two men. One of them strode to the parapet overlooking the stairs. The other stood at the center, hugging his cloak close against drafts, the lantern in his hand.

"All clear," announced the fellow at the parapet.

"Who'd be out on a night like this, anyway?"

"At least you can tell the captain that we did our bit and it won't be a lie."

"You're too honest for your own good. I'll catch my death in this weather."

"Least it ain't winter anymore."

"True. I hate winter."

"Not my favorite season either."

"Makes yer dick shrivel up to a button."

"I didn't know you still had one."

The two guards went back in the tower.

Stephen's fingers, meanwhile, had begun to fail with the strain. It would be a relief just to let go. But he couldn't desert Theo. He chinned himself on the parapet, threw a forearm upon the stones, and dragged himself up.

He returned to his place by the door, ear close, listening through the thunder in case the watch came back.

Despite Stephen's close attention to events on the other side of the door, its opening caught him by surprise.

"Startled you, eh?" Theo said as he slipped out and pulled the door closed behind him.

"I thought you might be the watch," Stephen said, his heart hammering. "They came out earlier."

"I saw. I was worried they'd spot you."

"Did you get them?"

Theo patted the leather pouch hanging from a thong around his neck. "No trouble at all. Let's get out of here. We don't have much time."

Theo led Stephen down to the wall encasing the stairs from the tower gate and Stephen acted as Theo's stepping platform as he had before. A spectacular flash of lightning spread horizontally across the sky, crooked fingers of white flame lashing out from the main bolt. Stephen would have marveled at the sight of it if he hadn't been so intent on keeping his footing on the slick stone as they scampered down the top of the wall toward the tower gate.

Stephen was halfway down when a bolt struck so close he thought it had hit right behind him. He was engulfed in searing white light; his hair seemed to stand on end. The impact of the accompanying thunder struck him like the hammer of God. He felt himself suspended in midair, and realized that he had been cast off the wall and was falling. He didn't know whether he was up or down, head first or feet first. He raised his arms to protect his head just in case, which turned out to be a good thing, because he struck head down. Fortunately, the steep slope of the motte rendered the impact a glancing blow and he tumbled down to the bottom of the ditch.

He stood up as the alarm bell at the top of the tower began to peel. "Shit," he said, glancing upward, the pelting rain obscuring his vision.

Theo said something altogether more harsh as he struggled to his feet and then collapsed.

"What's the matter?" Stephen asked.

"I think I've twisted my ankle."

Stephen pulled him up on one leg. "Can you walk?"

Theo tried to put weight on the injured leg. "No." He handed Stephen the pouch with the dies. "Get going, while you still can."

"No," Stephen said. He crouched, pulled Theo over his shoulder, and clambered out of the ditch, certain that at any moment a voice would call out to bring attention to them.

Instead, the voice at the top of the tower called out a different message over the ringing of the bell: "Fire! Fire!"

People had begun to spill out of the halls by the time Stephen reached its stairway. It would have drawn attention and perhaps questions if Theo remained on his shoulder, so Stephen put him down and supported him so he would not fall over. The crowd streamed toward the tower and its gate, which one of the watch pushed open, drawn by the yellow light glowing behind the tower's battlements.

Stephen and Theo limped toward the barn, as the towers and sleeping quarters emptied themselves of their inhabitants who raced toward the motte and the tower as well. No one paid Stephen or Theo any mind.

At last, they were in the barn and out of view. "Wait a moment, will you?" Theo asked. He climbed the ladder to the loft. There was the rustling of clothing, then a satchel plopped to the ground at Stephen's feet. "Take that to the missus, if you don't mind."

Stephen picked up the satchel. It held Theo's wet clothes. Stephen turned toward the door, where the yellow light of the fire had grown bright. "I wouldn't mind if it burned to the ground."

"Neither would I. Especially since I set it."

Chapter 16

Stephen watched the flames leap high above the parapets, a great torch that must have been visible for miles, with others from his sleeping quarters who had turned out in the wet to witness the spectacle. None of them made any effort to join the bucket brigade that had formed in an effort to fight the fire. That would have been manual labor. In any case, there were more than enough hands for the task, since the gate wards had thrown open the main gate and admitted the fire watch of the surrounding neighborhoods, who had flooded in at the alarm in such numbers that the motte and surrounding ground had seemed covered with ants.

The fire guttered out by morning, although a thick column of smoke continued to rise from the burned out shell.

Stephen, who had been up all night along with most everyone in the castle, collected his horse and rode away.

The streets about the castle were clogged with people who either had watched the disaster throughout the night or had collected in the morning for a view of the smoke-belching tower and to hear the gossip that circulated from every lip that emerged from the castle. Stephen was pelted with questions as he rode through the press, but he clutched the folds of his cloak about himself and said nothing except for the occasional, "Make way!"

The crowd thinned out at Hungreye Street, where there was some semblance of a normal workday, shops opening for business and cart and foot traffic beginning to increase as people headed toward the market that began by Saint Peter's Church, where merchants were setting up stalls and the congestion increased again. On any other day, it would have been a pleasure to meander through the stalls. A market day, especially in such a large town like Hereford, could almost be like a fair, with so many odd things for sale. But Stephen was preoccupied with his troubles as the mare plodded through the crowd on the way to Wydemarsh Street and the inn where he had left Harry.

He was so deep in his thoughts, playing over one way to deal with the kidnappers and then another, that he almost missed the sight of Will Thumper. He had not expected to see the Thumpers here, so far from Ludlow. He urged the mare closer to the Thumpers' stall. All sorts of odds and ends lay upon the table: a bolt of woolen cloth, pots and pans, knives and axes, wooden spoons and bowls, molds for baking cakes, tools for shaping wood, pliers that might have once belonged to a blacksmith, various hammers and drills, assorted spearheads and a small box of hunting points, a stack of blankets, folded linen sheets, an assortment of woolen stockings, and a pile of floppy hats. It was the sort of thing you often saw in a peddler's cart.

"Would you mind not blocking the way?" Will Thumper asked. "Keeps the paying customers away."

"What have you got there, Will?" Stephen asked, chewing on the last of the sweet bun.

"Stuff for sale! What does it look like? You don't have any objection to a fellow trying to make a penny, do you?"

"You know I don't. I just like it to be an honest penny."

"Come now, Sir Steve, you know I'm an honest man."

"That's true on some days. I heard you frequented the markets in other towns. Junk seller, or so they say, but that stuff doesn't look like junk." Stephen dismounted and fingered the roll of woolen cloth died a bright red, which was very expensive. "Where did you get this?"

"I bought it fair," Thumper said.

"Perhaps. And what of this?" Stephen picked up a heavy chain from which hung a heavy metal cross. It was hard to tell if it was made of gold or bronze. "I've seen the like around Felicitas Bartelot's neck every day I pass her house. Did you know her cross has gone missing?"

"Er, no, I didn't."

"Where'd you get this one?"

"Off a peddler."

"What peddler? Do you recall his name?"

"No, I don't. See him now and then. He stopped by the house for some drink and traded this bauble for it."

Stephen should have pressed further; in fact, duty required it. But the problem of the kidnappers had so taken over his thoughts that the questions died on his tongue.

"I think I'll show it to Mistress Bartelot. Perhaps she will recognize it."

Thumper scowled, but did not protest.

"If it's not her trinket, you can have it back."

"All right, then," Thumper said. "I'd like to avoid trouble, if I can."

Stephen weighed the chain in his hand, his mind making more sluggish headway than usual owing to his lack of sleep. "There is something you can do for me, I think, that will make your trouble go away."

Harry was at breakfast when Stephen arrived at the inn by Wydemarsh Gate. A thoughtful soul had even provided Harry with a pillow to sit upon and he looked satisfied with his bacon and hardboiled eggs as Stephen slipped onto the bench opposite him.

Harry's eyes narrowed. "What have you been up to?"

"Nothing."

"Of course. All that commotion at the castle last night — you had nothing to do with that, I'm sure."

"No. Of course not."

"Did you get them?"

"Keep your voice down."

"I will take your sour mood for a confession. How'd you do it?"

"Shut up, I said."

"Well, at least tell me about this terrible fire. Was anyone killed?"

"No, the watch got out, although they had to jump over the wall. One fellow broke a leg, I heard."

"A pity."

"What, that no one was killed?"

"No, that the fellow broke his leg. See? I am not without compassion for the unfortunate. Have an egg. You'll feel better. It's too early to get drunk."

Stephen took up one of the eggs from the bowl in front of Harry, who waved at a servant to fetch some more.

"You're not troubled by your conscience, are you?" Harry asked as Stephen chewed the egg.

"I have no conscience. Not any more, anyway."

"That's a good thing. They are such a burden. But what's bothering you?"

"Nothing. I said it's nothing."

Harry shrugged. "All right. But Father Harry will have this nothing out of you eventually."

"You are becoming irritating."

"Wouldn't be doing my job if I wasn't."

Harry paid the remaining bill while Stephen went out to tack up the other horse. Harry emerged and two servants kindly lifted him upon the mare. Harry grandly gave the servants a farthing.

"Shall we be off, my good man?" he said as Stephen secured him with the leather thongs they had brought for that purpose. "It is a long way home and I like to get an early start."

"It is a long way home," Stephen murmured, wishing that he had a home. He was unlikely to find a lasting one any time soon other than that wretched inn of the Wistwodes'.

He led the horses out to the street. Instead of going left toward the gate, he turned right into town.

"What is this, man?" Harry called. "You're going the wrong way!"

"No, this is the right way. Shut up and enjoy the ride."

"I do not enjoy riding any more than Gilbert does. It is far too dangerous an activity for the ordinary man."

"You only say that because you're too poor to own a horse. If you had one you'd think differently."

"If I had legs to hold on with perhaps I'd think differently."

They reached Jews Street. Harry rubbed his chin in thought but said nothing. They came to Theo and Sarah's house. Stephen stopped and dismounted. He knocked on the door. The elder daughter answered.

"Could you get your mother, please?" Stephen asked.

"Right away, sir," the girl said and ducked back into the house, leaving the door cracked.

Sarah arrived, wiping her hands on her apron. "I didn't think we'd be seeing you again, sir."

"I've an errand to run," Stephen said. "I'm leaving my horse and Harry with you for safekeeping." He handed the reins to his mare to the daughter and led Harry's horse through the doorway. "Mind your head, Harry."

"What are you doing?" Harry sputtered as they passed through the main room. "You didn't —"

He got no answer until they reached the back garden and Stephen untied the thongs holding Harry in place.

"It was Theo's price," Stephen said softly. "Don't let Sarah know. She thinks Theo's given up the business."

"You're leaving me here?" Harry asked as Stephen eased him to the ground.

"I'll be back for you and the tack once I've got Gilbert back."

"Don't get killed doing so. I don't want to be stuck here. Beggars' licenses are expensive in Hereford and I've just about run out of money. Although, you know, with a bit of silver we could make our own!"

Stephen straightened up. "Harry, I don't know what you're talking about."

Chapter 17

Edith Wistwode spotted Stephen crossing the yard of the Broken Shield. She leaned on the window sill and drew a breath, hand at her throat, wanting to call out, but her voice failed.

By the time she emerged from the house, Stephen had gone in the stable with his remaining horse. She thought it was odd that he had only the one — and no Harry in sight, either — but those thoughts left her mind as she hurried to catch up with him.

He was removing the saddle, the horse in one of the empty stalls, when she reached him.

"Do you have them?" she demanded. She noticed that he looked haggard, but she put that down to strain and the exertions of the journey.

Stephen did not answer. He put a finger to his lips, and went first one way down the stable and then toward Harry's stall to make sure there was no one within listening distance. He even climbed the ladder to the loft in case one of the boys was up there shirking work.

He nodded when at last he confronted her. "Do not speak of this again. Has anyone been by asking about me?"

"Only one of Henle's men. They've arrested Herb Jamesson. He passed bad pennies two days ago. Henle wanted to talk to you about it."

"Did you tell Henle's man where I'd gone?"

Edith nodded.

"At least you said it was to investigate the bad money, I hope."

"Yes. Although people have been talking. You and Harry were seen leaving together."

"What have you said about that?"

"What you told me to: that he has a sister in Hereford he wanted to visit. People thought it odd that you of all people would be the one to take him there."

"They'll just have to continue to wonder. We'll say he paid me to do it, I suppose, if further explanation is required. I'm going to bed. I've been up all night. Oh, and I suppose I should tell you, since everyone will expect it, there was a terrible fire at Hereford Castle. The tower on the motte burned to the ground, or the buildings within it did, anyway."

"I hope you had nothing to do with that," Edith said.

"Of course I didn't. I only watched."

As much as Stephen desired the luxury of catching up on his lost sleep, the opportunity eluded him. No more than an hour passed before an insistent pounding on his door awakened him. The annoying person at the door would not desist despite Stephen's shouts for him to go away.

When it was clear he would not be left alone, Stephen rose and crossed to the door, mindful of the roof beams on which he was prone to knock his head if he was not careful.

"What do you want, John?" Stephen asked, unable to suppress a snarl, when he cracked the door.

"Sorry to bother you, sir," said John, one of the hired guards at the castle. "Sir Walter would like to see you."

"Right now? I'm very tired. I was up all night. There was a great fire at Hereford Castle. Nobody could sleep through that."

"We've heard, sir. Can I tell him you're on your way?"

"In due time."

"Well, sir, Sir Walter wants to subject Jamesson to questioning, but he wanted to consult with you before he did so. I'm afraid that if you tarry . . ." John shrugged. "You know how impatient he is." John was one of those who frequented Jamesson's establishment, an inn at the Corve bridge popular for its bowls, so he and Jamesson were acquaintances.

Questioning . . . that could only mean the thumbscrew or some other device to encourage the disclosure of information that someone wished to conceal. "I'll be right down."

Herbert Jamesson was chained to a post in the castle's jail. Stephen noted that it was the same post from which Jamesson's brother had hung himself only the month before. Stephen wondered if Jamesson realized this, but he said nothing. The poor man's plight seemed bad enough without adding that tidbit for him to think about.

"Got yourself in a pickle, eh, Herb?" Stephen asked from the doorway. He had no desire to get any closer. A toxic ooze of shit, piss, the pungent reek of unwashed bodies, rotting hay and a hint of boiled cabbage was choking enough just at the doorway.

"Get me out of here!" Jamesson demanded. "Why is it the Wistwodes are let off scot free? Favoritism, that's why! The law works for those who have connections and against those who don't!"

"You know that isn't it. The Wistwodes washed their money and turned in the bad pennies they found. You apparently couldn't be bothered with that precaution from what John here tells me."

"This is how the Wistwodes will get rid of their competition. They passed some of their bad money at my inn, hoping that I'd be found out and accused of complicity in counterfeiting!"

"Whoever spent the money at your place wasn't connected with the Broken Shield. In the last few weeks have you had any unusual guests? A half dozen or so rough men, with the look of soldiers?"

Jamesson's brow furrowed as he struggled to remember. "I seem to recall such men. Kept to themselves. Didn't even try bowls, despite being challenged. I thought that was odd, but you get all sorts of strange people in my trade."

"I'm thinking of one in particular. Tall, broad shouldered, handsome in his rough way, but with a harelip."

"I remember a man like that."

"You don't happen to remember his name? Or that of any of his companions?"

Jamesson shook his head. "No, I don't."

"There you are!" a voice belonging unmistakably to Walter Henle interrupted from some distance across the bailey. "When I summon you, man, I expect you to come, not to dawdle about with the prisoners!"

Stephen stepped away from the doorway as Henle hurried his big square body toward him.

"I wanted to question Jamesson before I spoke to you," Stephen said as Henle drew up, breathing a bit hard from his exertions.

"And I wanted to speak you before you interrogated him. You have ruined my plan."

Stephen doubted that Henle had much of a plan; he wasn't a man for plans beyond the straight dash at something.

"Have you learned anything about the counterfeiters?" Henle asked when Stephen did not reply. "We've one of their confederates right here." He gestured toward the gaol.

"I don't think that Jamesson is involved. He's an innocent victim."

"Oh, come now, he had almost a shilling in bad money which he was at pains to conceal."

"Wistwodes discovered they had bad money and he is no more guilty than they are."

Henle harrumphed at this, for no doubt he wished for a reason to strike out at Gilbert. "What proof do you have of that?"

"One of the chief suspects in the ring stayed at the Pidgeon. I have no doubt he is the source of the bad money."

"Chief suspect? What chief suspect? You never said anything about a chief suspect before! Did you learn anything in Hereford?"

"Not in Hereford. This fellow of whom I speak was seen in the yard of the Broken Shield the night Feyn was murdered," Stephen lied.

"This is the first I've heard about this. Who saw him?"

"Harry," Stephen said, mentioning the first name that popped into his head, glad that Harry was gone so this claim could not be checked.

"I think I should speak to Harry then. I've had my people speak to everyone who might know something while you were gone — in case you left a stone unturned."

"That's good to know," Stephen said. "Harry, I'm afraid, is not available for questioning. He is in Hereford."

"What the devil is he doing in Hereford?"

"Visiting relatives. He has a sister there. He fancied an opportunity to see her."

"Harry? Has a sister? In Hereford?"

"That's what I said."

"How on earth did he get to Hereford?"

"Since you ordered me to go there, I took him."

Henle looked at Stephen as if he were mad: as well he might, since conveying a beggar like Harry anywhere was a mad thing for a person of Stephen's station to do. Henle waved a hand. "You are altogether too friendly with the likes of him. Well, no matter. Fellow like that can't be believed anyway."

"You'll let him go then?"

"Who?"

"Jamesson."

"I am not convinced he's innocent. We'll keep him in hold until we know more. Are you satisfied that you've got out of him all you need?" Henle glanced at the doorway, clearly glad not to have to approach it but probably yearning to apply more vigorous questioning methods than Stephen was known to employ.

"Yes, I think so," Stephen said. "Are we done here? I was up all night, thanks to that fire at the Hereford Castle. No one could possibly sleep through the racket."

"I suppose we are," Henle said. "Keep me apprised of all developments. I say, though, tell me about this fire. I hear it was catastrophic."

Chapter 18

Henle's interest in the fire was so consuming that it was some time before Stephen could get away. He suspected he would be required to tell the story quite a few more times. Such spectacular events were rare and people wanted to know every lurid detail.

Yet Stephen managed to reach Bell Lane without being waylaid to tell the story, although John Spicer the Younger had beckoned from the wine shop at the top of Broad Street with an invitation to stop for a cup of wine. Stephen waved him off. It was too early in the day for wine in any case.

As he neared the Broken Shield, he looked up to see Felicitas Bartelot gazing down from her open window, as she did most days when the weather allowed it. Although Edith told him that she had not paid her rent this month, she had not yet been evicted. That could happen any day, however.

"Good day, Sir Stephen," Mistress Bartelot called down as their eyes met.

"And to you," Stephen said. "I just remembered. I have recovered your cross. You must forgive me that it slipped my mind until this moment."

"Nothing about my spoons?"

"I am afraid I have not made progress on that score."

"Who was the thief?"

"I've not established that yet. But I found by chance someone the thief had sold it to."

"Will Thumper," she said with malice.

Stephen shrugged, intending neither to confirm nor deny.

Mistress Bartelot was not deceived. "Why would you protect that rascal?"

"First, I have not said it was Thumper. I found the cross in the Hereford market of all places. Second, these things can require more delicacy that you might imagine at first."

"I don't see why. A bit of the thumbscrew should get a confession out of him. The town would be better for it."

"You'll have to settle with the return of your property, I'm afraid. That part of it, at least."

"That is a disappointment. I shall be right down."

"I have to fetch it." Stephen entered the inn, crossed the hall and climbed the stairs by the fireplace to his room.

When he came down and headed back through the hall, he spotted two men he had not expected to see again. One of them rose from their table in the corner and intercepted Stephen at the door.

"My lady would like a word, sir," said Walter, a broad-shouldered man with a quick smile whose mistress presented him as a servant but who carried himself like a soldier.

"She's here?" Stephen tried to sound disinterested in the fact that Margaret de Thottenham might be somewhere within ten miles.

Walter pointed skyward. "In the front room."

"I will see to her straightaway," Stephen said. "Thank you."

But Mistress Bartelot could not be ignored, so he went back to her house, where Dungon was peering out the window for his approach and opened the front door before he could knock. Stephen glanced back at the Broken Shield. The windows to the front room were open, as they usually were in good weather, but no one was visible. He could call to Margaret if he wanted to, but he did not.

"You really have it?" Dungon asked.

Stephen showed her the cross.

"It is the one," Dungon breathed. "My lady will be very pleased. It is a pity about the spoons, but she put more store in this bauble, I think, even though it's only made of bronze. I keep it polished so that it shines. People mistake it for gold because of that."

"Why would that be?"

"Her husband gave it to her before he died. It is all that is left of him. He was a decent man, even if a little distracted. It's funny, isn't it, sir, how the memories of the dead slip away? I can hardly recall his face."

"Tell me something, Dungon. Why are you still here if she has no money? She can't be paying your wages."

"I have been with her twenty-five years. It's hard to go. But I shall have to eventually, I suppose. The end of the month is soon enough."

"You'll deliver the cross to Mistress Bartelot?"

"I thought you might want to do that yourself. I'm sure she wants to thank you."

"I have other business, urgent business. It just came up. Tell her I am sorry about the silver, but I'm glad to have done this much."

Stephen spun about and almost ran back to the inn.

A woman's voice called "Come!" at Stephen's knock on the door. He pushed the door open and entered. The Lady Margaret de Thottenham was seated on the cushioned chair by the window, working on some embroidery. The embroidery fell to her lap at the sight of him. She looked better than he remembered: a small woman who barely came up to his shoulder, slender hands and arms, a long graceful neck, a heart-shaped face with a bud of a mouth that lighted rooms and hearts when it smiled, her wheat-colored hair bundled under her wimple with only an errant strand over an ear to betray its brilliance, blue eyes capable of dancing with amusement or flashing with steely determination watching now. She looked as delicate as any flower such that a breeze could blow her over, but he had learned in his brief and dangerous acquaintance with her that her spine held more iron than those of most men.

"I'm surprised you didn't see me from the street," Margaret said. "What were you doing with that old woman?"

"Returning something she had lost."

"And no reward for you, either, I don't doubt. Sometimes I think you are a fool."

Stephen shrugged. He didn't like that she might think him a fool. "I'm sure many think so."

"To their misfortune. Christina," Margaret said to the maid seated on a stool by the bed, "please leave us for a while. I have something I wish to discuss with Sir Stephen that is for his ears alone."

"Yes, my lady," Christiana said. She glided to the door and eased it shut behind her.

Margaret put aside her embroidery and crossed the room. She rested her hands on either side of Stephen's face. "You look tired and careworn. What have you been up to?"

"Nothing of consequence."

"I doubt that. Shall we pick up where we left off?" she asked as she drew his lips to hers.

When they were done, they lay together in the bed, her back to him, he curled around her slight body, hand cupping one of her breasts. Her breathing was music. He tweaked a nipple. She swatted the offending hand.

"Stop that," she said. "I shall have to put you to work again if you keep up, and I am spent too much for the exertion."

Stephen's hand resumed its cupping. "What are you doing here?"

"Passing through."

"And you just thought to pay me a visit?"

"Well, I don't know anyone else in Ludlow whom I'd like to visit, so why not?"

"You always do as you please."

"Mostly. As a widow I have greater freedom than many women." She turned her head to see him out of the corner of her eye. "Mistress Wistwode says our friend Gilbert is in trouble."

"You consider him a friend?"

"Your friends are my friends."

"Now I know you aren't being truthful."

"Well, I'd like to consider Gilbert a friend after what we went through over the Pentre affair." She sat up. "Edith said he had been kidnapped and that you were to ransom him. What could he possibly be worth in money? And where will you get it?"

"They don't want money."

"What do they want? Maybe I can help get it, whatever it is."

"It's already taken care of."

"That's a relief. It must be a very precious thing. Some jewel or other, like those emeralds of the saint you tracked down last month?"

"You heard about that?"

"I like to know what you're up to. You should write more often. Or I should say, you might write."

"I'm not much at letters. Anyway, the thing isn't a jewel but it's precious enough to kill a man for."

"You can't tell me what it is?"

"I'd rather not."

Margaret pouted but did not pursue the point. "What now?"

"I wait for the kidnappers to contact me to arrange the exchange."

She drew a deep breath and sank down on the pillow. Her fingers made little circles on his chest. "Be careful, Stephen. Whatever you do, please be careful."

"I will," he murmured, sleep, which he wished to push away, drawing his eyes closed as it stole upon him, almost unaware of her lips brushing his forehead as she brought his head to her shoulder.

"Poor Stephen," she said. "Poor, poor Stephen."

Chapter 19

Margaret de Thottenham left before breakfast the following morning. Stephen, who had groped his way to his garret room sometime before dawn so as not to be seen leaving the front chamber, almost missed her departure, for she had not informed him of her plans. He knew something was afoot when he pushed open the shutters and saw James, her other body guard, lead out a string of horses and tack them up just as the sun was rising. He threw on his clothes and hurried down to the yard in time to be there as Walter gave Margaret a leg up to the saddle.

"You were going to leave without saying good-bye?" Stephen asked.

"It's not good-bye, Stephen," she said. "We'll meet again, I'm sure." She reined her horse toward the gate. "Take care. Perilous times are coming, I'm afraid."

The times were always perilous; people constantly lived on a knife edge with death looming about in many forms: disease, crop failures and starvation, random acts of criminal violence. One particular peril loomed larger than these others. Stephen wondered if she had some special knowledge about it. "What are you talking about?"

"Just be careful." She pressed her heels to the horse and rode out of the gate, followed by Walter, James, and her maid.

Toward evening, as the inn began to fill up and Edith and Jennie prepared the tables for supper, the inn's front door opened and admitted two fellows that Stephen had seen before. They spotted him in his corner by the fireplace and wound through the tables until they reached him.

"Well, Harelip," Stephen said, giving his nearly empty tankard a swirl, "I was wondering if you'd show up after all."

Harelip settled on the bench across from Stephen. He scowled at being called Harelip. "You can call me Otto."

"That's not an English name."

"Runs in the family."

Otto stroked the tabletop with the fingers of one hand. Stephen noticed that the other was out of sight. He almost wished Otto would pull his dagger; he felt like killing someone. But Otto said, "You have them?"

Stephen extracted one of the dies from his belt pouch. He rolled it across the table to Otto. Otto examined the engraved end. He rolled the die back to Stephen and stood up. "On the Shrewsbury road, two miles or so north of Onibury. There's a crossroads that leads to Stokesay. Tomorrow, at the third hour. Come alone. If you're not alone, I'll cut his throat."

"If you hurt him, I will find you and hunt you down. I'm good at finding things and people. Ask anyone in Ludlow. It may take some time, but I'll get you in the end."

"Haven't found Wattepas yet, have you?" Otto grinned and strode toward the door.

Jennie was bringing out a platter laden with bowls of soup and bread when Stephen finished off the last of his ale. He stared out a window at a party of men and horses entering the yard. One of the horses paused in the middle of the yard, drew up its tail and defecated. Edith noticed this event as she filled a guest's tankard in the hall. She went to the window and called for Mark to clean up the pile and returned to serving ale.

Normally, of course, a pile of horseshit was something that was not to be noticed other than to step around it, but this horseshit tickled at Stephen's mind. There was something important about horseshit that he was missing and the thought of what he had missed was a burr that would not go away.

Jennie passed by his table and was about to put a bowl of soup down when it came to him and he stood up. He drained the bowl as if it were a cup as Jennie's eyes grew round at the impropriety of it; while it was not unknown for ordinary folk to drink their soup like ale, people of Stephen's class were not often caught doing so, and certainly not in public where others could observe and remark about their bad manners.

"Sorry," Stephen said, "I've just thought of something."

"My word, sir!"

"It's good."

"Your thought?"

"No, the soup."

"Cook will be glad to hear you thought so," Jennie said to Stephen's back as he hurried toward the door. "Would you care for some bread as well to go with it?"

Stephen stopped and turned. "Certainly."

Jennie threw him a round of bread as if it was a stone without spilling a drop from the soup bowls remaining on her tray — it was known throughout Ludlow that Jennie could throw a rock as well as any boy. Stephen bit into it: day old but not yet stale. "Thanks!"

The brisk walk to Galdeford Gate and the bread cleared Stephen's head and sobered him up, although he was still a bit sleepy from all the ale.

It was still not quite sundown and the gate was open as Stephen passed through, waving to One-eye Dick and the gate ward, who were throwing dice upon a blanket.

He turned left at the stone cross and the village well, which threw long shadows across the ground, and turned onto Upper Galdeford Lane.

Presently, the large oak outside the Makepeese house came into view and shortly after the Makepeese house itself. The oldest of the Makepeese children, Sally, was chasing a goat about the yard in an attempt to shoo it into the house. They exchanged waves and Stephen crossed the ditch on the opposite side of the street to the house of Mistress Gwenllian.

She was visible through an open window leaning over a pot suspended above the hearth in the center of the floor. She spotted Stephen as he crossed the yard. But he did not head for the door, but swerved around the corner to the back garden. He stopped at the corner and gazed about, searching in the tall grass.

Gwenllian emerged from the back door, wiping her hands on an apron. "What is it, sir?"

Stephen came forward a few steps and knelt by the fenced vegetable garden. He unsheathed his dagger and prodded the thing that had tickled his memory: a pile of horseshit, brown now with age. There was a faint curve in the dirt that had to come from a horse's hoof beside the pile. He looked up at Gwenllian. "Horseshit in your garden," he said. "What's it doing here? It didn't come out of Wattepas' ass, did it?"

Gwenllian fell back a step. A hand flew to her throat and fear glittered in her eyes, but she said, in an effort to brazen over this incongruity, "I suppose it came out of a horse, like it usually does."

"Fertilizing the grass, are you?" Stephen stood up and crossed to Gwenllian, whose eyes fell to the dagger that remained in his hand.

"Must have fallen out of the trolley," she said. "It's good for the cabbage, you know."

"I doubt it." He was before her now, staring down into her eyes. They were light brown eyes, and quite pretty. He put a hand on her throat and pushed her up against the house. It was against the law to lay hands on a woman who was not your wife, but Stephen's temper had begun to fray as he thought about how he had been lied to; but the truth was, he was angry more with himself for having been stupid.

"It came from a horse, all right," Stephen said, "a horse that was in your yard. A horse that took Wattepas away."

"You are imagining things," Gwenllian said. "And if you don't let me go, I shall call out. I shall say you tried to rape me."

"And the neighbors can come and hear my accusation against you. Go ahead."

Gwenllian's lips worked but she did not cry out after all. "You have no accusation to make."

"He came here to meet those fellows and rode away with them of his own accord, didn't he."

Stephen could feel Gwenllian trembling. At last she nodded.

"Where did they go?" Stephen asked.

"Don't make me tell! Please! That man with the harelip, he'll kill me! He swore he would if I talked!"

"Something is going on. Something to do with counterfeiting. And you know what."

"I don't know!" she cried. "Really I don't! Why would I? I'm just a woman!"

"But you are caught up in it nonetheless and will be punished like they will be when the truth comes out — unless you confess to me now."

Gwenllian's chin trembled and her body shook beneath Stephen's restraining hand. Finally she said, "All I know is that they went to Bishop's Castle! I don't know why! Leofwine never told me anything about his business! You must believe me!"

Stephen's hand fell away from Gwenllian's throat. He took a deep breath, glad that he had not had to go any further. He had done some terrible things in his life and they weighed heavily on the scale of his conscience. He did not wish to add one more crime to the balance.

"I believe you now," he said.

He sheathed the dagger and left her.

Chapter 20

The meeting place lay nine miles north of Ludlow on the Shrewsbury road. The crossroad was surrounded by open farmland running up to low wooded hills on either side, which made it a good place for the exchange because any body of men intent on a surprise could be seen from far away.

Stephen, who had arrived early, paced from one side of the road to the other. He was in mail and carried his longbow on his shoulder. He had not liked that helpless feeling staring down Otto's crossbow, and he wanted something to equal the odds.

The fields about the crossroads had been planted in beans and wheat. Sprouts had already begun to poke upward and the field seemed covered with green fuzz. A few men and women were visible pulling weeds, and a dog and a boy chased birds, which flew up in a cloud, swirled in the air, settling some distance away, where the process was repeated. Some of the people stopped their work to look at Stephen. It was an odd thing to see a man pacing at the crossroads where there normally was no one, especially an armored man with a longbow.

Although it was now almost midmorning, Stephen had not seen a soul on the road. It was quiet.

At last, he saw horses approaching on the road from the north. Stephen slung his shield on his back, strung his bow and nocked an arrow.

As the horsemen drew closer, Stephen was relieved to see Gilbert's stout form sitting awkwardly upon a horse, clutching the high pommel of the saddle, a sack over his head. They halted about fifty yards away.

Otto dismounted and pulled Gilbert from the saddle. This caught Gilbert by surprise and he fell down. Otto kicked Gilbert and said, "Get up, you idiot."

Gilbert, whose hands were bound, struggled to his feet with protests that were muffled by the hood over his head.

Otto must not have liked what he said, for he clouted Gilbert on the side of the head, sending him staggering so that he almost lost his footing again.

Otto grasped Gilbert by the shoulder, and marched him toward Stephen. "You're a suspicious fellow."

"I'm dealing with you. I've good reason," Stephen replied.

"You can put that thing down."

"I fancy that I'll kill you first if anything goes wrong," Stephen said.

"What could go wrong? We're just a pair of mates doing a little business. You first."

Stephen pulled the dies from his pouch, and tossed them to the ground about half way between him and Otto.

Otto shoved Gilbert toward Stephen. If he expected Stephen to catch Gilbert's dangerous lurch, he was mistaken, for Stephen stepped out of the way. Gilbert blundered by, tripped on his own feet and fell again with a cry of "Oh, my heaven!"

Otto stooped and collected the dies. "Nice doing business with you." He backed away, turned about and jogged back to the other men waiting on their horses.

"Until we meet again," Stephen said, not relaxing until they had all gone back north and ridden out of sight.

Gilbert had not attempted to rise again. He sat in the road, legs splayed.

Stephen cut the bounds securing his wrists and pulled the sack from Gilbert's head.

Gilbert rubbed his face. He looked haggard. What hair he had left stood out every which way as if flung about by the wind and then frozen in place. "Dear Lord, I never thought I'd see you again."

"Nor did I, frankly."

"You have no idea how close it was," Gilbert said as Stephen helped him to his feet. "There was quite a debate over whether they should just kill me out right to save them the trouble of feeding me. And they were afraid that perhaps I had seen too much, although what that too much was, I have no idea. They never really thought you'd get the dies back. The whole thing was almost a joke to them, a cruel joke, and at my expense. However did you manage it by the way — getting them back?"

"I'd rather not say," Stephen said. "It wasn't easy, I'll tell you that, or legal either." He set down the bow and arrow and pulled the mail shirt over his head. "Where did they take you?"

"It was a town of some sort. They kept me locked in a cellar of some house with the bacon and ham, that's all I know. It was more torture to be tied to a post with bacon and ham over my head and me not being allowed any, than being confined to the cellar. I'm afraid that isn't much help."

"How many were there?"

"I can't be sure."

"Did you hear anything?"

"What do you mean?"

"About what was going on."

"I have no idea what was going on, though I heard talk through the door. They were planning something big. I have no idea what, but it had them all very excited."

"How big?"

"I only heard bits and snatches, and not all of that clearly. I got the impression, though, that they were not all there was to the scheme."

"Did you hear anything about Wattepas?"

"Why would I have heard of him?"

"Because he wasn't kidnapped. He went away with this Otto fellow of his own accord."

Gilbert's brow furrowed. "That means he's part of this, somehow. How do you know this?"

"His mistress told me."

"Wattepas has a mistress? Ah — the woman Gwenllian. You had it out of her, eh? I should have liked to see that."

"Undo these ties, will you?" Stephen turned so that Gilbert could get at the ties along his spine that secured the gambeson.

Gilbert fumbled with the ties. "What are we to do now?"

"You're to return straightaway to Ludlow. Edith is beside herself with worry, and I don't want her torture to go on any longer than it must."

"But what of you?"

"I must see about those fellows. I've done a terrible thing. Hanging won't be good enough for me if it gets out. And with that sort, it always gets out."

Gilbert's eyes ranged south toward Ludlow. "I should like to see how this turns out. That fellow with the harelip was very rude. I don't think I shall go straight home. I will take a detour. Help me with this, will you?" Gilbert grasped the saddle on the rented horse. "It will not cooperate."

Stephen gave him a leg up. Gilbert plopped in the saddle and took up the reins.

"Dear Lord, I curse the man who invented horse riding," Gilbert said. "It's such an unnatural way to get around."

"But faster than walking."

"I'll give you that, although I hardly think that risking your life just to get around a little quicker is a good bargain."

"So you insist on coming?" Stephen asked as he folded the mail shirt and gambeson and put them in a canvas bag with his helmet.

"There won't be any fight, if my eyes are any judge." Gilbert eyed the canvas bag. "I want to see what bit of magic you intend to use to save us. My life apparently is in the balance, after all."

Stephen mounted his mare. "Just be careful how you ride. She has a sensitive mouth, that mare, so don't pull on her. And keep your legs still, otherwise she's likely to run away with you. Just give her enough of a tap to encourage her to follow me. And don't fall off."

"Don't fall off — the best advice for riding a horse that I've ever heard!"

They rode north at a slow walk, watching the sign left in the dirt by the kidnappers' horses.

A half mile or so beyond the crossroads, the road crossed the River Onny at a ford, and about two hundred yards beyond the ford, another road came in from the left. The tracks turned left and went west along this branch. Stephen breathed easier at the sight of this. He had guessed they would go that way, for at the end of the road some eight or ten miles away lay the town of Bishop's Castle.

The road west was not heavily traveled and in many places was no more than a cart track — three grooved paths, two for the cart wheels and the center one made by the horse. It followed the route of the Onny, on gently rising ground, flanked by wooded hills on either side.

As Stephen followed the road, he grew more anxious and worried that things had gone wrong. But at last at another ford of the Onny, which flowed over the rocks of the stream bed, he came upon Tad Thumper.

"We was wondering when you'd show up," Tad said, rising from the fallen tree trunk that had been his seat by the side of the road.

"Good Lord!" Gilbert exclaimed. "Tad Thumper! What are you doing here?"

Tad spit into the road. "Wistwode, you fat old sod. You look better with a sack over your head. You should wear one more often."

"What is he doing here?" Gilbert asked Stephen. Gilbert's eyes narrowed. He looked about at the forest, which pressed close in at this spot. "Where's your father? Where's Will Thumper?"

"Enjoying the fruits of our hard labor," Tad said.

"Hard labor?" Gilbert asked.

"Is it done, then?" Stephen asked.

"This way," Tad said, heading off into the woods that bordered the ford.

Stephen followed on horseback for perhaps fifty yards before they reached a stand of long-haired ponies tethered to some elms. Will Thumper came round the ponies.

"Sir Steve," Thumper said, tossing a quarter loaf at Stephen, "have some dinner. Murder sure makes a man work up an appetite."

"They were no trouble?" Stephen asked.

"Not a bit. It was like shooting fish in a barrel. Never knew what hit 'em."

"I shot one!" Tad said.

"First time, too," Thumper said. "That's my boy. Drilled him straight in the back. Not a moment's hesitation." He smiled with pride.

"I daresay, that boy's enough of a ruffian already," Gilbert said. "Introducing him to murder is not my idea of setting a good fatherly example."

"If I was to raise him to be like you," Thumper said, "he'd be beat down in a week. You're lucky to be walking around, flapping your mouth the way you do with nothing to back it up."

"Don't think it will always be so easy," Stephen said.

"You've shown us a thing or two on that score, you sure have!" Thumper said.

By this time, all the Thumpers, more than a dozen men and boys, had paused in their dinner to gather around so that Stephen might hear their stories and admire their handiwork. But he stopped the babble that broke out with an upraised hand.

"Where are they?" he asked.

"That way." Will pointed beyond the ponies where six horses were tethered to a line strung between two trees.

Stephen, taking a bite out of his bread, went to see for himself. There, near the horses, the corpses of six rough-looking men were laid out side by side. Otto the harelip's body was among them, one eye partly open, mouth slack. Stephen dug into Otto's belt pouch and retrieved his purse and the dies.

"That's it, then," he said. "I suggest that you not tarry. They'll be missed soon and someone might come looking."

"And we get to keep the horses and all their tack? And their weapons, too?" Thumper asked.

"That was the deal."

"Hear that boys? We're rich!"

"I'd sell them far from this part of the country if I were you."

"Good advice, but we know our business. Mount up, boys. Our work here is done."

The Thumpers and their loot had disappeared down the track at a brisk trot by the time Stephen and Gilbert returned to the road.

"A devil's bargain," Gilbert said. "Nothing good comes from dealings with that man."

"It couldn't be helped. He was our only chance."

"A frightening thought. What happens when they talk?"

"The Thumpers are different. Most thieves sing like pigeons, but the Thumpers know how to keep silent when need be."

"You are more trusting than I."

"We don't have a choice."

"I shall be glad to get home. I hope my dear Edith has not died from worry."

"Are you sure you want to go back now? That town's not far."

"What town would that be? I never did catch its name."

"Bishop's Castle."

"Ah — I have heard it is a lovely place. Such a disappointment to be denied its pleasures. Must we go there?

"We should find out what Harelip was up to."

"Henry, his name is Henry."

"Really? He told me his name was Otto. A lie."

"Obviously."

"You are determined?"

"Quite."

Gilbert's shoulders sagged. "I should have known you'd say something like this. Well, let's get on with it.

Stephen nodded and turned his mare toward Bishop's Castle.

Chapter 21

Stephen buried the dies along the side of the road, using his helmet as a shovel. He chose a spot behind a large oak where it could not be seen by the casual passer-by. He covered the disturbed earth with leaves and placed a marker in the form of a white rock over the spot so he could find if and when he came back.

Gilbert got up from his seat at the base of the tree as Stephen stood back and pried the dirt from beneath his fingernails with the point of his dagger.

"I feel as though I should say a prayer," Gilbert sighed. "So you'll leave them here?"

"It would have been amusing to make my own money."

"Scruples are such a burden. But it is good to see that you have some left, after what's happened."

"Life would be easier without them. My mother worked too hard to pound them into me, though, to give them all up now."

They rode for another hour before town came abruptly into view from behind tall hedges on the right intended to keep the sheep in their field on the hill above the road. There was no wall or embankment and palisade, which was an oddity this far in the west of England, where the savage Welsh were prone to pour out of their mountain fastnesses to wreak havoc. The people of Bishop's Castle might one day rue their decision to forego the expense of a wall, but then the presence of just such public works had not protected the town of Clun last autumn, which had been overrun and burned.

A road came down the hill from the right that led to the back part of the castle. The peak of the motte peeped above the top of the castle's stone wall. It should have been capped with a tower, but, as had been the case he was last here, only bushes and a few saplings occupied the summit where the tower should be. Stephen continued down High Street which lead downhill.

It wasn't far to a wide and somewhat level spot where two streets came together that served as the town market. At the corner, where High Street continued its precipitous journey downhill, was an inn, but Stephen passed it by. It was sure to be an expensive one, since it had a chimney, which indicated a fireplace, a rare and expensive feature. He continued down High Street, which ran a good two hundred yards before the town ended. As he remembered, there was a more modest inn here with a stable alongside it. They stabled their horses, storing Stephen's baggage in the shed, and went into this inn, where dinner was just being served, to Gilbert's relief, since he had not eaten since the day before.

The inn's hall was half the size of the one at the Broken Shield, but there was a fire in the hearth in the center of the floor, a bar well-stocked with small barrels of wine and ale, and the aroma of boiling beef from a kitchen at the rear. Stephen and Gilbert sat down, beckoning to the serving man behind the bar, thinking about the featherbeds they were going to ask for in place of the usual pallet filled with hay. Stephen's purse bursting with stolen money was a temptation to indulge himself more than he knew he was entitled to. He felt a pang of conscience at this thought but he suppressed it with the explanation that Henry-Otto had been a bad man and the money, if it was even good money, had to come from some evil enterprise.

The servant came over, wiping his hands on an apron. "What can I get you?"

"Ale and a bit of that beef I smell, if you don't mind," Stephen said.

"Very good. Cook makes it good and tender. Nothing like a bowl of fresh boiled beef, but I gotta warn ya, it comes expensive."

"I think we can manage it. Say, I'm looking for someone. I wondered if you could help me find him."

"Who's that?"

"Fellow name of Henry. Big, tough looking. A soldier. Has a harelip."

The servant squinted at the far wall. "I don't know any such person. Why do you ask?"

"He owes me money."

"That is unfortunate. Sorry I can't help you." The waiter turned to Gilbert. "And you? What will you have?"

"The same."

"I'll be right back." The servant brought over cups of ale and retreated to the kitchen in the back of the house.

"I don't believe that for a minute!" Gilbert said. "In a town this size!"

They had hardly finished their ale when the servant was back with bowls of stew, the beef swimming in gravy with carrots and leeks and a few errant beans and peas, and a half loaf of black bread so heavy that you could knock a man out with it, but it performed well for soaking up the gravy.

"Quite satisfactory," Gilbert murmured. "Tender, moist, salty. Just the way it should be. If only there were butter for the bread I would be in heaven."

"I'm glad you approve. I'd hate to see you get in a fight with the cook after you had criticized his work."

"I might steal the cook away if I didn't already have a good one." Gilbert swabbed more gravy with a chunk of bread. "I had thought finding this Henry's lair would be easy. He stood out, I'll say that for him. What are we going to do?"

"Ask at every shop in High Street, I suppose. I can't think of anything else to do."

"I was afraid you'd say that. I was hoping to finish this business in a day and be gone. One or two questions, the gang pin-pointed, and we're off for the sheriff. Let him do the hard work of apprehending the evil doers. I don't like it here."

Stephen and Gilbert worked their way up High Street, shop to shop, Stephen on one side of the road and Gilbert on the other as had become their practice. At each shop, Stephen asked after Henry the harelip and about Wattepas as well. But his questions had been received with the same caution as at the inn: evasive looks, pursed lips, and denials of any acquaintance with either man.

Half way up the street he turned to look at Gilbert with an expression of inquiry, and got a shrug in return. Gilbert was meeting the same blank unfamiliarity. Had Gilbert not been confined in Bishop's Castle after all? Was Henry's hideaway somewhere outside town, where he could come and go without anyone here being the wiser? Yet it seemed hard to believe that even if that was true Henry would not have ridden into town at least once. A fellow like that stood out and was hard to forget.

By this time, Stephen had reached the marketplace, where a butcher's shop stood to the right across from the expensive inn. A woman was outside holding a goat on a tether that she wanted the butcher to dispatch for her. She and the butcher were disputing the cost while the goat attempted to nibble at the woman's shoe. When she became aware of this, she gave it a kick, but it started again as she returned her attention to the butcher, who seemed to want more than the single swipe of a knife was worth to her. Perhaps it was a charge for her squeamishness, since most people slaughtered their own goats.

Stephen was thinking about whether to ask the butcher about the location of the town's whorehouse, which might be a better source of information, rather than bother him with questions about Henry or Wattepas when a child's voice behind him called, "That's him!"

Stephen turned to find out who the "him" was. The boy was pointing at him. At the boy's back were six burly fellows with swords.

Stephen could not imagine why some boy he did not know would point him out on the street, and he glanced around to see if there might be someone else about who could be the target. But there was only him, the woman with the goat and the butcher. The boy and the appearance of the soldiers interrupted the negotiation, and the woman and the butcher fell silent to see what was going to happen. The goat did not seem interested, while Gilbert turned his back, suddenly preoccupied with pairs of gloves offered for sale at a shop across the street.

"He's the one been asking about Henry!" the boy said as the soldiers came around him and surrounded Stephen.

"What you want with Henry?" one of the soldiers demanded as they surrounded Stephen.

"Why, he, uh, owes me money," Stephen said.

"Fat chance of that. Who're you?"

"Nobody."

"You got a name, don't ya?"

"Well, yes."

"Then spit it out."

"Uh, Mark. It's Mark."

"Owes you money, eh, Mark?"

"From the bowls. He lost at bowls."

"When'd this happen?"

"A week or two ago. In Ludlow. At the Pidgeon."

One of the other soldiers said, "Henry *was* down there. Twice in the last month."

"But he don't bowl," said the man who had started the questions, who must be the leader.

"Well, he might have done," the second soldier said. "None of us were there."

"What you doing up here?" the leader asked Stephen.

"Just passing through. Thought I'd look him up. It was a friendly game. He don't have to pay up now if he can't."

"What's your business?" the leader asked.

"I'm an archer."

"Are you, now. Let me see your right hand."

The leader didn't wait for Stephen to offer the hand. He seized it and examined Stephen's first two fingers.

"Don't look like you're much of an archer to me," the leader said, letting go of the hand.

"I use a tab," Stephen said. "You know how much the string cuts the fingers."

"Yeah, we know. We're all archers." The leader offered his own right hand. The first two fingers, which drew the string, were heavily calloused. He said to the others, "Something's not right. Bring him along."

They marched Stephen up the hill to the castle. People in the shops and on the street gawked at the procession, no doubt thinking that he was some desperate evil-doer soon to pay for his crimes. A few people even came out of their shops to watch him pass by, muttering their disapproval of Stephen's presence in their law-abiding town. As they neared the bridge over the castle ditch, a curious young couple ceased their hand-holding and rose from their trysting place at the base of a tall beech tree growing out of the side of the ditch in a spot where no tree should be allowed to remain; proper ditches were to be kept clear. Its top reached higher than the castle wall and any enterprising boy could look down into the bailey from its branches.

The captors gave the lovers little time to stare. They pushed Stephen across the wooden bridge into the bailey and then to the hall. It was gloomy inside. The escort propelled Stephen straight across the floor to a collection of people seated by the hearth.

"My lord," the leader said, "we apprehended this fellow in the town asking after Henry. Claims to be an archer, but I have my doubts. There's something fishy going on, and I thought you should know about it."

One of the figures in the gloom turned in Stephen's direction.

"I'll say there's something fishy going on," Nigel FitzSimmons said. His mouth opened to say more, but he hesitated. Expressions of irritation, dismay and finally satisfaction played across FitzSimmons' face. "I never liked Henry's idea. I should have listened to your advice," he said to the woman at his side.

"Good afternoon, Lady Margaret," Stephen said to Margaret de Thottenham. "What are you doing here?"

"My duty," Margaret said. "As I warned Nigel you could be expected to do as well."

"Yes, you warned me he might turn up here," FitzSimmons sighed.

"It's not the first time you've disregarded my advice," Margaret replied to FitzSimmons.

"What has become of Henry and his boys?" FitzSimmons asked.

"They met with an accident," Stephen said.

The expression of irritation, now mixed with anger, returned. "I take from that they are dead."

Stephen shrugged.

"Damn it!" FitzSimmons snapped at no one in particular. "I warned him to be careful." He got control of himself again and asked, "How did you manage it? All by yourself?"

"I'll not give away my secrets any more than you will yours," Stephen said. "What makes you think I don't have the sheriff in on this?"

"Because you wouldn't be here alone if you did," FitzSimmons said. "Besides, you wouldn't want the sheriff to know about the details of our deal." He glanced at Margaret. "I know you must have the dies. What did you do with them?"

"I never had them. It was a trick to recover Gilbert."

"How is poor Gilbert?" Margaret asked.

"Roughly handled, but fine otherwise."

"I am glad to hear that," she said.

"I'll let him know," Stephen said.

"What will you do with Stephen?" Margaret asked FitzSimmons.

"Well, we can't very well let him walk around loose. He's caused us enough trouble already, and as we are almost ready we cannot afford the slightest interruption," FitzSimmons said. "Pity we don't have a proper gaol. You're acquainted with gaols already, I've heard. But I have just the thing." He turned to the leader of the soldiers. "Put him in the barn."

The leader grabbed Stephen's collar and yanked him toward the door.

"I don't want him hurt," Stephen heard Margaret say as he crossed the threshold.

"Not to worry," Nigel said as the door closed. "Now, let's get back to business. There is much yet to be done."

The soldiers chained Stephen to a post at one end of the barn.

"Why no gaol here, anyway?" Stephen asked as his escorts clamped on the collar. He would have welcomed imprisonment in a proper gaol, where he could lie down without a chain or collar.

"Haven't had much need for one since the tower fell down," the leader replied. "But don't worry. You'll be wretched enough here before long."

"Do you think you could find me a pot to piss in, at least?"

"Most folks dig a hole. Try that."

"I am not the sort for getting my hands dirty."

"Ah, well, suit yourself. Just don't complain when you roll in your own shit while you're asleep."

"I'll be careful. When is supper?"

"For you? Next week, I imagine."

Stephen made himself as comfortable as one can shackled to three feet of chain, and settled down against his post for the coming of the night. He should have asked for a blanket as well as a piss pot, but the response probably would have been the same in any case.

Night fell. The interior of the barn grew chilly. The sounds of voices carried from the hall, men and women laughing, a tune being played and then sung. At least people were enjoying themselves. Stephen was not. The chain did not stretch far enough for him to lie down, a common fault of gaol chains. There was nothing like being personally subjected to an injustice to appreciate it for what it was. Soon Stephen was shivering and hugging his legs.

Wind rattled the roof and the walls creaked. The patter of feet was audible nearby and something swift darted across Stephen's outstretched legs. He had the horrified realization that the feet he heard about him belonged to rats. He had heard once of a child being killed when rats got into her crib and chewed off her face. The prospect of such a thing happening to him filled him with dread.

Stephen heard the barn door open and close, and the shuffling sound of someone trying to make his way along in the dark. The shuffling got closer. Someone said, "Sir Stephen, where are you exactly?"

"Not much farther on, Walter," Stephen said, recognizing the voice of one of Lady Margaret's bodyguards.

"Thanks." Walter reached Stephen and knelt down. "My lady sends her apologies."

"For what? For deceiving me?"

"It is the game. Didn't you deceive her? In any case, she is sorry also for your present predicament."

"I have a feeling that there is more in store for me than being chained to a post."

"I am afraid that's true. We overheard earlier this evening that FitzSimmons plans to have you killed. You attempted escape, or something, and unfortunately, the guards were a bit too zealous in their efforts to recapture you."

"When is this supposed to happen?"

"Toward dawn. When everyone is fast asleep."

"How unthoughtful not to wake her up for a murder. Such things are so entertaining."

"He doesn't want Lady Margaret to be more upset than necessary."

"I see I have not given FitzSimmons enough credit. He is a caring man after all. And why are you here? To enable me to make my peace with God without being in a hurry about it?"

"No," Walter said. He grasped Stephen's hand and pressed a small knife into the palm. "My lady sends you this. Although we are on opposite sides, she does not wish your death. It is the best she can do, I'm afraid. The rest you'll have to manage for yourself. I best be going, sir. It's not safe."

"No, it isn't. Give her ladyship my thanks. And thank you, as well."

"There is one favor she asks."

"It is?"

"That you say nothing to anyone about what you saw and heard here."

"That might be difficult."

"It could put her life in jeopardy."

"I see."

Stephen weighed the knife in his hand. "And what about the wall? What am I to do to about that?"

"There's a tall beech not far from the east wall. You must have seen it."

"What of it?"

"How good are you at jumping?"

"You can't be serious."

"It's the best we can do. Can't have a rope left behind. FitzSimmons will know then that you had aid. It must look as though you got away yourself. Got to go now. Best of luck, sir." Walter retreated to the door. It opened and closed, leaving Stephen alone with the rats.

He wasn't sure what use the knife might be. Walter hadn't lingered long enough to share his thoughts on the matter. Stephen drew the short blade from its leather sheath. It was pointed and sharp, and it came to him — just the thing for chiseling out the pin securing his chain to the post.

Chapter 22

Stephen set to work, chipping and gouging away at the wood around the heavy iron pin. His shirt was damp and his hands were sore before he could work it free.

He gathered the chain in his fists so that it would not make too much noise and crept to the barn door. He cracked the door and looked about the bailey. The night was clear, the stars sharp, and moonlight fell across the bailey.

The question was whether there was a watch, and if so, how many men on duty. Some castles did not bother with a watch in peacetime, but this was the March, with the Welsh within a day's ride. The appearance of one man walking a circuit on the wall answered the first question. A few minutes later another man strolled into view, answering the second.

Stephen was considering a dash from shadow to shadow when one of the night watchmen climbed onto a crenellation and fumbled with his drawers to relieve himself over the wall: a common practice of guards not allowed the comforts of any of the towers. Stephen guessed the other man was behind the motte on the north side of the castle, which meant he could not see the bailey.

He slipped through the door and, clutching his chain, dashed to the wall at his left, which was in moon shadow. A wooden stair led up to the wall walk here. He crouched beneath the stair, listening for the slightest sound that he had been detected.

The guard across the way jumped back to the wall walk and resumed his stroll, coming in Stephen's direction. Stephen waited until he had crossed overhead, while the other guard came into view.

There would be no good time to make his move, but Stephen waited a while until the guard overhead had had a chance to move off a bit. Then he crept up the stairs.

At the top he was in full moonlight, except for the toothy shadows cast down by the crenellations. He pressed against the wall, hiding in one of those shadow teeth, breathing hard, trying to remember where that beech tree was. He darted upright and bent outward for a look. The tree was fifteen yards or so away to the right. He scuttled toward it, keeping in the shadow. He saw the branches of the beech above his head, dark etchings against the night sky. He chanced another look between the teeth of the crenellations. It seemed impossibly far away.

"Hey! You!" a voice called from his right: one of the night watchmen.

Stephen had no choice now but to jump or be captured.

He climbed to the top of the wall and gauged the distance. About ten or twelve feet separated him from the nearest branches. Footsteps pounded on the walls, approaching from left and right. Voices were raised in the gate tower.

Stephen leaped as far into space as he could just as the ward arrived to grasp at his heels.

He felt the wind of his passage through the air rustle his hair and hiss in his ears, chain tinkling as it writhed and tugged at his neck. His arms pin-wheeled of their own accord like the fans of a windmill and his feet raced along an invisible path in the air as if he ran across the gap rather than flew.

His trajectory was out and down, like the flight of an arrow, and he collided with the branches lower down. One branch clouted him across the face, knocking him backward so that he lay supine in the air for a moment, then his legs hit another branch and he flipped over. His hands grasped for a purchase as he crashed through the uncertain embrace of the tree. He caught a branch and hung there for a moment, then it snapped and gave way, and he plunged the remaining distance to the ground, rolling into the ditch.

Stephen stood up in the ditch, spending an instant to marvel that he had come through with only a battered and scraped face — the chain had not snagged to hang him, and he had no broken leg or turned ankle to hold him back now.

He wiped blood away from a cut on his cheek and was about to run when a figure that had crouched in the shadow of a fence stood up.

"I say," Gilbert said, "that was ungainly. Are you all right?"

"What are you doing here?" Stephen gasped, starting with fright and astonishment that there was anyone there and it happened to be Gilbert, the last person he expected to see lurking about in the night.

"Waiting for you, of course. Why else would I be here? Come on. If we linger, they'll catch us both. And I for one, have no appetite for imprisonment."

Stephen limped down High Street, bad foot aching with the impact of every pace. It was humiliating that he could just keep ahead of Gilbert, who waddled with unexpected speed at his heels. It must have been a funny sight, but Stephen did not take the time to enjoy it. He heard shouts from the castle and he knew there would be pursuit in moments. He thought about turning east and heading toward the hills that daylight would reveal lay in that direction. But he did not relish being chased while on foot. He had had an experience with that once before, when the pursuers had relied on hunting dogs to track him down, and he had only managed to make an escape through blind luck. He had no doubt that FitzSimmons would call out the dogs before long. He had no confidence that he could evade the pursuit this time.

They reached the marketplace where the road grew momentarily flatter and Stephen's bad foot landed in a rut, twisting his ankle, and he fell over. He stifled a cry and rolled to his feet. Gilbert gave him a rude push and snapped, "This is not the time to tarry!"

"Why couldn't you have thought to bring the horses?"

"And alert the town watch? There is one, you know. And we might have the good fortune to run into him any moment."

"I'd hate that."

"So would I."

"Where did you put the horses, anyway?"

"They're at the stable where we left them yesterday. Now do try to keep up."

The dash down High Street was exhausting and miserable, an event that one day might rival in his memory the flight from Warin Pentre's castle at Bucknell, when he had learned the identify of Rosamond, the girl found dead in the churchyard on Christmas day.

But at last after what seemed like a mile but was probably a mere two-hundred yards, it came to an end and they stood gasping in front of the stable. Like all such establishments, the stable lay separated from the street by a high wall and a sturdy gate, which concealed a yard surrounded by buildings.

The top of the wall and gate was too tall for Stephen to reach with a jump. Gilbert had his hands on his knees, struggling for breath, making more noise than a broken smith's bellows. It would be minutes before he had recovered enough to provide any assistance. Stephen had begun to feel the wings of panic, for he could hear voices raised in alarm up High Street. They didn't have moments to spare. He slammed Margaret's little knife into a post and, using that as a step, managed to leap high enough to grasp the top even as the knife gave way. He chinned himself and slipped over. Theobald the master burglar would have been proud. He threw up the bar and let the gate open itself for Gilbert and ran across the yard.

The interior yard was bathed in moonlight and deep shadow. He reached the stable proper, sure he would hear the voice of another watchman calling the alarm, and slipped inside.

The stable was like any other, with stalls for the horses running left and right. He groped to the right for the fourth and fifth stalls, where they had left the horses. Gilbert had tacked them up and put his canvas bag with his gear in the fourth stall along with his sword. Stephen led the horses back to the yard, where there was yet no sign of Gilbert.

Stephen was about to mount when a noise from behind caused him to turn his head to see a man approaching with a wood axe raised above his head to strike.

"Just what the devil do you think you're doing?" the fellow demanded.

"Recovering my horses," Stephen said.

The stableman squinted to get a better look at Stephen's face. "You're the fellow who was arrested."

"And now I'm free. So please get out of the way."

"I'll not be doing that. I'm arresting you again. Out! Out!" he began to shout, raising the hue and cry

The stableman seemed content to threaten with the axe rather than to use it: to cause delay until help arrived. But Stephen could not afford to wait. He stepped away from the mare so as not to endanger her, then darted at the stableman. The axe-wielder cut into this attack, but Stephen pulled back outside the arc of the cut, for the rush had been a feint intended to provoke the cut. As the axe fell toward the ground, Stephen reversed course and closed with the stableman. He punched the fellow in the face as hard as he could while grasping one of the fellow's arms. The stableman toppled onto his back. Stephen relieved him of the axe and clouted him in the head with the end of the handle.

"I am sorry," Stephen said. He cast away the axe as Gilbert finally staggered into the yard, having recovered enough to manage at least that. "Hurry up!"

"Is he dead?"

"No, now get on your horse."

"Would you mind giving me a leg up? I am quite spent and it is a long way to the saddle."

"Very well."

People were tumbling from the house inhabited by the stableman as Stephen boosted Gilbert to the back of the horse.

He leaped onto his mare, gathering the reins while fumbling to maintain a hold on his sword and the canvas bag, tugging her head toward the gate as he pressed her forward with his heels, urging her onward with his seat, the chain flapping against his back. The people from the house made no effort to close with him, owing to the sword in his hand.

Pursuers from the castle were turning the corner from High Street when Stephen and Gilbert emerged from the stable yard. They blocked the way east, so they galloped west. It was fortunate the castle folk were on foot, because they would have caught them for sure.

The road led westward, when he wanted to go south, and was lined on either side by houses, wicker fences or hedges. Had Stephen been alone, he would have jumped a fence, but Gilbert could hardly manage to stay on at a trot; jumping a fence was beyond him. However, they found a gate, which Stephen leaned far out of the saddle to open, and crossed the field behind a row of houses, cutting southeast until they encountered the Clun road.

A half a mile below the town, Stephen slowed the mare to a walk to allow her to catch her breath. He expected mounted pursuit before long and she needed to be able to run hard when the need arose. With luck the pursuers would have blown their horses in an effort to catch up, while the mare would be fresh again.

"How are you doing?" Stephen asked Gilbert, who by a miracle had not fallen off.

"Not well! Not well at all! Are we going to keep up that pace?"

"Only when they catch up with us."

"Oh, dear! You think they will?"

"I would not be surprised."

"I do not like this. Should we turn off to avoid them?" Gilbert waved at the forests on either side of the road.

"Our best bet is to get to Clun as quickly as possible."

"I do not like that plan. We are not well liked in Clun."

"But we are on the King's business. They will not interfere with us."

"You are more trusting than I."

"If they have dogs, the forest will not protect us. I can tie you to the saddle as I did for Harry, if you like."

"No, that will not be necessary. I cannot bear the thought of being treated like Harry."

"I'll not tell."

"Oh, yes you will. It will slip out in some unguarded moment, and then I'll be a laughingstock."

"Aren't you already that to some people?"

"Perhaps. But let's not make my lot any worse than it already is."

Stephen asked for a trot — a slow one because the trot was the most punishing of the gaits, and merely sitting upon a horse was torment enough for Gilbert. Anything faster either risked pitching him to the ground or provoking another volley of complaints. As it was, Gilbert endured the jolting silently. so that Stephen could listen for the sounds of pursuit. The night was quiet and peaceful beneath the harsh moonlight, the road a silver ribbon stretching ahead.

A mile passed and then another in tranquil quiet, and Stephen began to think that FitzSimmons wasn't coming after all. But then he heard the sound of horses approaching fast on the road behind him, round a bend.

"Back to work," Stephen murmured to the mare as he asked her to a slow canter.

The pursuit came into view within moments. A shout told Stephen that he had been seen. The pursuit urged their horses to greater speed.

Stephen asked for a gallop, as much speed as he could get out of her.

"Oh, God in Heaven, help me!" Gilbert shouted as his horse burst forward to keep up.

Stephen looked over his shoulder at Gilbert, who had dropped his reins and was clutching the saddle pommel. "Stand in the stirrups!" Stephen called. "It's easier that way! And get those reins back!"

"Who knew that riding a mere horse could involve so much trouble," Gilbert said as he fumbled to regain the reins.

The horses ran flat out for at least a mile along a road that rose and fell over gentle hills, but gradually the hill climbs took their toll and the chasers began to tire and fall behind. When Stephen noticed this, he slowed the mare so that she would have something in her if needed. He didn't need to pull away and lose FitzSimmons, he just had to stay ahead and reach Clun first — in fact, it was surprising that FitzSimmons had come this far, for they were now well into the Honor of Clun and the lands of Percival FitzAllan.

Finally, the enemy's horses blew out and the pursuit collapsed to a walk. Stephen slowed to a walk as well, careful to leave at least a hundred yards separating them in case FitzSimmons brought along a crossbowman. Stephen kept an eye on them over his shoulder — there were six that he could see. If they stopped that would be a sure sign they had a crossbowman, who could not shoot accurately from the back of a moving horse, but might risk a shot while halted even at this extreme range.

After a quarter of an hour, Stephen judged that the mare had recovered enough, and he picked up a trot. They rounded a bend on the road, which he remembered from his previous visit to Clun. He had climbed the wooded hill to the left and ridden over it to come at the time from the east. They were was only a mile away. When the bend concealed them from the pursuit, he broke into an easy canter. He felt safe now. The horses could cover the last mile at a gallop if need be and there was nothing FitzSimmons could do.

The rise of the road around the shoulder of the hill ended and the road descended toward the town, invisible in the distance except for a pall of smoke hanging ahead between two hills.

Stephen heard the pursuers galloping behind as they'd speeded up when he disappeared. He urged the mare faster, confident that the pursuit would break off when they realized the town was near.

The town announced its presence by the appearance of rows of houses on either side of the road leading to the castle gate on the northwest corner of the walled part of Clun. A few were only timber frames, not yet completed, since all the houses here — as well as in the town — had been burned by the Welsh during the attack last autumn.

The castle, the walled upper bailey visible over the rooftops, lay apart from the town to the west at a bend of the river. Stephen dipped into the town ditch and urged the mare on the last few yards to the castle gate, certain that he was out of danger.

It was an unusual castle in that it had three baileys, each upon its own motte and apart from the others, surrounded by its own wall and connected by wooden bridges. The lower two had been walled with timber, which had burned in the attack. The palisades on the lower baileys had been rebuilt, but hastily, without towers of any kind. The gate was protected only by a walk above it.

There was no guard on the wall even though the March was still in turmoil, with raids by the Welsh being launched without respite. No one knew where a Welsh army would pop up next. Only last month a second attack on Clun had been blunted in a battle just west of Newcastle no more than three miles off, with heavy losses on the part of the Welsh.

Without dismounting, Stephen banged on the gate with the pommel of his sword and called out, "Hello! Hello! Open the gate in the King's name!"

But no one answered or showed himself above.

He thought he heard noises within, but those sounds diminished in importance because there was a new one from his rear: horses coming up. He glanced back and saw three horsemen clamber out of the town ditch.

"At him!" FitzSimmons snarled, and they charged, swords drawn and pointed.

Stephen sat stunned, disbelieving that FitzSimmons would pursue him to the gates of Clun, which was enemy territory to him and as unsafe as any place could be, since FitzAllan was an ardent a supporter of the king.

His mare was a peculiar mount. She had been a cow pony in central Spain before he bought her, and she knew what to do when charged almost without being asked: only slight leg pressure on her left side behind the girth sent her dancing sideways at the moment when the attackers reached striking distance. She danced a canter in a semicircle, bringing Stephen to the unprotected left side of the man on the far left, and Stephen cut him down with a swipe of his sword, a wound that severed the man's spine.

FitzSimmons and the other attacker yanked their horses about, while Stephen applied his right leg so that the mare now danced to the left in order to keep the attackers on the right where he could use his sword to defend as well as attack.

FitzSimmons' companion delivered a frightful blow at Stephen's head, rising up on the stirrups to give as much force as he could to it. Stephen parried in the left hanging guard and cut at the man's thigh. The sword went through his leg and stuck for a moment in the leather panel of the saddle before the mare's dancing carried Stephen away and dislodged it. The companion, his leg attached by a thread of flesh, sagged over his horse's head as it trotted away.

Stephen thought that deprived of his support FitzSimmons would break off, but he was wrong. FitzSimmons attacked furiously, and the horses circled each other, each man trying to get to the other's back or left side, exchanging and defending blows one after another in quick succession, the *ting!* of clashing swords filling the air with the music of death.

Stephen marveled at the agility and responsiveness of the mare. He had exercised her in this way now and then in the paddock, but had never considered her for this deadly work, yet it was as if she directed the battle rather than him — needing only leg pressure and shifts in his seat rather than reins to guide her.

It was hard to tell how long this went on. It seemed like forever but could have only been a minute or two. Then the three missing companions emerged from the ditch, their delay probably from the fact they rode lesser horses which could not keep up.

Stephen saw the arrivals out of the corner of his eye. Dismay and a realization that this was his end filled his mind. He could barely stand up to FitzSimmons, let alone four at once, and with all so close he could not run — he would be cut down right away if he tried.

"Belay that now!" a voice called from above their heads. "Or I'll fill you all full of shot!" There were five men on the wall above them glaring down over drawn crossbows.

Stephen and FitzSimmons drew apart and the newly arrived companions halted beside their leader.

"What's going on here?" the voice demanded.

Stephen pointed his sword at FitzSimmons. "They are enemies of the King. I bring word of their misdeeds, and they would kill me to silence my message."

"Who are you?" the voice asked.

"Stephen Attebrook, deputy coroner of Ludlow."

"You don't say. And who are they?"

"Nigel FitzSimmons, follower and servant of Simon de Montfort. The others I do not know. But they are with him."

"Is this true?" the voice demanded of FitzSimmons.

In answer, FitzSimmons wheeled his horse and rode into the town ditch. In a moment he and the others were out of sight.

"Well, I suppose it is," the voice said. "You! Throw down that sword and get off the horse. I'll not open this gate until you do."

Stephen dropped his sword and dismounted. The gate swung open. Three armed men emerged, one carrying a lighted lantern. The man with the lantern held it close to Stephen's face.

"You're Attebrook, all right," said the man who had called down from the wall. "I remember you from your last visit. Lord Percival will be glad to get his hands on you. Hold him tight, boys. We'll be certain he doesn't slip away again."

Stephen looked about, expecting Gilbert to be ordered off his horse as well. But there was no sign of the clerk.

Chapter 23

Stephen was a prestigious enough guest to bring out the castle's constable, Richard de Dageworth, to see to his welfare.

"This is him, eh?" Dageworth asked the guards, peering closely at Stephen in the flickering candlelight, for during Stephen's last visit they had not met.

"It's him, sir," one of the guards replied, giving Stephen a shove.

"Lord Percival will be glad to get his hands on you after all the trouble you've caused," Dageworth said. "For my part, I was a friend of Warin Pentre's and I'll not soon forgive you for his death. I'll be there when you pay for it."

"It wasn't my doing," Stephen said. "Blame for that lies elsewhere." This was not exactly truthful. He had played a role in the attack on Pentre's castle at Bucknell, just not a direct one. However, what he had done was damning enough if the full truth ever got out.

"So you say. But a murderer's words cannot be believed. Put him in hold."

"Whatever your grievances, you are commanded not to interfere with me," Stephen said as the guards grasped arms and one took up the chain which still dangled from his neck. "I am on crown business of the most urgent sort."

"I doubt that, traitor," Dageworth said.

"I've uncovered a ring of counterfeiters of the king's money. Report that, at least, when you tell FitzAllan of my capture. He'll want to know about it."

"I might."

It seemed that those rebuilding the lower baileys had not yet got around to providing for a gaol, although some thoughtful person had arranged for the erection of a set of stocks in the yard of the middle bailey. The guards led Stephen to the stocks. Stephen wished now for his post at the barn of Bishop's Castle, for he could at least sit down there. Here he had to stand up. It would be a long, sleepless night.

"You'll be comfortable here, I'm sure," Dageworth said with relish before he turned away.

A messenger set out for Hereford at dawn to inform Earl Percival of Stephen's capture. Stephen wished the messenger a swift and safe journey, for he had not got a wink of sleep during the night, and the prospects for any were dim.

Shortly after the messenger's departure, the castle's children were let out of doors by their mothers, and it wasn't long before they spotted Stephen. The children gathered round and amused themselves for some time by hurling insults and pelting him with cow and horse shit before the mothers intervened and put them to their chores.

Breakfast came shortly thereafter, evidenced by the disappearance of everyone into the bailey's timber hall by the gate to the upper bailey. The hall's windows were open and Stephen watched the activity with some envy because no one had given any thought to his breakfast, except for one of the castle wards who plucked off a piece of fresh horseshit which had clung to Stephen's cheek and pressed it to Stephen's mouth before walking on to a more tasty meal. "Needs salt!" Stephen said to the man's back as he spit out the bits that got in his mouth.

The morning wore on without incident apart from one boy who flung a stone at Stephen's head. Fortunately, the aim was off and the stone succeeded in only nicking one of Stephen's hands.

About noon, when dinner had concluded, a young woman crossed from the kitchen with a clay jug and something wrapped in a cloth. The cross expression on her face suggested that she did not like the chore she had been given. Yet she let Stephen drink from the jug, spilling a good bit of the water it contained, not very concerned whether he got any of it. The object wrapped in the cloth proved to be a butt of moldy bread, which she delighted in forcing into his mouth. Not being particular about the condition of his bread — glad in fact that there was any — Stephen chewed the hard crusts that made it past his lips. Some fell to the ground. At first, he thought the woman might feed him that too, dirt and all, but she flung the scraps into the pigsty and departed. The commotion among the pigs indicated that they enjoyed the treat more than Stephen had done.

The afternoon, full of the misery of aching feet and back, chafing neck, cramps in the shoulders, and a desperate desire for sleep, dragged on far longer than it had any right to do. Supper arrived for the servants in the middle bailey, but no one stooped to feed the prisoner.

Then there was the interminable wait for nightfall, any hope of being released to take his ease upon the cold, hard ground dashed as castle folk gathered for some singing and dancing in the hall before the candles were blown out at last and everyone retired for a night that grew increasingly chilly, despite the fact that spring was supposed to be underway. Clouds crept across the stars and a wind arose, carrying the scent of rain.

With the departure of the day, Stephen lost track of time. He surprised himself by being able to doze off standing up and leaning his weight upon the stocks, a discovery for which he was grateful even if the sleep he obtained was not very refreshing.

Sometime well into the night a commotion in the lower bailey awakened him: voices shouting, muffled by distance. The gate to the middle bailey creaked as it opened. At least ten riders trotted through the wooden gatehouse and headed up the bridge to the upper bailey, where the constable and his officers made their residence.

Hours seemingly went by. Then figures emerged from the dark and stood before Stephen.

"What's that God awful smell?" Dageworth demanded. "Have you shat your drawers, man?" He laughed and the men accompanying him laughed with him.

"What do you want? You're interrupting my sleep."

Dageworth did not reply. He said to the men behind him, "Unlock him, and get him cleaned up before you bring him into the hall. I'll not expose the ladies to that filth."

It took the support of a man on either arm to help Stephen reach the stone hall in the upper bailey. The escorts stripped him of his clothing at the foot of the steps, doused him with buckets of freezing well water, then forced him to wash with soap before they gave him a change of fresh clothes. To be fair, Stephen was glad for the soap and the clothing, although he wished for warmer water, since it took some time before he was able to stop shivering. This sharp discomfort was the reason few people took regular baths.

Dageworth was still up when Stephen entered the hall, a candle burning on the high table at his elbow, his deputy at his side. Stephen made out several feminine faces peering at him round the corner of a stair.

"Those riders came from the earl?" Stephen asked.

Dageworth shook his head. "No, they are from Walter Henle in Ludlow. I am ordered to turn you over to them. I am disappointed."

"You poor fellow."

Dageworth drummed on the table. "I would appreciate it if you do not speak of your reception here when you see the earl."

"We'll talk about that after I've had a night's sleep. Where is my bed, anyway?"

"That way." Dageworth gestured toward the stairs as the women, who had been watching there, ducked out of sight.

Chapter 24

Stephen reached Ludlow late in the afternoon, having got a late start from Clun. Stephen would have liked nothing better than to creep off to the Broken Shield and his garret room, for he had not recovered from the rough handling he received during the preceding days, but his escort insisted that they proceed directly to the castle.

He surrendered his sword to a servant at the doorway to the hall and entered the vast chamber. As was often the case when a high functionary was in residence, the hall was filled with people: various petitioners seeking favors, hangers on and lesser officials, with servants hurrying about seeing to their needs while the visitors loitered around waiting to be noticed or to be called upon.

Henle was standing by the fireplace at the far end of the hall. He looked up at Stephen's entrance and turned away from the cleric who had occupied his attention. He beckoned Stephen to approach.

"Your man Gilbert reports that you've discovered the den of the counterfeiters," Henle said.

Stephen's promise of silence came to mind. But that promise had not applied to Gilbert, and it appeared he had made as full a report as he could. "I think so."

"In Bishop's Castle, it seems."

"The trail seems to lead there. It is curious. Nigel FitzSimmons is at the heart of it. I cannot say why."

"I'd like nothing better than to clap him in irons. We shall ride there directly and put a stop to it."

"But it's outside our jurisdiction."

"We have an obligation to the King to take action immediately. No one will care."

"Well, the sheriff of Shropshire might take exception."

"It will be done and over before he knows of it." Henle smiled. "And we will get the credit. We will ride first thing in the morning. Now, go get some sleep. You look terrible. Off you go. I have much to do to prepare for this expedition, and I haven't any more time to waste with you."

"I don't see why Gilbert needs to go too," Edith said as she set a platter of sliced beef on the table for Stephen.

"We need to find the evildoers who had me in their cellar," Gilbert said, helping himself to some of the beef even though it was not yet dinner time and the meal had been brought out for Stephen's benefit, a sign of Edith's appreciation for having returned Gilbert to her. "They must be brought to justice along with the others."

"I'm sure Sir Stephen can find the house," Edith said. "He's so good at that."

"He's only good at it because he has my advice," Gilbert said with a mouthful of beef.

"Swallow before you speak, my dear," Edith said. "You aren't in the monastery."

"We weren't allowed to speak at all there," Gilbert said.

"A rule that ought to be observed here from time to time," she replied. "We would all be better off for it." She gathered up the platter and returned to the kitchen.

"You're sure you want to come?" Stephen asked.

"I want to see the expressions on their faces when they are arrested."

"I did not think you were a man given to vengeance."

"Normally I am full of forgiveness, but I am making an exception here."

"It will mean another long ride."

"It will be in daylight, thank God. Not another night ride. I got lost twice on the way back to Ludlow. It was miserable. You cannot thank me enough for it."

"Well, it's a good thing you made it back. Otherwise I'd still be in the stocks. So tell me," Stephen asked, "there wasn't a chance to ask on our ride, but how did you happen to be at the tree? The last I recall, you were trying to hide behind a rain barrel."

"That is unkind, though I did try to remain inconspicuous. I first thought of running away, but instead, I followed you to the castle gate. They wouldn't let me in, of course, not that I tried. Lady Margaret's man Walter saw me there. He exchanged good days, which I must say, gave me quite a fright. I expected him to call the alarm and have me arrested. But he merely asked why I had turned up in Bishop's Castle. So I told him."

"All of it?"

"No, of course not all of it. I'm not that mean spirited or daft. Just enough to make my presence plausible."

"That is a relief."

"He told me to go back to the inn. He came later with the plan. And here we are. His plan worked out splendidly, something I cannot say for yours."

Henle's party consisted of four knights besides Stephen and thirty-five or so sergeants from the garrison and called up from manors about Ludlow. Forty armored horsemen made an impressive sight trotting two-by-two, so much so that many people, alerted to the spectacle as they rode through Bromfield flocked to the roadside to watch them pass. Even Gilbert's unassuming presence and bumpy horsemanship did not mar the magnificence of the procession.

It was a good twenty miles to Bishop' Castle, a full day's ride for most people, but they traveled at the army pace when unencumbered by infantry and reached it by midday.

A forty-man troop was still reckoned by some to be an army, since many raiding parties in the borderland failed to muster that many, and the shops of Bishop's Castle emptied as they went by, the people watching silently and with some apprehension, for no one ever expected anything good to come from a gathering of armed men.

They passed up High Street at such a brisk pace that the castle gates were still open when they reached them, and were crossing the bridge even as the gate wardens hurriedly closed the portal.

Henle had not expected to be shut out, and he shouted to be let in, even adding he had come in the King's name. No one answered his summons for many moments. Then figures appeared at the top of the gate tower.

Stephen recognized the under-constable, Martin Pico, as he called down, "What do you want?"

"I have come for Nigel FitzSimmons!" Henle called back.

"Whatever for?" Pico asked in response.

"He is here?"

Pico's eyes wandered to Stephen as he considered his reply. "He was. He is no longer."

"Open the gate so I can establish this fact for myself."

"Have you a warrant for Sir Nigel's arrest?"

"I have." And the ink had hardly dried on it, since it had been drawn up only that very morning before they had set out, issued by none other than Henle himself.

"The last I heard you were a mere undersheriff of Herefordshire. You have no jurisdiction here."

"I have jurisdiction wherever the King's business takes me. Now open the gate."

Pico was quiet for a moment. "Very well. I will allow you and one other in."

Henle's mouth tightened. He did not like this condition. But he nodded. "Attebrook!" he said as he dismounted. "Come with me."

The gate cracked wide enough to admit a man on foot and the wardens pushed it shut and dropped the bar, which landed with a great thud.

Although Stephen and Henle had their shields on their backs, they kept a hand on the pommels of their swords, for there had been nothing friendly about Pico's reception, and given the political climate, anything might happen, most of it not good. However, there were only the wards of the gate to receive them, armed with sword, shield and spear, to be sure, but lacking mail and helmets, menacing enough to the ordinary man, but not to Stephen and Henle even if they were outnumbered.

They waited in the bailey for several moments, then Henle struck out toward the hall just as Pico emerged from the gate tower.

"What do you want with Sir Nigel?" Pico called to Henle's back as he hurried to catch up.

"They kept you in the barn, you said," Henle said to Stephen as they reached the hall.

"Yes."

Henle rounded on Pico. "Assault of a King's officer for starters. For which I've a mind to arrest you as an accomplice."

Pico blinked. Apparently he had not expected to be vulnerable to accusation himself. "And that would be for the unfortunate events surrounding Sir Stephen's visit?"

"It would," Henle snapped as he entered the hall.

"It was a personal matter," Pico said, "between the two of them. There is some bad blood between them, the death of one of Sir Nigel's relatives, I'm told."

"And you did not interfere," Henle said.

"I'm afraid not. FitzSimmons is a formidable man. One is not wise to cross him."

"What was he doing here?"

"I'm not sure. Paying a visit. He wasn't here long."

"Hmm," Henle said. Only servants were in the hall, so he headed for the stairs to the upper chambers. "Come along, Attebrook."

It did not take long to search the upper chambers, including the servants' rooms in case FitzSimmons was skulking in one of them. Then they went outside and looked into every outbuilding, down to the kitchen, smithy and barn, leaving the pig sty and cattle shed since no one of FitzSimmons' stature could be hiding there, although those are exactly the places Stephen would have picked and for that very reason. The search of these buildings did not take long either.

"We should question the servants," Stephen said to Henle as they stood in the yard. "We'll get more out of them than Pico."

"No need," Henle snarled, his disappointment plain at not having caught FitzSimmons out or of having seen anything to do with a counterfeiting operation. "What could they possibly tell us?" He gestured toward the main gate. "Open up!"

Pico looked relieved until Henle added, "We'll pitch camp in one of the fields to the south of town. I'll expect food and drink to be sent down to us. At your expense."

"Of course," Pico said.

"Decent food, you hear? None of the scraps meant for the pigs."

Henle proposed to remain the day and a night not because he thought the delay might reveal some secret that would put FitzSimmons into his hands, but out of consideration for the horses. Asking more than twenty miles in a day of them was too much except in urgent circumstances.

Stephen and Gilbert had no tent of their own, and were forced to share one with eight of the sergeants. They sat on folding camp chairs while the sergeants put up the tent. The sergeants were pounding in the last of the pegs when a caravan of carts appeared from the town and turned into the field where they had made camp. Pico had not tarried in sending down the promised food and fodder for the horses, although the food was not cooked. However, he had sent cooks to take care of that, and they set to work building fires, hanging slabs of meat and cutting vegetables for a stew that would be ready in a few hours' time. Meanwhile, a servant passed out loaves of fresh bread and hard boiled eggs to tide them over.

"I would wager that FitzSimmons decamped as soon as he got back from Bishop's Castle," Stephen said as he tucked into his ration of bread and eggs. "The question is, what was he up to and where has he gone?"

"Somewhere he cannot be traced, I would imagine," Gilbert said. "That's that, I suppose. I thought you had lost interest."

"If we find FitzSimmons, I may be accused of the theft of the dies. They have no proof, but an accusation itself could be my undoing."

"Ah, yes, I had not thought of that possibility. I'm sorry."

"But I would like to know — for my own sake."

Gilbert sighed. "I would as well."

"So then —there is the place where you were held. Now that we've come back, it makes sense to finish what we started. It wasn't at the castle, at least you did not give me that impression."

"It wasn't. I'm sure of that."

"But you don't know where it was."

"I am afraid not. It was close by a market, though, I am fairly sure of that now. I have thought a lot about it on our rides and I believe I heard men haggling over prices — and the scent of fresh buns. And there is another thing: the cellar that was my home away from home was on the ground floor. An odd place for a cellar."

"Was it cold and musty?"

"Your usual cellar."

"Perhaps it was dug into the side of the hill."

Gilbert looked thoughtful. "That could be."

Stephen rose from his chair. "Let's see if we can find it."

"But supper will be ready soon."

"Supper is still several hours away. You can't wave a wand and make water boil."

"No, you can't."

The horses had been untacked and tethered on a line for feeding and watering, so there was nothing for it but to walk.

High Street was no less steep this time than when they first made the climb. It went faster though because they did not stop at any of the shops to ask after Henry. So it was only a matter of minutes before they had retraced their steps to the door of the butcher shop below the peak of High Street where Stephen had been arrested. He exchanged glances with the butcher.

"Could I interest you in a chop, sir?" the butcher called.

"You might send a boy down to that field below town," Stephen replied. "We're camped there. The undersheriff might be interested."

"Very good, sir." The butcher spoke to his boy who dashed into the street, pausing at the sight of Stephen.

"Is it true, sir, that you leaped from the castle wall?" the boy asked.

"Yes."

"Landed on your face, then?" the boy asked, grinning.

Stephen felt the cut on his cheek throb. It had closed up once Edith picked out the embedded bits of bark and it only pained him when he thought about it. "I'd have broken my neck, wouldn't I?"

"Of course, sir." The boy raced away downhill.

Stephen gestured at the street that came in from the left, which was level compared to the other streets in town and joined High Street at a wide junction. "This is the market."

Gilbert looked around as if seeing it for the first time. "Not much room for a market."

"It's a small town. There probably isn't much to sell."

"Odd place for a butcher shop. Ordinarily those things are kept out of sight."

"Perhaps the people of Bishop's Castle like seeing their dinners slaughtered. Some people do. Cheap entertainment."

"I'm not aware of any such people. It's almost like consorting with tanners."

"You said you heard men haggling. Are you sure it couldn't have been someone at a shop?"

Gilbert pulled his lip. He closed his eyes. He opened them. "We were going down a hill, not a steep one, certainly not as steep as the one we've just climbed. And we weren't that far into the town. We went right as I heard the noise. It stopped as we approached and there was murmuring."

"What sort of murmuring? What did they say?"

"Just murmuring. You know, muttering of some sort."

"But you couldn't make out the words?"

"What difference would that have made? Besides, I had a sack over my head. It is hard to hear clearly with a sack over your head, not to mention the way it interferes with one's vision. I do remember that the road was not steep. It seemed to have leveled out."

Stephen gestured up Market Street. "It levels out here."

"So it does."

Stephen entered Market Street. It curved gently to the right and was lined on both sides by shops and houses shoulder to shoulder so that there was no telling how far back the buildings ran and whether, on the right, they bunched against the hillside.

They were nearing the intersection with a street that came in from the left to plunge downhill, with the market expanse out of sight behind the curve of the road when Gilbert stopped short.

"Do you hear that?" Gilbert asked.

"Do I hear what, your stomach growling?"

"That tapping."

"I don't hear any tapping unless it's your guts clanking together."

"Here now! I'm being serious!"

"Why should tapping matter?"

"Because I remember now! I heard the same sound."

"Now or then?"

"Then!"

Stephen listened. He heard nothing. Then he caught the sound of faint tapping, not as if on wood, but as if on metal.

"It's coming from here!" Gilbert hurried to a shop a few steps ahead. Unlike the normal business in town, the shutters were closed. Gilbert pressed his ear to the shuttered window and pointed. "It's here!"

"All right, so you heard tapping. Then what?" Stephen asked.

"Well, it stopped. And I was taken into a house and marched directly to that cellar I told you about, and locked in."

"So you're saying that this house was near the sound of the tapping."

"That's exactly what I'm saying."

Stephen pounded on the door of the shop which was the source of this mysterious tapping.

The tapping stopped. A few moments later a short bald man wearing an apron, in his hand a small hammer not unlike the sort Leofwine Wattepas, the Ludlow goldsmith, was known to use.

"May I help you, sir?" the little bald man asked. Then he caught sight of Gilbert to Stephen's rear. His eyes widened in shock and surprise.

"Do you know him?" Stephen asked.

"I-I-I-," the bald man stammered, "I can't say that I know him."

"But you've seen him before."

"Not his face. But it is hard to forget a belly like that." The little bald man motioned with his hands, contouring a stomach that was rather larger and more impressive than the one Gilbert possessed, although it was impressive in its own right.

"I take exception, sir," Gilbert said. "I am not fat."

"Right," Stephen said. "We do not refer to Master Wistwode as fat. He is stout. But you have seen his," Stephen mimicked the contouring gesture, "before."

"Indeed I have."

"Under what circumstances?"

"He was . . . shall I say, a guest in this house."

"That is a polite way of putting it," Gilbert muttered.

"And why was he a guest in your cellar?" Stephen asked.

"Oh," the bald man said, "it isn't my cellar. I merely rent the shop."

"You don't live behind?"

"I could not afford the rent. It is quite a grand house and this is an exclusive district."

"What is your business?"

"I am a tinsmith."

"A tinsmith." Stephen considered this answer for a moment. "You wouldn't know anything about the minting of money, would you?"

The tinsmith looked away, eyes darting. "I have nothing to do with that!"

"You mean, there was the minting of money going on here?"

"At the castle. Not here."

"But the people who live here are involved."

The tinsmith drew a deep breath and let it gust out. "Yes."

"Of course they were," Gilbert said from behind. "How involved?"

"Henry is a castle guard," the tinsmith said. "He does the constable's bidding."

"How is it that a castle ward enjoys the use of a house like this?" Stephen asked.

"I don't know," the tinsmith said. "The constable must like him, I suppose. He is useful at getting people to pay their rents, I'll say that for him. All he has to do is show up at their doorstep, and most people pour the contents of their purses on the ground. Please don't say to anyone that I spoke ill of him. He has a bad temper."

"Is Henry home now?" Stephen asked, even though he already knew the answer to that.

"He'd be at the castle now, wouldn't he? Or out and about on some chore for the constable," the tinsmith said.

"I'll speak to his wife, then."

"The family isn't home."

"Where are they?"

"I don't know. They left in a bit of a hurry."

"Like Nigel FitzSimmons and all the folk at the castle who were involving in minting money?"

The tinsmith hesitated. "Yes."

"Do you know where they went?"

"No. They didn't say. Somewhere into England, is what I heard. It is a secret, or so I was told."

"Secrets are notoriously hard to keep."

"People are keeping that one. So far, anyway. Pico said he'd have the head off anyone who spoke out." The tinsmith glanced up and down Market Street. "Are you done? I've work to do."

"Did they leave any servants behind?" Stephen asked.

"Did who leave servants behind?"

"Henry and his family when they left."

"I didn't say Henry left with his family."

"But you did say the family left."

"Well, yes. I did say that. And no. There are no servants. There's only —" The tinsmith stopped short and clamped his lips together.

"There's only, who?" Stephen pressed.

"Only the grannie. She's old and frail and was not up to the journey."

Stephen pushed by the tinsmith into the hallway that ran by the shop into the depths of the house. "I'll speak to grannie, then."

"Please, sir. Don't make trouble! Go away before anyone sees you!"

Stephen grasped the little man by the collar and drew him close. "Fetch grannie, or I'll have your head off."

"That would create such a mess," Gilbert said. "I'm sure your wife wouldn't want that."

"All right! All right!" the tinsmith fairly shouted. He retreated into the house.

Stephen followed him to the hall, suspecting he might slip out the back or a side door. But the tinsmith got as far as a bent figure in a chair by the central hearth without making a break for it.

"Grannie," the tinsmith said, "you've a visitor."

"I heard the racket," the old woman said. "You woke me up. Do you always have to shout?"

"I wasn't shouting."

"You were! I know shouting when I hear it! I may be feeble, but I'm not deaf. What do they want?"

"The fat fellow whom Henry put in the cellar. He's come back."

"What? Does he need accommodations again?"

"No, I don't think so. They're asking about the . . . you know what."

"Oh, dear. This is a pickle. I knew that business would be more trouble than it's worth. I told Henry not to get involved. But that fool boy never listens." The old woman squinted at the tinsmith. "Who is the 'they' you speak of, Lutelheed?"

"Them." Lutelheed pointed to Stephen and Gilbert, who had remained at the entrance but now advanced across the hall.

The old woman looked Stephen up and down, gauging his social status at a glance. "Pardon me, sir, if I do not get up. I am infirm."

"I see that," Stephen said. There were two canes leaning against the arm of her chair.

"Lutelheed has no manners. He should have asked your name — you can go, by the way, Lutelheed. I shall take care of things myself from here on."

"Of course." Lutelheed hesitated as if he wanted to hear more despite this direct order, but under the old woman's formidable gaze, he retreated to the entrance and shut the door.

"There!" the old woman said. "Now we can talk. You are?"

"Stephen Attebrook. This is my friend and colleague, Gilbert Wistwode."

"I know this Wistwode, by sight if nothing else. And I have heard of you. I am not surprised that you turned up. Where is Henry?" When Stephen did not respond, the old woman said, "He's dead, isn't he."

"I am afraid so."

"Did you kill him?"

"Not directly, no."

"But you had a hand in it."

"Kidnapping is a rough business. Anyone involved in it cannot expect gentle handling."

The old woman sighed. "I know that. I am not surprised to hear this. I warned him against it, in fact. But he was always eager for the main chance. If it wasn't one scheme it was another."

"Was he your son?"

"Grandson. So now why have you come? You have your prize back." She flicked a finger at Gilbert. "I don't know how you put up with him. Always complaining about the food."

"I think you know. This business you mentioned."

"Of course." But instead of going on, the old woman's lips clamped shut.

When she did not go on, Stephen said, "At first I thought it was Henry's plot. But I have since learned there seems to be more to it than that."

Again, the old woman did not speak. She stared into the fire. At last she said, "It is not for me to talk about it. They are ruthless, those people."

"You mean Nigel FitzSimmons."

She waved a hand before her face, the same motion as swiping at a bothersome fly. "Him, the people around him. They'll be back eventually. And when they are, they'll settle with anyone who's crossed them. Even little old women like me are not safe from them." She motioned toward the door.

"No doubt Lutelheed is listening. He wouldn't mind a reward for betraying my betrayal."

"Would it be a betrayal? They are against the King."

"FitzSimmons is a friend of the lord of this place. Of course it would be a betrayal."

While they had been speaking, Gilbert crept toward the door to the shop. He opened it, closed it and turned around. "Master Lutelheed has returned to work."

"Has he? How out of character," the old woman said.

"You can speak then without being overheard," Stephen said. "If you've a mind to."

She smiled. "You'll not bring out the thumbscrew?"

"I left it at home. Sorry."

"Well, the two of you could beat it out of me, I suppose."

"You look like a match for both of us."

The old woman chuckled. "That would have been true fifty years ago. I'll tell you what I know, on condition."

"Which is?"

"Tell me where you left Henry, so I can have him fetched and buried proper."

"All right." Stephen described the spot of the ambush.

The old woman nodded, as if gathering her thoughts. "It is a close held secret, this thing of theirs. And unlike most secrets it was kept. But Henry did overhear things while he was up at the castle. Bits and pieces here and there. If one put them together and thought about them, one could get a picture."

"And you did?"

"Of course I did. I'm no dolt, unlike most people in this town. They are so frightened of the castle folk that they prefer to look away and pretend that nothing is happening."

"Go on."

"Even as I think about it now, it takes my breath away with its audacity."

"You have piqued my interest."

"I am not the one who did that." The old woman rubbed her thighs. "War is coming. They are planning for it. They are minting money for the war. I understand that armies are expensive. Montfort needs an army. This is how they propose to pay for it."

"I thought that might be it. Where have they gone?"

"I don't know. That piece of information was not shared with me when my grandson and his family left in such haste."

"Your grandson?"

"I have a full dozen. It's hard sometimes to keep them all straight. Two live, or lived, here, with their families." The old woman clapped her hands. "There you have it! That's all I know. Precious little, isn't it? You could have figured it out for yourself, as you are well acquainted with Sir Nigel, or so I was told." She laughed at having got what she wanted at so cheap a price.

"There is one thing that puzzles me," Gilbert said as the pair trod slowly down High Street toward the encampment on account of Stephen's bad foot, which had begun to ache again and caused him to limp. "Why would FitzSimmons mint bad money? We found quite a lot of it. You don't want to pay soldiers with bad money. They'd rebel."

"I was wondering the same thing," Stephen said.

"No, you weren't. I got there first."

"You only spoke first and in haste. I was waiting for evidence to support my suspicions." Stephen picked up the pace. "Come on, supper might be ready by now. If you're as hungry as I am, we could eat a horse between us."

Chapter 25

Supper was not quite ready when they got back to camp, but nearly so, vapors rising from the cooking pots and fragrant smells wafting across the grass.

Stephen sat on a camp stool, his conscience at war with itself. There were so many interests and concerns each pulling in its own direction that he thought he might fly apart. Most of the time, his conscience kept to itself so the experience was novel and unwelcome.

A servant poured wine into Walter Henle's wine cup a few steps away before another tent. I should let it lie, Stephen thought. That was the sensible and prudent thing. But by themselves his legs forced him up and across the gap.

"Where are you going?" Gilbert asked in surprise, for one of the cooks began calling that supper was ready.

"I won't be a moment."

"This can't be good," Gilbert said as he put down his wooden bowl and followed Stephen.

Henle regarded Stephen and Gilbert over the rim of his wine cup. He swirled the cup and motioned for his servant to refill it.

"You expect me to believe that some old woman in the town knows what FitzSimmons is up to?" Henle asked when Stephen finished giving his brief report of what he and Gilbert had learned. "Some crone on the street?"

"She was in a position to hear things," Stephen said.

"Rumors and innuendo," Henle snorted. "Guess work, gossip, nothing more."

"I don't think so. I think her news is reliable."

"Whatever it is, it isn't much." Henle's teeth ground together. "What do you expect me to do with this intelligence, if we can even call it that?"

"Report it to the sheriff. He'll want to know. The King and his advisors will want to know."

"FitzAllan," Henle muttered. "He'll put no more stock in this gossip than I do." He wagged a finger at Stephen. "No, I'll not stake my reputation on this. I've my position to think of."

"Of course you do," Gilbert was heard to say.

"What was that?" Henle asked.

"Nothing, my lord," Gilbert added hastily. He tugged at Stephen's sleeve. "Let's leave his lordship to his wine. Our supper is getting cold, if there's even any left for us."

"By your leave, sir," Stephen said.

"Go," Henle said.

Stephen turned away, Gilbert at his side.

"I thought you were afraid that FitzSimmons will be caught," Gilbert said.

"I am. But I think the King would like to know that his enemies are preparing to move against him, and soon, if I read the signs correctly — no matter the cost to me and to —   "
He broke off.

"To whom?"

"Margaret's involved in this."

"I knew she had to be. She seems to be everywhere, her finger in every pie. You saw her again? Here?"

Stephen nodded. "I owe her a debt which I am afraid I will not be able to repay."

"Well, I don't think you owe that woman anything. She's using you, like she uses everyone."

A rebuke came to Stephen's lips, for Margaret's less appealing qualities were balanced by others that Gilbert had not seen or did not sufficiently appreciate, but he suppressed it. Gilbert was right in the main, of course, although Stephen didn't like to hear it.

"That may be," Stephen said. "One betrayal deserves another, I suppose."

Chapter 26

The gossips of Ludlow had moved on from counterfeiters and unfathomable plots by the time Henle's party returned from Bishop's Castle to the more titillating news that the marriage of Adele Wattepas to Sir Maurice Crauford had been postponed, cancelled some said while others maintained that it had merely been put off. The argument raged.

"I for one am glad to hear it," Edith said as the Wistwode family gathered about the fire at the end of the day, their work done, taking the weight off their exhausted feet before retiring for the night. "That woman has been scheming to climb back into the gentry since I first knew her."

"You should not be so unkind, my dear," Gilbert said staring into the fire.

"Well, it's the truth!" Edith said.

"Yet doesn't Adele have a right to some happiness?"

"That marriage isn't about Adele's happiness, although I don't doubt she would be happy enough to climb out of her pit of mediocrity."

"That we inhabit," Gilbert finished for her.

"I am quite happy where I am in the pit, and you should be too."

"I am happy because I have you, my dear."

Edith smiled. "And you should be."

"I wonder what brought it about," Stephen said who was as prone to indulge in gossip as anyone although he would not have admitted it.

"Well," Jennie Wistwode said, "I heard that Crauford has fallen ill."

"It must be serious to put off the wedding," Edith said. "I've no love for that man, but I wouldn't wish illness on anyone."

"You are delighted at Lucy's unhappiness, though," Gilbert said.

"I am weary of her pretentions," Edith replied, "and her insistence that she is better than everyone else, when we are all in the same boat."

"You're going tomorrow?" Gilbert asked Stephen to change the subject.

"Yes," Stephen said. "It's time to get Harry back. Ludlow is out of sorts without him around."

"You're sure you couldn't leave him there?" Edith asked, throwing a surreptitious glance at Jennie. "After all, he's with family now. As he should be."

"I'll ask him if he wants to stay," Stephen said. "But I would be prepared for bad news."

"I am sick of bad news," Edith said. "Wars, disease, people dying — it would be good to hear something good for a change. You know, this business with Adele Wattepas has got me thinking. Perhaps it's time we found a husband for Jennie."

"Don't you think it's too soon, Mama?" Jennie asked with some alarm. "I'm still only sixteen. There's time yet."

"No," Edith declared. "There's not. People will be calling you a spinster before long. Can't have that. We need to get you properly settled."

"I don't want to be properly settled."

"My dear, you have no say in the matter. You'll do what you're told and that's that. Isn't it, Gilbert?"

"As you say, my love."

Edith came in from the street, not a place she could normally be found first thing in the morning, spotted the groom Mark tarrying over his breakfast as he was known to do in order to put off work as long as possible, and called, "Mark! You're needed outside!"

"Now, mistress?" Mark answered, perplexed that duty could call him into the street rather than his usual haunt in the yard and stable.

"This very minute!" Edith declared. She turned and marched back out to Bell Lane.

When the door opened for her, Stephen heard over the murmur of guests in the hall enjoying their repast of yesterday's bread and cheese, some with a few strips of bacon, the sound of a woman sobbing. Sobbing women in the street were unusual enough to spark his curiosity, foreboding and a pang of guilt at something important left undone, since he had a hunch what it might mean. So he followed Mark out the door.

A pile of household belongs lay outside the door to Mistress Bartelot's house: dismantled bedsteads, rolled mattresses and bedding, several benches and stools, cooking pots and a box of spoons, knives and other utensils. Burly working men were going into and out of the house adding to the pile, which was not large in any case. Mistress Bartelot stood beside the pile, clutching her heavy bronze cross. She was the woman sobbing. Dungon, her housekeeper, was dividing the big pile into a smaller one.

"Take Mistress Bartelot's things to the shed," Edith ordered Mark, gesturing back toward the yard of the Broken Shield.

A one-horse cart came round the corner from Broad Street and approached them.

"Ah, Gerald," Dungon said to the young man leading the horse. "These are my things."

"Right, mum," Gerald said. He started loading the contents of the smaller pile onto the cart while Mark retreated to the yard to fetch the handcart.

Edith patted Mistress Bartelot on the shoulder. "We'll find room for you, Felicitas, until you can make other arrangements."

Mistress Bartelot nodded.

"I'm sorry," Stephen said. It was the usual thing one said in such circumstances, and utterly inadequate.

Mistress Bartelot nodded again.

Edith took her arm and led her back to the inn.

When Stephen left Ludlow for Hereford later in the morning, instead of crossing the Teme at the bridge below Broad Gate, Stephen turned upon the path that ran eastward along the river. It occurred to him that he ought to talk more to Thumper about certain thefts. He had meant to do so long ago, but one thing or another kept getting in the way of his intentions.

No one emerged from the house to greet Stephen as he entered the Thumpers' ample yard. He put this off to the fact that he had become such a frequent visitor no one bore any curiosity for his visits any longer.

The deserted yard and back garden with its broad vegetable patch and pig sty gave the impression that no one was home, but Stephen heard voices from within the rambling house. He knocked on the door and presently Tad Thumper opened it.

"What do you want?" Tad said, hooking his thumbs into his belt.

"New shirt you have there, eh? And that looks like a new knife," Stephen said. "Sold the horses already, have you?"

"Got a good price for them, too," Tad grinned.

"I'd like a word with your pa."

"He ain't up yet."

"Sleeping like a lord now?"

"We could almost be lords with all that money!"

"Be a good lad and wake him for me."

"He'll be in a foul mood."

"I'll take the risk."

Tad retreated down the entrance hall to a side room, where the younger Thumper children were chasing each other around the hearth. Two of the Thumper women were carding wool beside the hearth. Neither of them made any effort to warn the children about playing near the fire, and they even said nothing as one of the boys, who couldn't have been more than six, leaped over the hearth with a whoop.

It was some time before Will Thumper made an appearance, and Stephen spent the time chafing in the entranceway, for Tad never returned to invite him into the hall. Nor did the women, who noted his presence but continued with their work.

Will came through the door to the hall, rubbing his face. His eyes were bloodshot and had gray bags beneath them.

"What is it now?" Thumper asked.

"I need to know how you came into possession of that cross."

"I thought we had an understanding that we'd not speak of it."

"We did. But I'd like you to reconsider."

"All right, then, what are you offering?"

"I've nothing to offer."

"Not even a threat or two?"

"No threats. Consider it a favor."

"Me! Do you a favor?"

"Yes. I appeal to your good nature. I'm sure you have one somewhere. The fact that you haven't killed that boy Tad is evidence of it. A lesser man would have done."

"I've come close once or twice, I'll admit. He's a handful."

"Well?"

Thumper stroked his chin, which badly needed shaving; it had avoided the razor for at least a week. He sighed. "I suppose. Although I'll have you know I didn't know it was stolen goods."

"I believe you."

"You do?" Thumper seemed surprised. "You can't let on that you heard from me, though. It might be bad for business."

"Cross my heart."

"It was in Hereford."

"I thought as much."

"Just after we got there. Fellow came by with it and offered it for sale. I took it cheap. He wanted to be rid of it.

Said his wife didn't like it. I can understand that. It's a heavy awkward thing."

"I know."

"You could knock a man out with it. I don't understand how Bartelot can hold her head up with that thing round her neck."

"Probably from years of practice. Did the man have a name?"

Thumper hesitated. He nodded. "Theo. His name is Theo."

"Is he in the business?"

"He was, years ago. But he got married. His wife made him get out. That's why I thought nothing of it."

"That wouldn't be Harry's sister, Sarah, would it?"

"You know them?"

"We met."

"I'll be damned. I didn't think you traveled in such circles."

Stephen smiled. "We're friends, aren't we?"

"That's one way of putting it. You won't let on that I told you?"

"How can it matter, if he's not in the business? Or so he says."

"I'll do no business with anyone if it gets out that I've blabbed."

"You're rich now. You don't have to worry about the business."

"Well, the money's not going to last forever."

"I reckon not. I'll be careful not to let on that we talked."

The house was quiet now that the children had been packed off to bed, except for the cracking of the fire as it burned down, the sigh of the wind in the eaves, the creaking of the timbers and the occasional faint stirring of very small feet in the dark crannies.

Stephen had not had a chance to speak to Theobald alone since he had arrived in Hereford, and it did not look as though he would have any better opportunity than at that moment. So he said, "Theo, you were in the business once. Tell me about it."

"I don't know what you're talking about," Theo said. He locked eyes with Sarah for a moment.

"Yes, you do — the business you were in before you went to work at the castle. The climbing business."

Theo was quiet. Then he said, "I'm not doing that stuff anymore."

"I'm not saying you are. But you know people, you must know people who are still involved."

"I won't say nothing about that."

"Let it lie," Harry said.

"I'll not give you away," Stephen said. "But there are things I need to know. Answer if you can, or not. I won't press you any further."

Theo sat without speaking.

Stephen took that as assent to move ahead. "There were two break-ins at Ludlow last month. In both, the culprit got into the houses through upper story windows. I have no idea how, but I imagine it involved climbing and the use of ropes."

"Harry mentioned something about that," Theo said. "I don't know why you're asking me about them."

"It is an unusual style, rather like your own."

"I had nothing to do with them."

"But you might know who is responsible. There can't be many who employ that method."

"I had a partner. He's the only one who comes to mind. But he's dead now."

"His bad ways caught up to him," Sarah said.

"One of the culprits fell from a roof and was killed," Stephen said. "A boy, about fourteen, red hair. I wonder if you might know who he was."

"That is one way they go," Sarah murmured.

"There's lots of boys with red hair in England," Theo said.

"But I doubt there's many who climb for a living," Stephen said.

"I might know one such. Haven't seen or heard of him in a while."

"You wouldn't have since he's dead. What's his name?"

"What are you going to do with this?"

"Find who he works for."

"What's your interest?"

"They stole some things from a friend of mine. She'd like to get them back."

Theo chuckled without humor. "That stuff has probably been sold by now. People in the business don't hang long onto the take."

"Nonetheless, I intend to see what they have to say."

"You're an honest man now, Theo," Sarah said. "Tell him what he wants to know. You don't owe them anything."

"You know them. They're the sort who'd cut your throat if they think you crossed them," Theo said.

"You're not crossing anybody," Stephen said. "You're just giving me the name of a boy who died."

Theo still hesitated.

Instead, Sarah spoke: "Ollie. His name's Ollie. He lives with his father on Grope Lane."

Hereford was a large town and it took the better part of ten minutes to walk from Theobald Tennet's house to Grope Lane through muddy and crowded streets. While there were many grand houses in Hereford, for it was a wealthy town, this area was occupied by smaller, ruder houses, none taller than a single floor, of the kind you would find in any village, many of them in need of repair or even replacement, roofed with thatch instead of shingles which was gray and patchy, the plaster flaking from between the supporting timbers to reveal the underlying wattle that itself looked scrofulous.

Theo pointed out Ollie's house to Stephen and then hurried away before anyone noticed him.

An elderly man was seated on a stool beside the door to Ollie's house, a clay pot on his lap. He noticed Stephen staring at the house from across the street. "You want something?" the elderly man shouted.

"No," Stephen answered.

"Then move on and quit your staring." The elderly man raised the pot to his mouth and drank, spilling brown ale on his shirt front. He pointed a finger at Stephen as he returned the pot to his lap. "I said, move on, you!"

If Ollie was involved with a master thief, he had not got rich off it, Stephen thought. He had intended to question the people living there about Ollie's associations, but the look of the elderly man and Stephen's reception, suggested that he would meet with the same degree of resistance he had encountered in Theo and in the old woman at Bishop's Castle. While there might not be much loyalty among thieves, there was just enough to make things difficult.

Stephen wandered Hereford's streets, struggling to think of what to do now. He paid so little attention to his surroundings that he almost failed to react when a hooded figure bumped into him and muttered, "Yer pardon." This by itself might not be very extraordinary or a matter of concern, since people were always bumping into one another in towns, but Stephen felt light tugging at his purse and he just managed to grasp the hand holding the knife that was about to cut his purse.

He twisted the wrist and deprived the hand of the knife. A boy of about ten or eleven was attached to the hand, which Stephen continued to twist. The boy squirmed and kicked while Stephen maintained his hold on the hand.

"Leave off, you!" the boy shouted.

The commotion attracted the attention of those passing by and a crowd began to collect about Stephen and the boy. Stephen looked around for the boy's companions, especially the hooded man, who might make trouble, as cutpurses did not act alone. They always worked in packs.

"I've caught a thief," Stephen said to the crowd.

There were grins here and there among the crowd. Something about them that suggested to Stephen that the boy was known, and they were eager to see what happened now.

"Quit your squirming," Stephen told the boy, "or I'll break your arm."

"You wouldn't dare."

"I've a short temper," Stephen said in a mild tone that belayed this boast, "and no patience for thieves."

"I ain't no thief! You've attacked me! Without reason!"

"Is there trouble, sir?" a voice said behind Stephen.

He turned to locate the voice, for it had seemed reasonable and carried authority. The man who had spoken was a hefty fellow with a truncheon under his arm. A similar man with a similar truncheon stood beside him: no doubt bailiffs of the parish if not of the town.

"That boy bothering you, sir?" the bailiff asked.

"No," Stephen said. "He bumped into me. I thought he might be trying to cut my purse."

The bailiff regarded the boy. "Your mum know where you are, Alf?"

"That sot's too drunk to find her own feet," Alf the boy spat.

"You be sure to stay out of trouble in my parish," the bailiff said as Stephen let go of Alf, who wasted no time in ducking between to spectators and making his escape.

Without the prospect of any beating, the crowd broke up, leaving Stephen standing with the two bailiffs.

"There is one thing you can do to help me," Stephen said.

"And that is, sir?"

"I'm looking for someone."

"Who might that be?"

"I'm not sure, exactly."

"Well, that might make finding him a bit difficult."

"I am aware of that. However, I know one of his associates."

"His associates, eh?"

"A boy name of Ollie. He's about fourteen, red hair and so high." Stephen indicated with his hand, estimating as best he could from his memory of the dead boy's body.

"Ollie?" the other bailiff said. "There's an Ollie of that description what lives in Grope Lane."

"That's the one," Stephen said.

"What would you want with the likes of him?" the first bailiff asked. "He's more trouble than that little scut Alf."

"Ollie has gone into the burglary profession," Stephen said. "I'm sure he had time to regret his choice before the end."

"I do not catch your meaning."

"He fell off a roof trying to burgle a house and broke his neck."

"When did this happen?"

"Last month, in Ludlow."

"You don't say. I'd not heard that. No wonder we haven't seen him about lately. But if he's dead, why are you asking about him?"

"I'm looking for his partner in crime."

"What would you want with a burglar, sir?" the first bailiff asked.

"To catch him, of course, and to recover some of his loot, if that's possible."

"Fat chance of that."

"I feel obligated to try nonetheless."

The bailiffs put their heads together in a whispered consultation.

"Your most likely prospect is a fellow named Theo Tennet," the first bailiff said. "He's rumored to be quite the burglar, though no one's ever been able to prove anything against him."

"I've already talked to Tennet, and I've ruled him out."

"Hmm, well then, you might try Hugo Horwood."

"Where can I find him?"

"That could be a problem. He's an elusive fellow. But he rents a house on the other side of town on Wye Bridge Street. He's a knife-maker, or claims to be."

"We've always had our doubts about that," the second bailiff said. "Lives too well for a common knife-maker."

"Tell me," Stephen said, "did Tennet and Horwood ever work together?"

"You mean in the burglary trade? No, but we've always thought Horwood was an apprentice to a fellow named Parfeter. He was hanged a few years back for thievery. Tennet and Parfeter were long-time friends."

"Well," Stephen said, "that sounds about right. Thank you."

"Good day to you, sir. And good luck with Horwood."

Percival FitzAllan laid the parchment back on the table and rested his hands on either side of it. His fingers tapped the tabletop, the rings on his fingers knocking when they struck the wood as he stared across the great hall of Hereford Castle.

"You've no idea where FitzSimmons has gone?" he asked Stephen, who stood before the table.

"No. No one would say."

"And you think he's minting money for the barons? Why are you bringing me this accusation? The evidence seems rather thin."

"Henle does not put any weight on it," Stephen said. "But I cannot think of any other reason why FitzSimmons would do such a thing."

"If it's true, what do you make of it?"

"I think that Montfort is planning to rise soon. Perhaps this summer."

FitzAllan was quiet again for a time. "You may be right. It can't hurt to be on the lookout. I shall write to the King straightaway." He pushed the parchment aside, a signal of dismissal. When Stephen did not yield his place to the next supplicant, FitzAllan looked annoyed. "Is there more?"

"I'd like a favor, my lord."

"What is it?"

"I'd like you to prevail on the chief bailiff to issue a beggar's license to someone."

"A beggar's license?" FitzAllan asked, astonished. "That's absurd." He smiled without humor. "Is that someone you? I had no idea you were in such dire straits."

"Well, I am desperate. But I think this is the only way to solve the problem of some recent thefts. Oddly, they are of silver. Perhaps there is a connection with FitzSimmons."

"You don't say. All right then, I'll have my clerk speak to the bailiff. Are we done now?"

"Yes, my lord. Thank you."

Stephen stopped the handcart a hundred yards down Wye Bridge Street from Horwood's house and shop. He lifted Harry from the back of the cart and set him on the ground with a grunt. This act attracted some attention, for legless beggars riding in carts was not a normal occurrence. It would have attracted even more attention had Stephen worn his usual clothes instead of a woolen shirt and stockings borrowed from Theo so that he appeared to be just another common working man. But after a few stares, people went on about their business and it was almost as if they were alone in the street.

"Theo will be back for you in the evening," Stephen said.

"So you're leaving me after all," Harry grumbled. "Abandoning me to a cruel fate."

"It's not much different that your old fate."

"But I'm known in Ludlow, and respected. Here I will be the butt of children's jokes and the pranks of any idle passerby. I put a stop to that in Ludlow. I'll have to start over. This had better be worth it."

"I don't know if it will, but I don't know what else to do." Stephen gestured toward Wye Bridge Gate, a squat stone edifice in the distance. "Horwood's is the shop under the sign of a sword surrounded by a sprig of holly. You have your cup?"

"Never leave home without it."

Stephen had asked the question from anxiety because Harry's cup dangled from a thong about his neck.

"Here's your license, then." Stephen handed Harry a rolled patch of vellum which he had obtained from the city clerk.

"This is a foolish plan," Harry muttered, thrusting the license beneath his shirt. "Surely there must be a better one."

"It's the only plan I've got."

Harry laughed. "If you're depending on me to save you, you are truly desperate." He wagged a finger in the air. "If it works, and that's a big if, my fee will be commensurate with your success."

Stephen did not want to contemplate the odds of success, for Harry, as often was the case, was right. "Off you go. Holiday's over. Back to useful work."

"Just like that? Off you go? That's all you have to say after subjecting me to this indignity? After leaving me alone again in this cold-hearted town? You're not the one who will suffer these muddy streets in the cold rain! You're not the one who will be pelted with clods of horseshit! Well, be away, then, if you must! This is the last favor I do for you!"

Harry strapped on his leather mittens, which protected his hand from the rough ground, and swung toward Wye Bridge Gate.

Stephen watched him for a few moments, regretting the imposition. "Sorry, Harry, you poor bastard," he said, but not loud enough for Harry to hear. He wished he could do something for Harry, but he could not think of a thing that would help.

Bad Money

Then he took up the handles of the cart and headed back to Theo's house, the first stage on his return to Ludlow, where he expected this mad plan, if it worked, to ripen.

Chapter 27

Stephen cracked the shutters of his garret room at the top floor in the Broken Shield Inn, and settled on his cot, the straw filling the linen bag crinkling beneath him. The air was cool and crisp. The aroma of smoke from the many fires in town was absent, carried off by a light breeze that whispered under the eaves. Something fluttered by in the darkness, a bat perhaps. The upraised voices of a man and woman came over the fence from a neighbor's back garden; the woman complaining about the need for butter and the man replying that they must wait until he was paid. A child said something Stephen could not make out. He had been told that when the River Teme, which flowed around two sides of Ludlow, was low you could hear the rushing of the water over the rapids even here in the center of town. The water had dropped from the spring floods, but there was no rushing that he could make out. The moon, just past full, should have risen by now, but an overcast hid it from sight, and it was pitch dark beyond the sill.

It was like any other night. Nothing was happening; nothing seemed likely to happen. Soon it would be time to give up, admit defeat and retrieve Harry from Hereford. Stephen kicked off his boots but did not remove his clothing. He lay down and pulled his blanket to his chin. Sleep was a long time in coming.

Sometime during the night, Stephen awoke to a thump on the roof above his head. When the thump was not repeated, he dismissed the noise as a false alarm. Then after a time, there was another thump followed by a series of thumps, well, not exactly thumps, but surreptitious bumps. He glanced toward the window. The clouds had broken and moonlight shone hard upon the roofs of the houses on the slope below the inn. Something flickered out there; he wasn't sure what.

Then the figure of a man squirming as if in midair was silhouetted against the moonlight: a man climbing down what had to be a rope.

Stephen held his breath, fearful of making any noise, for his bed was noisy and in the quiet of the night, the slightest sound might alert the fellow beyond the window that all was not as he expected it to be.

The climber swung back and forth until he was able to get a purchase on the window sill with a foot. He crouched on the sill and slipped into Stephen's room.

Stephen's heart beat fast — this had to be Horwood! He let the figure get three steps in before he burst off the bed and tackled the intruder.

The force of Stephen's rush drove the pair into the opposite wall. Stephen hit his head and saw stars. His grip weakened, but he managed to hang on somehow, but ended up on the floor with the intruder straddling him. The man's hands closed about Stephen's throat, cutting off his wind, forcing Stephen's tongue out as he gagged for breath.

With his remaining strength, Stephen clamped a forearm down upon the intruder's arms collapsing them and loosening the grip. He rolled, carrying the intruder away, and reversing their positions so that Stephen was now on top, although between the intruder's legs. The intruder squeezed his legs down in a body lock and fumbled at his belt for a dagger, which he drew and struck at Stephen.

Stephen caught the blow, grasped the dagger's blade and disarmed the intruder, the dagger flying into a corner.

He had no weapon himself, having taken off his belt and put it on the floor beside the bed: a stupid oversight. So he did what he could, slamming an elbow in the intruder's stomach. Although Stephen put his full weight behind the blows they seemed to have little effect, and as he rose to deliver another, the intruder released his body lock and kicked Stephen in the face.

It was a glancing blow, however, otherwise that would have been the end. Even so, it propelled Stephen backward.

Free from their embrace, the intruder slipped to his knees and glanced around, no doubt looking for the dagger, which was out of sight in the shadows.

They rose to their feet as if by mutual agreement and began an exchange of punches, pummeling each other like mad drunkards, so carried away that the blows felt no more serious than raindrops.

Somehow during this exchange they had pivoted about the chamber so that Stephen now faced the window and the intruder the door. Stephen struck with an elbow meant for the intruder's head, but it hit the shoulder, yet with enough force that the intruder staggered backward, encouraged by a punch in the face, one step . . . two . . .

There was not space enough for a third. The intruder's thighs collided with the window sill and he toppled out, cartwheeling the four stories to the ground where he landed with a pronounced thud that sounded remarkably like a grain sack falling from a wagon.

Stephen gasped for breath, leaning upon the sill, gazing at the body in the yard below. The first word that came to mind escaped his lips: "Fuck."

His great plan lay in ruins.

"Hugo!" a voice called from above Stephen's head. "Are you all right?"

Horwood's accomplices were still there — right above his head! Desperate to salvage something from the shambles, Stephen leaped for the rope that dangled in space before his eyes.

For some insane reason, he thought it would be nothing to pull himself up, but he discovered that he didn't have the strength and he thought that he'd join Hugo in the yard below. But with a herculean effort fueled by panic, he put one hand above the other and repeated this torture until at last he had a grip upon the roof. He chinned himself and got a forearm up. The dark figures of a man and a boy were crouched there.

"Shit!" the man exclaimed. "You're not Hugo!"

The sensible thing for them to do would be to push Stephen off the roof. But they were some distance away anchoring the rope to the roof and sat transfixed long enough to enable Stephen to climb up. With Stephen no longer dangling on the edge and having no appetite for murder, they bolted toward the neighbor's house, jumped down to its roof since it was not as tall as the inn and scrambled up toward the peak.

It took everything Stephen had to get up and follow them.

The race was on, one stumblebum who could barely keep his feet staggering across rooftops after burglars who slipped and slid on the shingles, and as they came nearer to Broad Street and turned south toward Broad Gate, the stumblebum was able to close the gap, scrambling up to a peak and sliding down on his bum, heedless of splinters. Stephen had been in quite a few chases in his time, both as the pursuer and the pursued, but none had been as inelegant as this.

Several houses down Broad Street, Stephen grasped the peak of a roof where a hook, resembling the kind used on ships, had been fastened onto the crest. A rope snaked down the other side and disappeared into a narrow gap between the houses. The man was just disappearing into the gap, using the rope to make his descent.

Stephen heaved on the rope to gain some slack and unhooked the grapple. He dropped them both. Grapple and rope tumbled toward and into the gap. There were cries of pain and fear from the chasm, but Stephen was beyond sympathy. Theft often was a life-and-death business, the victim cast into suffering and poverty, as Mistress Bartelot had been.

He edged down the roof to the gap and looked in. It was too dark to see anything in there even though his eyes were well adjusted to the night. The man cried, "Raymond! Don't leave me!"

But Raymond did not heed the call. Stephen saw a figure at the head of the gap enter Broad Street and limp toward the gate. Groans of despair filtered from the darkness.

Another man might have quailed at an attempt to clamber down the gap, but Stephen had experience in such climbing. In Spain, they had climbed up and down such shutes while in full armor as an exercise in strength and agility. The only difference now was that he had no toes on his left foot for purchase on one of the walls. But there was nothing for it except to try. He edged into the gap, his right hand and foot on one wall and left on the other. It wasn't as bad as he had feared, and he was able to make it to the bottom without killing himself.

The man had reached the street on hands and knees. He turned at Stephen's approach.

"Please!" the man cried. "I surrender!"

Stephen panted, hands on knees to recover his breath. At last he knelt on one of the thief's arms and unbuckled his belt, which had a dagger hanging from it that might be used against him. Stephen said, "On your stomach, hands behind your back."

The thief rolled over as ordered and did not resist when Stephen brought his wrists together. Stephen secured the thief's arms with the belt and pulled him to his feet, an act that required almost more strength than Stephen had left, for the fellow was solidly built even if he came up only to Stephen's shoulder. But the effort met failure as the thief collapsed with a cry.

"My leg! You've broken my leg!"

Stephen felt the leg in question. "I don't think it's broken. It's probably only a sprain."

"I'll be able to walk to the gallows after all," said the thief, who seemed to be recovering from his panic. "What a relief."

Stephen sat in the street beside him as much to recover his strength as to consider what to do now. It was not that far to the Broken Shield, but seemed an impossible distance if he had to carry the thief.

"What's your name?" Stephen asked.

The thief hesitated. "Ralph."

"Ralph, how would you like to avoid the gallows?"

"How would that miracle come to pass?"

"I have a few questions. If you answer them, I'll see what I can do to save you."

"What could you do, an ordinary bloke like you?"

"I'm the deputy coroner of this town. Small a job as that is, I have some influence."

"So this whole thing was a trap."

"Of course it was a trap."

"That beggar in Hereford we got the word from, Harry, or whatever his name is, you put him up to it?" Ralph asked in disbelief. "Dropping that there was silver at the inn?"

"Let's just say I let information slip knowing that it probably would come to you."

"That's too clever."

"Thank you. Cleverness is a trait I have always admired."

"So, you're clever enough to see that I'll not be hanged?"

"I'll make no promises about that. You never know what the undersheriff here will do. But I think I can manage it."

"I'm not telling you the lad's name."

"I don't want to know his name. That was Horwood who tried to get in my window, wasn't it?"

"Tried? You say he only tried? That's not how it sounded to me."

"That's what we'll say."

"It was."

"Were you up here last month with him? With a red-haired boy?"

Ralph nodded.

"That was Ollie, wasn't it? He was one of Horwood's boys?"

"Sad thing, that. It happens now and then," Ralph said, with a nod. "He's not the first boy we've lost."

"I had no idea burglary could be such a dangerous business."

"It do have its perils."

"You broke into an old woman's house across the street from the inn."

"Yea."

Stephen went on, "You took a horde of silver spoons. Where are they?"

"Long gone."

"Sold, I suppose."

"No, they wasn't."

"Horwood still has them?"

"Course he don't have them."

"What became of them then if they weren't sold?"

"Somebody else's got them."

"A dealer in stolen goods?" Stephen thought of Will Thumper. There must be many more like him.

"No, we work for a gentleman who likes to collect silver."

Of all the things Ralph could have said, Stephen had not expected this. "You steal silver for a gentleman? Would his name happen to be FitzSimmons? Nigel FitzSimmons?"

"No, his name is Crauford."

"*Maurice Crauford?*"

"The very same. Do you know him?"

"We're old friends."

Chapter 28

"So," FitzAllan said when Stephen finished his report in the King's hall of Hereford castle, "you expect me to invade Crauford's house, just because you accuse him? What is your evidence?"

"If you do not act quickly, the stolen goods will be gone," Stephen said, "once word gets here that Horwood's dead."

"I asked, what is your evidence besides this Horwood's dying gasps? Your say so isn't enough. It didn't work at Bishop's Castle. Why should I take a chance here?"

"Because I think there is a link between Crauford and FitzSimmons. FitzSimmons needs silver for his plan. Crauford has been getting it for him."

FitzAllan waved a hand before his face as if batting at an irritating insect. "A guess."

"But they're friends."

"We're all friends, or acquaintances, anyway, on both sides. The fact people might know each other doesn't make them accomplices in crime. Or rebellion either, for that matter. I know Crauford, for God's sake, and FitzSimmons, too. Will you accuse me next?"

"No, my lord. But what else can explain Crauford's sponsorship of these thefts? There have been quite a few of them. He must have fifty pounds in silver by now."

"He does have a house, here in the bishop's quarter," FitzAllan said in a softer, more contemplative tone. "Your informant is right about that. Look, the problem is that if we invade Crauford's house, we will offend him. He has Prince Edward's ear. It's the only reason he got his command in the first place. Nobody else would trust him with men. He's an idiot. He cuts a fine figure on a horse and at the dance, but I wouldn't trust him to swing a sword or to stand fast in battle. Yet he is the Prince's friend, and so in the end, we risk offending the Prince, not mention the bishop, who resists the authority of anyone to arrest his tenants but his own bailiffs.

Are you willing to do that? On the word of some person from the streets whom you've not even had the courtesy to identify? Other than this Horwood fellow?"

"Well, perhaps you can lend me a half dozen bailiffs. If I fail, you can say I acted without your authority."

FitzAllan smiled thinly. "Better it should fall on your shoulders than mine. You've enough enemies already, young fellow. I suppose it can't hurt to have a few more."

Crauford's house lay in the middle of Broad Caboches Lane. It was an impressive three stories of red stone, flanked on either side by equally prosperous houses belonging to canons of the cathedral, which was visible at the end of the street. It ran almost a hundred feet along the street and reared up with such grandeur that it fairly shouted that its possessor was a man of great wealth. It was not what Stephen had expected.

"What now, sir?" the leading bailiff asked at Stephen's hesitation.

"There won't be but a caretaker, his wife and a boy, according to my informant. Crauford's gone off to Windsor and his command." Stephen waved at the front door. "Proceed."

The bailiff nodded, stepped around the cart they had brought with them and pounded on the door. When no one answered, he pounded again. "Open up! In the King's name!"

"Coming! Coming!" an elderly man's voice called from beyond the door. "No need to knock it down!"

The door opened. The elderly man stood in the crack. His gray hair was neat and combed straight back from his forehead, which was high, square and regal. Blue eyes stared at his visitors without the slightest degree of anxiety at this unexpected event. He wore a fine red linen shirt with a silver badge in the shape of a hart on his left breast.

"What can I do for you?" asked the elderly man, whom Stephen took to be a steward and who did not bother to introduce himself.

"We've come to inspect the house for stolen goods," the lead bailiff said.

"Stolen goods!" the steward said. "Nonsense. By what right?"

"By the King's right. That's all we need. Now, out of the way or be knocked aside."

The elderly man's eyes flicked to Stephen, who by the cut of his clothes, even if they were careworn and had a few threads hanging loose, had to be in charge. "All right, all right. No need to be rude. We've nothing to hide."

The door eased open and the steward backed away.

The door, which opened on the south end of the house, was separated from the hall to the right by a wooden partition.

"You know the master isn't here," the elderly man said to Stephen as he passed through the door. "You're not one of the sheriff's men. I don't recognize you."

Stephen answer was a nod as he strode to the passage into the hall which was midway down.

"The master's not going to like this."

Stephen paused. "We won't be long."

What he sought was not in the hall, but he had to pass through it to get to the buttery, where food was stored. The passage to it was on the other side beneath the stairs to the upper floors.

Two female figures were standing by the hearth in the center of the floor, their eyes on him.

Stephen stopped short at the sight of them. "Mistress Wattepas. Adele. I did not expect to find you here."

Adele's answer to this was to break for the stairway.

Stephen gestured at her. "Go get her."

A pair of burly bailiffs rushed across the hall and snared Adele halfway up the stairs.

"I see I can kill two birds with one stone," Stephen said. "I was wondering where you two had got to. Don't let them go anywhere. We'll take care of our first business first."

Stephen expected bluster from Mistress Wattepas like he had received from the elderly steward, but she looked away, eyes flinty, her lips a hard line. Adele looked frightened.

The buttery, where the food was kept, held crates and sacks along one wall. A long and high cupboard occupied the other. A pair of pheasants hung upside down at the open window, which looked out into the back garden, where the corner of a wooden kitchen could be seen.

At the far corner by the window, barrels of wine sat on top of a pallet. It was not unusual to rest things upon pallets, especially sacks of grain, to keep them off the dirt floor and the moisture that could contaminate the contents.

"Move those barrels and then that pallet," Stephen ordered the bailiffs who could be spared the task of keeping hold of Mistress Wattepas and her daughter.

There wasn't room enough for Stephen in the buttery while this work went on, so he retreated to the passage way to wait with the steward.

Although the barrels had been full, or nearly so, it did not take that long to roll them aside and pull the pallet away from its corner.

"We've found it," one of the bailiffs said, sticking his head out of the pantry.

"Very good," Stephen said and reentered.

The pallet had concealed a wooden door in the ground, which had been thrown up. Stairs led down to a cellar. It was dark down there.

"I'll need a candle," Stephen said to the steward.

"Of course, you will, sir," the steward said.

He went out and came back in a few moments with one.

"A lighted candle," Stephen said.

"How stupid of me," the steward said, and retreated again.

This time he brought a copper pan in which lay some tinder, and a flint and steel. The steward handed the pan to one of the bailiffs. He struck sparks into the tinder. When one caught at last, Stephen lighted the candle.

Holding the flame before him, Stephen descended to the cellar. Things sparkled in the darkness, shadows creeping about.

"Anything down there, sir?" called one of the bailiffs, who had remained above owing to the crampness of the space.

"I've found what we're looking for," Stephen said.

He climbed out the cellar and handed the candle to a bailiff. "Have it all brought up and put on the cart."

"This is an outrage!" Mistress Wattepas snapped when Stephen returned to the hall, having recovered her sense of indignation.

"We'll see," Stephen said. "Sit down. The both of you."

The two women sank into chairs by the fire after some hesitation.

"I am afraid your wedding plans have hit an obstacle," Stephen said. "I presume by your presence here that the talk of a postponement was premature, or not accurate."

"What sort of obstacle?" Mistress Wattepas demanded.

Before Stephen could reply, Adele burst into tears, face in her hands.

"Stop that, you silly girl!" Mistress Wattepas snapped.

Stephen waited a moment for Adele to stop sobbing. She raised her head, no longer making any noise, but tears streaming down her cheeks.

He said, "It seems that Sir Maurice is the center of a theft ring."

"That is preposterous!" Mistress Wattepas said.

"There is the proof." Stephen gestured to the first of the bailiffs who had appeared carrying an armload of the stolen silver. "We will take it to the castle and have the owners come to identify it. With that, he will be condemned. I cannot imagine he will escape a serious sentence, perhaps even beheading."

"No!" Adele cried. "Please, no!"

"There is something else I want to discuss, though," Stephen said. "Your husband."

"What about him?" Mistress Wattepas asked in a dismissive tone, but something about her bearing suggested wariness and perhaps anxiety.

"You know that he was not kidnapped. He made it look like a kidnapping to cover his departure for Bishop's Castle. Your engaging me was part of that ruse. What was he doing there?"

Mistress Wattepas did not reply.

"I know that something was going on at Bishop's Castle, something to do with the minting of money. Apparently a certain Nigel FitzSimmons had come up with a plan to mint money without license. A clever plot to help finance a rising by the barons. Or so I am told by a knowledgeable source."

"A lie," Mistress Wattepas spat.

"Your husband worked at the mint here in Hereford during the Long Cross coinage," Stephen said. "He was one of the engravers of the dies."

"I know nothing of such things."

"Of course you do. It couldn't have escaped your conversation, especially since you were already married at the time if the ages of your children are any guide. In fact, I suspect his work was widely known to people interested in such things. I have no doubt that's why FitzSimmons approached your husband and tried to recruit him into this plot. The thing is, evidently Nicholas Feyn was the better engraver. In order to avoid direct complicity in case things went wrong, your husband instead recruited Feyn for the business. But something went wrong. Feyn ran away, carrying off a set of dies. And he came to Ludlow. A strange thing to do. Why was that?"

"I have no idea."

"But I think you do. He came to see your husband. But why?"

Stephen's inquiry met silence.

"You stand to lose everything you have," Stephen said. "The only way to save anything from the wreckage is to help me."

"You can't make such promises," Mistress Wattepas said. "You are but a little man, of no account."

"I know you think little of me because your family was higher than mine," Stephen said. "But you must attend to your present circumstances. Crauford is beyond her reach now. But other suitors might not be, if you keep some means and don't lose all to the crown. Which you will do when your husband's collusion becomes known to the authorities. So you must gamble upon the King's mercy."

Mistress Wattepas stared bitterly into the fire. "Feyn came to see Leofwine," she said at last. "He was to deliver the dies to Leofwine, you see. They were Adele's bride price."

"Bride price? You mean, they were to be given to Crauford?"

"Yes."

"He demanded them?"

Mistress Wattepas nodded.

"Why would Crauford want a set of dies?" Stephen asked.

"I don't know, but I surmise from all this silver your men are carrying off that he planned to mint his own money as well." She looked around. "Houses like these cost a lot of money. He was short of it. But we're all short of money. Perhaps that was his way out of the dilemma. Simpler than borrowing, you have to give him that."

Stephen had an inspiration. "Leofwine wanted to use Feyn's dies because they were less likely to be detected as forgeries, and thus less likely to threaten your daughter's happiness."

Mistress Wattepas nodded.

"And how did Feyn end up in the privy?"

"That greedy little man!"

"Mother! Don't!" Adele said.

"What's the use?" Mistress Wattepas said. "He'll work it out himself anyway."

"That your husband killed Feyn?" Stephen asked.

"There was an argument," Mistress Wattepas said in a tired voice. "Feyn demanded more than was promised. Without the dies, Crauford wouldn't go through with the marriage. So Leofwine struck him. He didn't mean to kill him. It was an accident."

"And for his pains, he didn't find the dies."

"That miserable cripple in the stable heard the altercation and came to the door," Mistress Wattepas said. "Leofwine would have been seen, so he hid until that monster went back to his bed. By the time Leofwine came out, Feyn had dragged himself into the privy, thinking he might hide, I suppose. I expect he fell in on his own account. Leofwine had nothing to do with his death."

"There will be a price for the blow, if your story is to be believed."

"It isn't my story. It is Leofwine's. He will stand by it under oath if need be."

"Hmm," Stephen muttered, digesting what he had heard. "Crauford is a friend of Fitzsimmons. Does he know about that plan? He must, if he thought to mint his own money. Where else would he have got the idea?"

There was another long pause before Mistress Wattepas nodded. "He knows. He's part of it."

Stephen was speechless for a time. "What possible part could he have to play?"

"The plan isn't merely to strike money to pay for the baron's soldiers. It's also meant for the King's men."

The full impact of her words dawned on Stephen. "The bad money. FitzSimmons is going to give the bad money to Crauford who will pay it out to the King's mercenaries."

"Yes."

Bad Money

"And they'll discover this and, having been paid in bad money, they will leave service, weakening the King considerably when war breaks out."

"So Leofwine has told me."

Stephen hurried toward the doorway. "I must go. Bring them along when you're done loading the cart! The servants too!"

Chapter 29

Percival FitzAllan rode straightaway for Windsor Castle when Stephen brought him word of what he had learned at Crauford's house. He covered the distance, one-hundred-twenty miles, in two days of hard riding.

He spent an hour closeted with the King, Prince Edward and several of their closest advisors. Stephen was not privy to this meeting. He remained in the passageway outside the chamber, however, in case any of the great men wanted to question him.

The participants in this secret meeting emerged with grim faces, which suggested that they took seriously the news that FitzAllan had brought.

A force was sent to the mercenary encampment outside town to arrest Maurice Crauford. He was put to questions upon his arrival at the castle, a little roughly, resulting in the loss of two fingers and part of a thumb before he confessed.

A scratch force of knights and sergeants was put together and rode off that very day for a certain manor about forty miles east of Bishop's Castle, where Crauford said the minting operation had been relocated. Stephen's horse was so exhausted by the ride from Hereford that she could not make this one, and no one thought to give him another. So he remained behind.

He spent several anxious days until a messenger returned with word that the raid had been successful: the minting operation had been broken up, dies and other materials captured along with a party of workmen, although FitzSimmons and Leofwine Wattepas had managed to escape. Stephen was relieved that nothing was said about Margaret de Thottenham.

Shortly afterward, Stephen received a summons from the Prince. Like most visitors to the sprawling castle, he had been confined to the west bailey and not allowed in the east one, where the King's hall and apartments sat along one wall below the huge round tower on its great motte. The messenger who had brought the summons conducted him through the gate, across a wooden drawbridge over a ditch north of the motte and through a fortified gate into the eastern bailey. Stephen could not help gauging the prospects for scaling the walls of that tower on the motte, and felt chagrined when he realized he was doing it. The messenger led him then to a chamber in one of the buildings near the gate rather than to the hall itself and left him at the door. The messenger knocked, entered the room, then came out again.

"Wait here," the messenger said. "The Prince will call for you when he's ready." He went away.

Stephen waited in the corridor for more than an hour, listening to the murmur of voices beyond the door. There was not a bench or stool in sight, so he could only pace back and forth, fretting that he might have done something wrong.

Finally, the door opened and a familiar figure emerged: Ademar de Valence, one of the King's justices. A tall thin man who concealed the spare scaffold of his body in heavy maroon robes lined with ermine, he scowled at the sight of Stephen.

"You!" de Valance spat. "I've warned him this is a mistake."

"What's a mistake?" Stephen asked, surprised to be addressed. He and de Valence had not got along from the first moment they had met and their aging acquaintance had not improved things.

"Just stay out of my way in future," de Valence said, and strode down the corridor to the stairway, followed closely by a clerk whose arms were burdened with scrolls.

A servant stuck his head out the door. "The Prince will see you now."

The Prince stood looking out a tall window. He turned when Stephen stopped at the table separating them which was covered by more scrolls.

The Prince was a tall man — taller even than Stephen who was six feet in his stockings — with auburn hair that fell in cascades about his head, looking today like it needed a combing. Stubble covered his cheeks and prominent chin: he was known to dislike the attentions of barbers and only shaved once or twice a week. He smiled at Stephen, lighting up his open, handsome face.

"Attebrook," Edward said, "thank you for coming."

"My pleasure, my lord," Stephen said, glad at least that there seemed to be no reprimand on the horizon. "How may I serve you?"

Edward's fingers wandered among the scrolls on the table until he found the one he wanted. "Our friend Geoffrey Randall has resigned his commission. His wounds, you see. They are rather serious and there is no prospect for recovery soon. We need a replacement. He has recommended you for the position. The King has accepted this recommendation. Here is your appointment." Edward handed Stephen the scroll.

Stephen accepted the scroll, feeling light-headed. He read the words with a struggle since they were in Latin. "I'm to be appointed coroner?"

"That is the idea."

"Thank you, my lord."

"The appointment comes with a stipend, of course. It's not a lot, but in your case it should keep you in bread and beer well enough. I'm sorry that we're not in a position to do more."

"That is well enough, my lord. I am grateful."

Edward turned toward the window and Stephen thought he had been dismissed. But Edward beckoned. "There is one thing that occurred to me," Edward said. "Come on, man. Don't put down roots there."

Stephen crossed round the table and stepped to Edward's side. Edward was looking out into the bailey so Stephen looked out as well. Edward waved at someone outside one of the stables lining the southern wall. The groom drew out a horse and led him on a halter across the yard. Stephen's heart beat faster at the sight of that horse, an Andalusian stallion he knew very well. He had paid the horse to Edward some months ago to avoid a prosecution for homicide.

"FitzAllan told me the part you played in defeating this plot involving bad money," Edward said. "A knight shouldn't be deprived of his best horse."

"Thank you, my lord."

"War will be upon us soon. We'll need every lance we can muster."

"There are dark times ahead."

"Times of struggle. But we will see it through, God willing. I hope you will be ready when the call comes. Now," Edward clapped Stephen on the shoulder, "if you will excuse me, I have a lot to do. Correspondence! You'd think that being a prince meant lolling around drinking wine with beautiful women, but no, it's mainly correspondence."

Chapter 30

The move into Stephen's new house began at dawn. There was not much to move of his things: a borrowed bed, a second-hand chair, a stool, a washstand, the bench Harry had carved upon and a basin — not enough to fill a single chamber let alone an entire house. But as generous as his stipend had been, it was now almost all used up in rent, Gilbert's back wages, pasturage for his horses, and a few other odds and ends.

Mark the groom and another of the servants carried the parts of the bed into the house and upstairs to one of the upper chambers along with the stool and washstand, having deposited the chair and bench by the hearth in the hall.

Mistress Bartelot's belongings took longer, and she fussed quite a bit making sure that the servants and Jennie Wistwode got things in their proper places. The process was not without aggravation. Mark whispered to Stephen as he hurried by, "Are you sure you want to share a house with that woman?"

"You should be asking her that," Stephen said. "It was her house to begin with." Although in fact it was not now her house, since Stephen had taken over the tenancy. Mistress Bartelot had not yet gone down to Hereford to recover her stolen spoons, so she had no money. But she had been happy to move back even if she had to share the place with him.

Stephen saw Harry plodding to work at Broad Gate, and he went out and called before Harry got too far away, "Why don't you come in and have a look around?"

"Why would I want to do that?" Harry asked. "I've seen the inside of a house before. There's no reason to think this one is different from any other."

"Well, this house is a little different. There's something I want to show you."

"I can't imagine what that might be," Harry said. But he followed Stephen through the door and into the vacant shop that occupied the front of the ground floor.

A new chest stood in a far corner, the pinewood still shiny and yellow.

"So," Harry asked, "what am I supposed to see? A lot of dust?"

"There's that chest."

"What about it?"

"It belongs to you."

"What would I do with a chest? Besides, I can't carry something like that back to my stall."

"You won't need to carry it anywhere. Why don't you open it?"

Harry glared at Stephen with suspicion. "What's it got in it, snakes?"

"Not snakes, although I suppose the contents might hurt someone if he isn't careful."

"And you still expect me to open it?"

Nonetheless, Harry dragged himself to the chest and flipped up the lid. The chest held an array of tools: chisels and carving knives of various sizes and shapes, drills, and other assorted things that an expert woodcarver had a use for.

Harry glanced back at Stephen. "What is this?"

"It's so you'll have a true craft now," Jennie said from the doorway where she had been watching round the corner. "Sir Stephen bought them for you! With his new stipend!"

"You knew about this?" Harry asked, incredulous that such a secret could have been kept in the Wistwode house.

Jennie nodded. "I helped pick them out. I hope they're all you need."

"You did?" Harry said. He rested a hand upon the tools.

"I can't believe this," Gilbert said from behind Jennie. "Harry speechless! We need more witnesses to this extraordinary event!"

"We've spoken to the carpenters' guild," Stephen said. "They have agreed to admit you, especially since you won't truly be in competition with their members. It's not like you'll be building houses and making carts, or that sort of thing."

Harry's mouth hung open and still nothing came out. At last he managed to ask, "And this," he waved about, "will be my workshop?"

"Yes," Stephen said. "And your home. You won't have to live in the stable anymore."

"I am quite comfortable there," Harry said, his face screwed up with emotion that he could not contain. "But I suppose it will do."

"Well, then," Stephen said, "come in while we get the fire started and have a cup of ale."

And so the two of them went through to the hall, followed by Jennie and Gilbert. The house did not yet feel like home, but it soon would.

CPSIA information can be obtained
at www.ICGtesting.com
Printed in the USA
LVOW13s0240190117
521490LV00009B/331/P